Queridos amigos roedores,
bienvenidos al mundo de

TENEBROSA TENEBRAX

Tenebrosa Tenebrax

Nosferatu

Bobo Shakespeare

Abuelo Ratonquenstein

Científico despistado, experto en momias egipcias.

Periodista del Valle Misterioso, resuelve misterios con Nosferatu, su inseparable murciélago doméstico.

Escritor famoso, amigo de Tenebrosa Tenebrax.

Escalofriosa

Abuela Cripta

Ñic y Ñac

Kafka

Sobrina preferida de Tenebrosa.

Apasionada de las arañas, posee una tarántula gigante llamada Dolores.

Gemelos latosos, expertos en informática.

Cucaracha doméstica de la Familia Tenebrax.

Poldo

Mayordomo

Bebé

Adoptado con
amor por la Familia
Tenebrax.

Fantasma que
mora en el Castillo
de la Calavera.

Mayordomo de la
Familia Tenebrax. Esnob
de los pies hasta la punta
de los bigotes.

Señor Giuseppe

Entierratón

Madam
Latumb

Ama de llaves
de la familia.
En su moño cardado
anida el canario
licántropo.

Lánguida

Cocinero del Castillo
de la Calavera, sueña
con patentar el
«Estofado del señor
Giuseppe».

Papá de Tenebrosa, dirige la
empresa de pompas fúnebres
«Entierros Ratónicos».

Planta carnívora
de guardia.

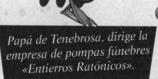

Geronimo Stilton

MISTERIO EN EL CASTILLO DE LA CALAVERA

3 1336 11129 3206

Textos de Geronimo Stilton
Inspirado en una idea original de Elisabetta Dami
Coordinación artística de Roberta Bianchi
Cubierta de Giuseppe Ferrario
Ilustraciones de Ivan Bigarella *(lápiz y tinta china) y* Giorgio Campioni *(color). Con la colaboración de* Christian Aliprandi *(coloración del mapa de las páginas 122-123)*
Diseño gráfico de Yuko Egusa

Título original: *Mistero a castelteschio*
© de la traducción: Helena Aguilà Ruzola, 2011

Destino Infantil & Juvenil
infoinfantilyjuvenil@planeta.es
www.planetadelibrosinfantilyjuvenil.com
www.planetadelibros.com
Editado por Editorial Planeta, S. A.

© 2010 - Edizioni Piemme S.p.A., Via Tiziano 32, 20145 Milán – Italia
www.geronimostilton.com
© 2012 de la edición en lengua española: Editorial Planeta S.A.
Avda. Diagonal, 662-664, 08034 Barcelona
Derechos internacionales © Atlantyca S.p.A., Via Leopardi 8, 20123 Milán – Italia
foreignrights@atlantyca.it / www.atlantyca.com

Primera edición: abril de 2012
Tercera impresión: noviembre de 2014
ISBN: 978-84-08-11149-8
Depósito legal: B. 7.674-2012
Impresión y encuadernación: Unigraf, S. L.
Impreso en España - Printed in Spain

El papel utilizado para la impresión de este libro es cien por cien libre de cloro y está calificado como **papel ecológico**.

Stilton es el nombre de un famoso queso inglés. Es una marca registrada de la Asociación de Fabricantes de Queso Stilton. Para más información www.stiltoncheese.com

Una sombra
en la noche...

Era de noche y aún estaba en mi despacho de
El Eco del Roedor. De pronto, a través de
la ventana creí ver la SiLUETA
de un murciélago volando.
¡Qué RARO! Miré
el cielo negro, en el
que brillaba la luna
LLENA, y
me limpié las gafas
para ver mejor...
Pero no vi nada.
Seguí trabajando
mientras me bebía
mi manzanilla. Te-

nía la sensación de que alguien me observaba. ¡Realmente **RARO**!

Un escalofrío me **erizó** el pelaje.

Intenté continuar con mi trabajo, pero sentía una extraña inquietud. No lograba concentrarme. Al final, apagué la luz y decidí volver a casa. Pero… ¡qué **RARO**!, tenía la impresión de que alguien me seguía. **APRETÉ** el paso. Llegué a la puerta de mi casa corriendo. Entré, cerré con llave y, con un suspiro de alivio, eché el cerrojo para sentirme más seguro.

Luego me dirigí a la cocina y preparé otra **TAZA** de manzanilla triple y unos tacos de queso.

Acababa de ponerme el delantal cuando un soplo de viento me hizo **vibrar** los bigotes. ¡La ventana estaba abierta de par en par! ¡Qué **RARO**! No recordaba haberla de-

jado abierta. Me apresuré a cerrarla y, en ese instante, oí un suave aleteo.

De repente, algo me rozó los bigotes y me lanzó un bulto sobre la cola.

Yo solté un grito, asustado:

—¡Ayyyyyy!

Me volví y vi un paquete muy grande, envuelto en papel **violeta**. Una vocecilla resonó en mis oídos:

—¡MENSAJEPARATI.
MENSAJEPARATI.
MENSAJEPARATI!

Entonces lo reconocí.

Era **Nosferatu**, el murciélago doméstico de la Familia Tenebrax.

Me masajeé la cola magullada.

—¡Abre el paquete! —chilló el murciélago—. Es para ti.

Rasgué el papel violeta y… ¡vi una **LÁPIDA**! Bajo dos corazones enlazados, se leían dos iniciales: R y G. ¡Qué **RARO**!

El paquete también contenía un CD con una etiqueta color violeta que decía «Misterio en el Castillo de la Calavera» y un mensaje: «Querido amigo, en este CD te mando una nueva aventura. Tienes que publicarla en seguida. Es una historia de amor… ¡escalofriante!

Dentro del **PAQUETE** violeta encontrarás una participación de boda. Lee la historia y averiguarás quién está a punto de casarse en el Castillo de la Calavera».

ME MORÍA DE CURIOSIDAD, Y EMPECÉ A LEER…

MISTERIO EN EL CASTILLO DE LA CALAVERA

TEXTO E ILUSTRACIONES DE TENEBROSA TENEBRAX

Querido amigo.

En este CD te mando un... tura. Tienes que publicarla en...

Es una historia de amor... ¡escalofriante!

Dentro del paquete violeta encontrarás una participación de boda.

Aquí hay algo raro...

—¿Tía?

Tenebrosa abrió lentamente los ojos. Alguien le tiraba de la manga del camisón.

—¡Tía, despierta! ¡Tenemos un **PROBLEMA**!

Tenebrosa se incorporó, un poco A t o N - t A D A. Su sobrina Escalofriosa estaba en pie junto a ella. Kafka, la cucaracha doméstica que dormía a los pies de la cama, también abrió los ojos y levantó las **ANTENAS**.

Se acercaba el alba. En el Castillo de la Calavera, la enorme casa de la Familia Tenebrax, reinaba un silencio sepulcral.

—¿Qué pasa? —preguntó Tenebrosa con un enorme **BOSTEZO**.

La noche anterior, inspirada por una espléndida luna llena, había trabajado hasta tarde en un artículo sobre **HOMBRES LOBO** que quería enviar, en seguida, al *Diario del Miedo*, el periódico más famoso del Valle Misterioso. Y ahora tenía mucho sueño. Pero Escalofriosa parecía muy **PREOCUPADA**.

—A Remolino le ocurre algo... No apesta como antes, ha perdido su bonito color **VERDE LODAZAL** y... ¡se niega a comer!

—¿Qué dices? ¿Remolino no tiene hambre?

—exclamó bastante alarmada Tenebrosa y se despertó de golpe.

—**¡No es posible!** ¡Ese monstruo siempre ha tenido un apetito insaciable! ¡No me lo puedo creer!

REMOLINO

Monstruo del foso del Castillo de la Calavera.

PROCEDENCIA: Fétidos Pantanos Inaccesibles.

EDAD: entre 15 y 150 años monstruosos.

DIMENSIONES: variables.

COMIDA PREFERIDA: come de todo, pero le encanta la chatarra con óxido en adobo.

COLOR PREFERIDO: verde lodazal.

PERFUME FAVORITO: olor a calcetines sucios.

LECTURA PREFERIDA: los cómics del superhéroe Lodox.

MARCAS PECULIARES: burbujas verdosas por todo el cuerpo.

En el mundo sólo existe otro monstruo de esta especie y es de sexo femenino.

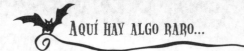
Se vistió velozmente y salió de la habitación **DE PRISA** y **CORRIENDO**. El mayordomo la esperaba en la puerta:

—Señorita, la situación es trágica. **¡SÍGAME!**

¿Lo ve?
¡No come!

Cuando llegó al foso, Mayordomo deslizó en el **FANGO** una bicicleta rota, uno de los platos favoritos de Remolino.

—**¡BLuIIRp!** —dijo el monstruo en tono melancólico y no se dignó mirar la bicicleta.

—¿Lo ve? Ya se lo he dicho, no come desde ayer. ¡No hace más que lanzar ese extraño **BLUIIIRP!**

¡Bluiiirp!

Tenebrosa negó con la cabeza, pensativa:

—Nunca lo había visto así.

¿Has intentado echarle un zapato **pestilente**?

—Sí, y no lo ha tocado. Mírelo, el zapato sigue ahí, **flotando**.

—¡Esto es grave! ¿Y si probamos con una sabrosa caja de clavos **oxidados**?

—Ya lo he hecho. No se ha tragado ni uno.

—¡Esto es muy grave! Y... ¿un bidón lleno de **BASURA** fermentada? ¡A eso nunca ha podido resistirse!

—Ya lo he hecho —suspiró Mayordomo, desconsolado—. Tampoco lo ha tocado.

—¡Esto es muy, pero que muy grave! **¡Gravísimo!** Sólo nos queda una solución...

—No estará pensando en...

—¡Sí! ¡Hay que convocar una Reunión Familiar urgente!

—Piénselo bien, señorita —dijo el mayordomo, muy PÁLIDO—. Recuerde que, después de la última reunión, hubo que RECONSTRUIR una ala del castillo.

—¡Es verdad! ¡Fue una reunión muy DIVERTIDA! Pero esta vez tenemos un problema muy serio… ¡Remolino está enfermo!

REUNIÓN FAMILIAR

El mayordomo subió a toda prisa los empinados escalones que llevaban a la cima de la torre más alta del Castillo de la Calavera, la **TORRE DE LOS MURCIÉLAGOS**. Allí estaban amontonados los primeros inventos que realizó el Abuelo Ratonquenstein cuando solamente era un aprendiz en el Taller del Genio Extravagante.

Entró en un cuarto oscuro y levantó una pesada tela cubierta de **moho** verdoso. Debajo había un curioso y gigantesco **ARTILUGIO**.

Era la Sirena Rompetímpanos, que se utilizaba para avisar a los habitantes del castillo en

casos de emergencia. Cuando el mayordomo empezó a **GIRAR** la manivela, el instrumento emitió un sonido **ENSORDECEDOR** que se propagó por todo el valle.

Uno tras otro, los miembros de la Familia Tenebrax se reunieron en el **SALÓN DE BANQUETES**.

ALARMA

ALARMA

ALARMA

—**Bienvenidos** —los recibió Tenebrosa, y luego añadió muy seria—: He convocado esta reunión porque tenemos un grave problema…

—¡REMOLINO ESTÁ ENFERMO! —exclamó Escalofriosa.

Los demás intercambiaron miradas de preocupación y temor.

—¿Está enfermo? —preguntó Madam Latumb—. ¿Qué síntomas tiene?

—Ante todo, un color rarito, un verdoso mucho más pálido que su VERDE LODAZAL de siempre —respondió Tenebrosa.

Entierratón

Abuelo Ratonquenstein

Escalofriosa

Ñic y Ñac

Señor Giuseppe

Kafka

Lánguida

—Bueno, con esta niebla es normal que esté pálido —comentó Entierratón.

—Ya, pero eso no es todo. No hace más que soltar un **BLUIIIRP** muy triste y melancólico. Al oírlo, entran ganas de **LLORAR**…

—¡Bah… tonterías! Será una mala digestión —dijo con sarcasmo Caruso, el canario licántropo, asomando por el moño de Madam Latumb.

—No, eso no es posible —intervino Escalofriosa—, no come **NADA** desde ayer.

—¡Cómo! —exclamó el señor Giuseppe—. ¿Ni siquiera mi estofado?

Tenebrosa **negó** con la cabeza.

En el salón se hizo un silencio lleno de preocupación, hasta que… se oyó una voz:

—Mmm… **PÁLIDO**… **MELANCOLÍA**… pérdida de **APETITO**… ¡Ya lo tengo! ¡Son síntomas clarísimos!

Era la Abuela Cripta, que se puso en pie y añadió:

—¡Ya sé lo que le pasa a Remolino!

Todos la miraban, incluidas la cucaracha doméstica Kafka y la planta carnívora Lánguida.

—Lo mismo que al protagonista de la última novela que he leído, *Sin ti mi corazón se enmohece*, de Bobo Shakespeare... ¡Remolino es un **enamorado** infeliz!

—Remolino... ¿¡¿enamorado?!? —exclamaron todos a coro—. ¿De quién?

—Ah, eso no lo sé...

—¡Nosotros lo sabemos! ¡Nosotros lo sabemos! —gritaron los terribles gemelos Ñic y Ñac—. Si os lo decimos... ¿tendremos doble ración de **TARTA**?

—¡Dejaos de tartas! —contestó Tenebrosa en tono severo—. Remolino está enfermo. ¡Decidnos lo que habéis DESCUBIERTO!

Ñac sacó una **POSTAL** del bolsillo de Ñic y la dejó sobre la mesa.

—La encontramos en el borde del foso.

—O sea que esto va muy en serio… ¡Remolino está enamorado! —exclamó Entierratón.

—Sí, de una **ESTRELLA** de cine —añadió el Abuelo Ratonquenstein.

PARA REMOLINO

BESOS LODOSOS

GOTELINA

Monstruo femenino, actriz de Horrywood.

ESTUDIOS: Escuela de Arte Dramático del Pantano.

EDAD: ¡no se le pregunta a una señora!

DIMENSIONES: grande, pero bien proporcionada.

COMIDA PREFERIDA: ramos de flores marchitas.

COLOR PREFERIDO: rosa pálido.

LECTURA PREFERIDA: *Corazón de lodo*, de Bobo Shakespeare.

MARCAS PECULIARES: un lunar violeta junto a la boca.

En el mundo sólo existe otro monstruo de esta especie y es de sexo masculino.

—Oh, qué **romántico** —suspiró Madam Latumb—. Cuando era joven, yo me enamoré del actor Mortimer Guaper.

—**AMOR**... ¡puaj! —se burló Caruso, el malhumorado canario—. ¡Qué gran pérdida de tiempo!

—¿Y lo dices tú? —le echó en cara Tenebrosa **SEÑALÁNDOLO** con el dedo—. ¿Acaso has olvidado tu obsesión por aquella lorita pizpireta?

El canario se **SONROJÓ** y se ocultó en el moño de Madam Latumb.

—¡El amor nunca se olvida! —exclamó emocionado el fantasma Poldo—. Es casi mejor que un antiguo castillo **REPLETO** de fantasmas.

—Sí, mejor que un **ATAÚD** forrado de terciopelo —opinó Entierratón.

—Mejor que un buen **estofADo** —murmuró el señor Giuseppe con aire soñador.

—¿Y tú, abuelo? —preguntó Escalofriosa—.
¿Te has enamorado alguna vez?

—¡Claro que sí! Todos los días… ¡de mis adoradas MOMIAS!

Todo el salón se llenó de suspiros.

¡¡¡AH, EL AMOR!!!

CARTA DE AMOR

Todos querían ayudar a Remolino a conquistar a su amada.

—Una bonita carta de amor nunca falla —aseguró la Abuela Cripta, experta en novelas románticas y en remedios para corazones ROTOS.

—Remolino es demasiado TÍMIDO para escribirla —objetó Entierratón y miró a su adorada hija—. Tenebrosilla… ¿por qué no le echas una mano?

—¡Lo haré! —dijo ella—. Voy a mi habitación a escribirla.

Tenebrosa se sentó a su escritorio, levantó la tarántula pisapapeles y cogió un pergamino

amarillento. Después, eligió un LÁPIZ de un bonito tono violeta e hizo que lo mordiera su coleóptero de mesa para SACAR-LE PUNTA.

—Ahora ya puedo empezar. ¿Cómo hay que dirigirse a una estrella monstruosa?

Su Lodosidad... **NO.**

DELICIOSO MONTÓN DE BARRO... **NO, NO.**

PUTRIDÍSIMA PRIMERA ACTRIZ... **NO, NO, NO.**

La chica negó con la cabeza, arrugó el tercer pergamino inservible y lo echó a la papelera TRITURAPAPELES con forma de boca de gato licántropo.

—¡Ya lo tengo! —exclamó al fin y empezó a escribir.

Lodosa de mi corazón:

Soy Remolino, tu fiel admirador.

He devorado todas tus películas. Incluso me he tragado los DVD con las carátulas.

Cuando veo tus ojos oscuros como noches de tormenta, se me revuelve el estómago y me da vueltas la cabeza.

Me gustaría enseñarte la puesta de sol en el foso del Castillo de la Calavera, mi amado reino.

Te regalaré todo lo que poseo: cucarachas y todo tipo de podredumbre.

Si respondes a esta carta, me harás monstruosamente feliz.

Fétidamente tuyo,
Remolino

Nosferatu planeó sobre el escritorio:

—¿*Hasterminado, hasterminado, hasterminado?* —gritó de un tirón.

—¡Sí! He escrito una carta monstruosamente **romántica**. ¡Ven aquí!

Lo cogió de la oreja y le tendió el rollo de pergamino.

—Llévasela a Gotelina, al plató de *Aullidos de monstruo,* en los estudios de Horrywood.

—Uf… Eso está muy **lejos**. ¡Tengo que volar mucho! —protestó el murciélago.

—Está bien… —resopló la chica.

Abrió un cajón del escritorio y cogió un paquete de **B O M B O N E S**.

Nosferatu abrió los ojos como platos, con aire goloso:

—¿Son de ala de **HORMIGA** roja? ¿¿¿Mis preferidos???

—Sí, toma —respondió ella y le lanzó un par de bombones.

El murciélago los cogió al vuelo y los devoró. Satisfecho, salió por la ventana con la carta entre los DIENTES.

Tenebrosa se concentró y empezó a escribir uno de sus artículos. Cuando levantó de nuevo la cabeza, vio que habían transcurrido un par de horas.

—¡Qué raro! Nosferatu aún no ha regresado... —dijo con aire preocupado—. A esta hora dan su programa favorito: *Los murciélagos también lloran.* ¡Y él no se lo pierde nunca! Tengo que ir a buscarlo.

UN PLATÓ...
¡ESCALOFRIANTE!

Tenebrosa saltó a su coche fúnebre, y se dirigió hacia los estudios de **CINE** de Horrywood.

El famoso director Escalofriosky estaba rodando su nueva película de **TERROR**. Salían varios monstruos y Gotelina era la protagonista.

Se comentaba que, gracias a esa interpretación, Gotelina conseguiría la anhelada **GARRA DE ORO**, el premio reservado a los mejores actores de películas de terror.

—¡**NOSFERATUUU!** —gritó Tenebrosa al llegar al plató de *Aullidos de monstruo*—. ¿Dónde se habrá metido?

A su alrededor, observó un montón de roedores muy ocupados: actores paseando muy **NERVIOSOS**, técnicos que transportaban todo tipo de luces, estilistas cargados con mucha ropa, maquilladores y escenógrafos que **CORRÍAN** de un lado a otro del plató...

De pronto, detrás de Tenebrosa, una voz profunda exclamó:

—Tus ojos son tan **bellos** como perlas de pantano.

Ella se dio la vuelta, pero no vio quién le había hablado.

—¡Gracias! —dijo de todos modos y parpadeó—. Debe de ser mi **sombra** de ojos de caparazón de cucaracha.

—Tus cabellos **BRILLAN** como serpientes de pantano —prosiguió galante el misterioso roedor.

—**¡Oooh!** —suspiró ella—. Debe de ser mi champú «Reflejos barrosos».

Y se acercó a un gran decorado, de donde parecía proceder la voz.

—… y tu **PELAJE** rubio brilla intensamente como la luna llena.

—Gracias, pero… ¡mi pelaje no es rubio!

Al mirar detrás del decorado, Tenebrosa vio a un actor ensayando las **FRASES** de una escena romántica. El roedor se interrumpió y la miró:

—¿Busca algo?

—Ejem… no, no. Bueno… sí. ¿Ha visto por aquí a un **murciélago** violeta? —preguntó.

—Creo que he visto uno en la sala de efectos especiales, ahí al lado.

La sala estaba completamente **OSCURA**.

—¡Uf, no veo nada! —dijo Tenebrosa al entrar—. Voy a encender la luz. ¡Aquí está el interruptor!

Pero cuando le dio al B O T Ó N, oyó un agudo maullido.

MIIIIIIIIIAAAAAAAAUUUU

Era la sirena lanzamaullidos que utilizaban en la famosa serie **GATOS LICÁN-TROPOS**.

Tenebrosa no se inmutó y empezó a buscar a Nosferatu.

En el desorden del cuarto, encontró:

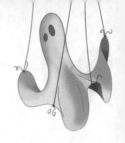

• Un disfraz de FANTASMA.

• Un par de **GUANTES** de hombre lobo.

• Una DENTADURA con afilados colmillos.

• Un morro de gato salvaje con bigotes **rizados**.

Pero ¡ni rastro de Nosferatu!

—Tengo una idea…

Al decirlo, Tenebrosa sacó de su bolsillo un PASTELITO relleno de mermelada de mosquito y lo agitó en la mano.

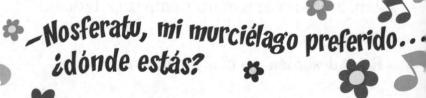

—Nosferatu, mi murciélago preferido...
¿dónde estás?

Se oyó el vuelo de unas alas, seguido de un chillido inconfundible:

—¡Hiiiiiiiiiiiiiiiiiiiiiiiiiiiiiiiiiiiiiiiiiiiiiii!

—¡Ah, estás aquí! —exclamó ella, mientras Nosferatu devoraba su pastelillo favorito—. ¿Has entregado la carta?

—**Ñam, ñam, ñam**... pues... llevo todo el día volando de aquí para allá... pero no encuentro a Gotelina. Y nadie la ha visto.

—Mmm... —murmuró Tenebrosa—. Este asunto huele a... **¡misterio!**

Y se dirigió hacia una caravana, diciendo:

—¡Ven conmigo! Tal vez el director pueda darnos alguna pista...

UNA ESTRELLA...
¡MOSTRUOSA!

El director Escalofriosky estaba sentado a una mesa, bebiendo tranquilamente una deliciosa INFUSIÓN de algas silvestres de pantano. Miraba con aire afligido un PÓSTER de Gotelina colgado en la pared de su caravana.

—¿Se puede? —preguntó Tenebrosa, asomándose por la puerta entreabierta.

Por toda respuesta, Escalofriosky suspiró y se secó una LÁGRIMA con un pañuelo. Nosferatu voló al interior de la caravana y empezó a dar vueltas sobre la cabeza del roedor:

—¿Quépasa, quépasa, quépasa?

El director no reaccionaba. Cogió un pañuelo más grande y se sonó ruidosamente la nariz.

—Señor director, estamos **BUSCANDO** a Gotelina —dijo Tenebrosa.

Al oír ese nombre, Escalofriosky se echó a llorar y hundió la nariz en el pañuelo:

—¡AH! ¡QUÉ DESASTRE!

¡QUÉ TRAGEDIA!

¡QUÉ DESGRACIA!

¡¡¡Soy un director acabado, destruido, fracasado!!! —Se dio con la pata en la frente y exclamó en tono dramático—: ¡Tendré que dedicarme a la cría de lombrices de carreras!

A Tenebrosa, que no le gustaban para nada los lloriqueos, dijo decidida:

—Vamos, vamos, seguro que no es tan **terrible**. A ver, cuéntemelo todo.

El director sorbió con la nariz y empezó:

—Se trata de Gotelina... la estrella de las estrellas. Ella ha... ha... ha...

—¿Ha...? —repitieron al unísono Tenebrosa y Nosferatu, impacientes.

—¡¡¡HA DESAPARE- CIDO!!! —gritó Escalofriosky y rompió a llorar.

—Ya sabía yo que aquí había un **MISTE- RIO** —dijo muy entusiasmada Tenebrosa, arqueando ligeramente una ceja—. Por suerte, tengo la solución.

Y dicho esto, sacó unas cuantas TARJE-TAS del bolsillo.

—Bueno, voy a ver... dónde la habré metido.

FONTANERÍA... mmm, ¡no! —dijo, tras leer la primera tarjeta y la tiró. Luego cogió otra:

—Tal vez ésta: **TRANSPORTES AÉREOS CATAPULTA**... no, no, no. ¡Ni hablar!

Aquí está: *Doctor Sarampionus* ... ¡Ah, no! Éste no entiende de **MONSTRUOS**...

El director observaba a Tenebrosa con

cara de sorpresa, mientras Nosferatu recogía las tarjetas que la chica iba **LANZANDO**.

—**¡AHHH!** ¡Ya está! ¡Mire esto! —gritó y agitó una **TARJETA** bajo el morro del director.

Míster M.L.

MONSTRUÓLOGO

Dejen los mensajes
urgentes en el Apartado
Murcielagoso número 117

—Pero... pero... ¿quién es **Míster M.L.**? —balbuceó Escalofriosky con desconfianza. Nosferatu le gritó al oído:

—¿Cómo que «quién es»? Pues es el insigne, famoso, inimitable y cualificado experto de **MONSTRUOS**, **MONSTRUITOS** y **monstruazos**.

—Seguro que él puede ayudarnos —añadió Tenebrosa. Luego escribió rápidamente un MENSAJE y se lo entregó al murciélago—: ¡Llévaselo a Míster M.L.!

Míster M.L.
MONSTRUÓLOGO

Según dicen, nació en el Pico Helado, en los márgenes del Valle Misterioso. Sus compañeros de juegos fueron los Yetis Blancos de las Cavernas. Se licenció en Monstruología Comparada con una tesina titulada *La importancia del idioma monstrués en la comunidad monstruosa de las montañas.*

Es autor del *Catálogo de monstruos* y fundador de la asociación «Salvemos de la extinción a los monstruos gelatinosos». Lleva diez años retirado de la vida pública.

P.D. ¡Nadie sabe qué aspecto tiene!

INVITAN A BOBO A CENAR

*Los conocimos en el libro «Trece fantasmas para Tenebrosa».

Entre tanto, en Villa Shakespeare, el timbre sonó repetidas veces, despertando a Bobo de su siesta.

El famoso*escritor* había heredado hacía poco aquella mansión plagada de fantasmas, y había tenido que adaptarse a las costumbres de sus inquilinos, los **TRECE FANTASMAS**.*

Cada noche, a las doce en punto, los trece hacían LIMPIEZA y lo despertaban. El pobre Bobo intentaba recu-

perar durante el día las horas de sueño perdidas, pero aquella tarde, una visita inesperada lo **SACÓ** de la cama.

—¡CARTA URGENTE PARA EL SEÑOR SHAKESPEARE!

—¿Qui-quién es? —preguntó Bobo con voz adormilada y el **gorro** de dormir puesto.

—Soy el mensajero del Palacio Rattenbaum. Estoy buscando al Distinguido Señor Roedor Bobo Shakespeare.

Bobo abrió lentamente la puerta y se encontró frente a un roedor ESTRAFALARIO. Llevaba un pelucón blanco y polvoriento y un uniforme con ribetes dorados, lleno de **ZURCIDOS** y de polillas.

—¿Usted es el Distinguido Señor Roedor...? —repitió el mensajero.

—Sí, sí, soy yo —lo **INTERRUMPIÓ** bruscamente Bobo.

El roedor le entregó un viejo sobre **AMARI-LLENTO** y se fue sacando pecho y levantando el morro.

Mientras Bobo daba vueltas al sobre, **APA-RECIÓ** junto a él el fantasma de su tataratío-abuelo Ratelmo, que vivía con él en Villa Shakespeare.

—Sobrino, ¿hay **correo** para mí? —preguntó.

—Pues, en realidad… es para mí… de parte de… Rattinbam… o Rottendam… Rittanbam…

—Ah, te refieres a Rattenbaum. Están en mi lista para la *BODA*.

—¿¡¿Bo-boda?!? —preguntó muy sorprendido Bobo—. ¿De quién?

—¡La tuya, naturalmente! He mirado todas las familias del Valle Misterioso que tienen roedoras en edad casadera. En casa de los Rattenbaum hay **TRES**.

—¿¡¿De-de qué-qué hablas?!? ¡Yo no me pienso casar! ¡Aún soy joven!

—¡De joven, nada de nada! Ya tienes bastantes **TELARAÑAS** en el morro. Venga, ¡abre el **SOBRE**!

Con un larguísimo suspiro, Bobo sacó la carta.

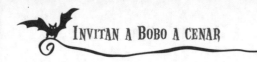
—¡Perfecto, sobrino! Así conocerás a las trillizas Rattenbaum. Según dicen, ¡son una *maravilla*! —exclamó Ratelmo. Luego añadió en voz baja—: Solamente tienes que sentar la cabeza y **casarte** con una de

Distinguido Señor Roedor Bobo Shakespeare:

Gracias a los chismorreos de nuestras fuentes más fiables, nos hemos enterado con sumo placer de que usted, un escritor famoso, se ha instalado en Lugubria. En esta ciudad de zoquetes, un roedor de su nivel sólo puede alternar con la antigua y aristocrática familia Rattenbaum. Por eso lo invitamos a cenar en nuestro palacio esta noche.

Háganos el honor de aceptar, porque no admitiremos un no por respuesta.
Cordiales saludos y reverencias,

La noble familia Rattenbaum.

ellas. Así me darás un sobrinito, que crecerá en esta bella mansión.

Bobo se vio obligado a ponerse su ropa más *elegante* y su tataratío-abuelo Ratelmo le puso una preciosa pajarita.

¡Listo para ir al Palacio Rattenbaum!

¿ARISTÓCRATA O NO?

Bobo llamó a la puerta del Palacio Rattenbaum. En vez de un TIMBRE normal, los dueños de la casa habían instalado un sonido de trompetas ensordecedor.

Bobo se sobresaltó y soltó un grito.

—Ah, no es más que el timbre…

Y miró a su alrededor, AVERGONZADO, esperando que nadie hubiera visto su reacción de miedica.

El parque que rodeaba el Palacio Rattenbaum estaba oscuro, SILENCIOSO y desierto. Aquí y allá se podían ver árboles secos, cubiertos de **moho** verdoso, con zarzas **ESPINOSAS** enroscadas en el tronco.

En la fachada, los marcos dorados estaban a punto de **CAERSE**, y el viento hacía batir las hojas desvencijadas de todas las ventanas.

—Me habré equivocado de dirección —murmuró Bobo—. Esta casa parece **DESHA-BITADA** desde hace años…

Iba a marcharse, pero oyó un chirrido siniestro y vio que la puerta se abría lentamente.

Luego, una **PATA** gris lo sujetó por la solapa de la chaqueta y lo arrastró al interior de la casa.

—Pase, rápido, que entra el **FRÍO** y la calefacción es muy cara.

En la gélida entrada, envuelta en la penumbra, Bobo se encontró cara a cara con un

Reloj parado

Teja caída

Cristal roto

Escalón partido

Jarrón a punto de caer

Pintura esconchada

Planta seca

PALACIO RATTENBAUM

Calle del Crepúsculo, 17
Lugubria, Valle Misterioso

Según la tradición, no documentada, el palacio empezó a construirse en 1313, por voluntad del gran capitán Ratoncio de Rattenbaum, que deseaba una casa acorde al poder y riqueza de su estirpe. A lo largo del tiempo, los gloriosos descendientes de Ratoncio adaptaron el edificio a las (presuntas) necesidades de la (presuntamente) noble familia. Así, hubo 217 remodelaciones, 513 reformas, 778 renovaciones, 212 ampliaciones, 471 rehabilitaciones, 228 modernizaciones, 1.213 obras, 215 restauraciones, etc.

Pero la familia Rattenbaum ha decidido suspender las obras de reconstrucción. Según la versión oficial, lo han hecho para conservar el aspecto aristocrático y crepuscular del edificio. En realidad, el motivo es que... ¡no tienen dinero!

No se aconseja visitar el Palacio Rattenbaum, ya que techos, paredes y cornisas pueden caer en cualquier momento.

EXTRAÑO roedor. Llevaba un traje elegante, aunque lleno de remiendos, y un sombrero de copa aplastado.

—Distinguido señor *Robo*, bienvenido a nuestro soberbio, LUJOSO e incomparable Palacio.

—Me llamo Bobo...

Sin escucharlo, el roedor prosiguió muy entusiasmado:

—Yo soy **AMARGOSIO RATTENBAUM**, el dueño de esta majestuosa casa. Y éstas son mis *maravillosas*, sublimes y encantadoras nietas.

De entre las sombras aparecieron tres guapísimas y elegantes roedoras con traje de noche.

Amargosio
Rattenbaum

—¡Hola! Yo soy TILLY.

—¡Hola! Yo soy MILLY.

—¡Hola! Yo soy LILLY.

Bobo carraspeó ligeramente y se presentó con educación:

—Ejem… Yo soy Shakespeare… Bo…

—¡Ya lo sabemos!

—¡Ya te conocemos!

—¡Lo sabemos **TODO** de ti!

Amargosio le explicó a Bobo:

—Mis nietas tienen SANGRE AZUL, la más azul que pueda imaginar. —Luego, se

acercó a él hasta rozarle la punta de los bigotes y añadió—: ¿Y usted? ¿Es duque, conde, marqués…?

—Pues… yo… la verdad… —balbuceó Bobo.

—No me lo diga. Deje que lo adivine… ¡es príncipe! ¡Se ve a la legua!

—Sí, por el pelo **DESPEINADO** —dijo Tilly.

—Y los bigotes **APLASTADOS** —añadió Milly.

—Y los ojos de **BESUGO** —concluyó Lilly.

Amargosio cogió de nuevo a Bobo por la solapa:

—¡Venga conmigo! Hay que comprobarlo en seguida.

Bobo se vio obligado a seguirlo por un tétrico **PASILLO**. Las paredes estaban cubiertas de grandes cuadros con marcos dorados. Eran retratos de roedores de expresión muy SEVERA.

—Ésta es la Galería de la Sangre Azul. Son los retratos de nuestros *aristocratísimos* antepasados. Modestamente… nuestra familia es la más **ANTIGUA** del valle, está escrito en el Libro…

—¿El Li-Libro? —preguntó Bobo, mirando a su alrededor.

—**SÍGAME** y lo verá usted mismo.

EL LIBRO

Amargosio se detuvo ante un **PORTALÓN** de madera maciza con un gran cerrojo. El roedor hurgó en sus bolsillos, sacó una **LLAVE** enorme y le dio varias vueltas en la cerradura hasta que el portalón se abrió.

Detrás había otra puerta cerrada con una CADENA. Amargosio la abrió y apareció una tercera puerta, más pequeña, cerrada con varios **CANDADOS**. El roedor los abrió uno tras otro y por fin entró en una sala.

—¡Pase! —le dijo a Bobo, que entró con cierto temor—. Vamos a consultar el Libro.

En el centro de la enorme sala, llena de extraños objetos de aspecto anticuado, había un libro abierto muy **GRANDE**, es decir, **ENORME**, mejor dicho, **DESMESURADO**.

Para consultarlo, Amargosio se subió a una escalera de mano, se puso las **GAFAS** en la punta de la nariz y empezó a hojearlo.

—A ver, a ver... Saker... Shafe... Shake... mmm, no lo encuentro...

—Pero ¿qué **BUSCA** exactamente? —preguntó Bobo, perplejo.

—¡Su nombre! Este Libro incluye los apellidos de todos los aristócratas del Valle Misterioso, con los árboles genealógicos, los linajes y los títulos adquiridos, regalados, intercambiados, heredados, obtenidos, inventados...

—¿Y por qué iba a estar mi apellido?

—Porque usted es **NOBLE**, es obvio. ¡*Tiene que* ser noble! Si no, ¿cómo voy a concederle la mano de una de mis **NOBILÍSIMAS** nietas?

Mecanismo hojealibros

Tarima
sujetalibros

Diccionario de términos nobiliarios

Mapa de antiguas posesiones

Baúl (vacío) de Ratoncio de Rattenbaum

—Ah, clar-claro... ¿¿¿Quééé??? ¿¿Cómo di-ces?? ¿La ma-mano? *¡Por mil tinteros!* —gritó Bobo, desesperado—. ¡YO NO ME QUIE-RO CASAR!

Amargosio Rattenbaum hizo caso omiso y le preguntó:

—¿Su nombre se escribe con **Y**?

—¡No!

—¿Con **Z**?

—¡¡Tampoco!!

—¿Con dos **X**?

—¡¡¡Que no!!!

—Espere, volveré a mirarlo.

A pesar de su empeño, no encontraba el nombre de su invitado, de modo que sacó un lápiz del bolsillo y murmuró:

—Siempre podemos añadirlo...

Y escribió de su puño y letra en el Libro:

Robo Cheskspir

—¡Mire! —exclamó—. ¡Aquí está la prueba! ¡Usted no es noble… es nobilísimo!

Y tras estas palabras, sa\tó de la escalera y abrazó a Bobo.

—¡*Bienvenido a nuestra familia!*

Él intentó soltarse.

—Es un gran placer recibir a un INVITADO como usted.

—Es muy generoso —susurró Bobo con un hilo de voz.

—¡No, no! El generoso es usted. Como todos nuestros invitados, es usted un H.P.M.R., **HONORABLE PATROCINADOR DE MANSIONES EN RUINAS.** Ejem… —Amargosio se aclaró la voz—. La estructura de esta inmensa casa necesita unas pocas REFORMAS…

—¿Unas *pocas* reformas? Yo lo veo todo en RUINAS —dijo Bobo, mirando un desconchón de pintura que COLGABA peligrosamente del techo.

En ese momento, una voz nasal resonó en el palacio.

—¡El Gran Chambelán se complace en anunciarles que la CENA está servida!

LA CENA INVISIBLE

La familia Rattenbaum al **COMPLETO** se reunió alrededor de la enorme e inestable mesa del comedor.

Doña Fifí, abuela de las trillizas, vestía un traje de seda REMEndadO que estuvo muy de moda en otra época. Se acercó emocionada a Bobo y le tendió la mano para que se la besara.

—En-encantado, señora —tartamudeó Bobo, e hizo una torpe *reverencia*.

—¡Por fin! —exclamó ella—. Hacía muchos siglos que no se acercaba por aquí un *gentil-ratón*. Esta noche serviremos una cena **especial** en su honor.

—Milly, trae el menú —pidió Amargosio.

—Tío, yo soy Tilly.

—Da igual, cariñito.

—Aquí está —dijo Tilly educadamente, y le entregó a Bobo un papel **GRASIENTO**—. Es la última moda en la alta sociedad: ¡la cena **INVISIBLE**!

Entre tanto, el Gran Chambelán, el mismo que por la tarde había ejercido de mensajero, empezó a servir la cena. Platos y bandejas es-

¡Por fin un gentilratón!

¡En-encantado, señora!

La Cena Invisible

ENTRANTES

TAPAS LIGERAS
(tan ligeras que han volado)

MOUSSE ESPUMOSA DE AIRE

PRIMEROS PLATOS

SOPA DE ALGAS DE MAR QUE NO ESTÁ

RECUERDO DE TALLARINES QUE HUBO ANTAÑO

SEGUNDOS PLATOS

DELICATESSEN DE PESCADO OCULTO
(tan oculto que no lo hemos encontrado)

AROMA DE QUESO OLVIDADO

POSTRES

TARTA FANTASÍA
(de quien desea comerla y tiene que inventársela)

BEBIDAS

IMPERCEPTIBLE NÉCTAR TRANSPARENTE

QUE CASI NO SE NOTA

taban **VACÍOS**, pero cada vez que les servían, los Rattenbaum exclamaban:

—¡Delicioso! ¡Exquisito!

—Amargosio, querido mío, sírveme un poquito más de néctar —pidió Doña Fifí—. ¡Me encanta!

Amargosio levantó la jarra vacía y fingió que echaba algo en la copa de su esposa. Bobo estaba **ANONADADO** y, además… ¡su estómago empezaba a quejarse de hambre!

En ese momento, sonó el **MÓVIL** que llevaba en el bolsillo del chaleco.

DRIIIIIN DRIIIIIN DRIIIIIN

Bobo aprovechó para levantarse y alejarse de la mesa.

—**¡Hola, Bobito!** —dijo una voz al otro lado del teléfono.

—¿Tenebrosa? ¿Eres tú?

—¡Pues claro! —respondió la chica—. ¿Estás en casa? ¿Qué tal con los **TRECE FANTASMAS**?

—No, ahora estoy en…

—Da igual, Bobito. Estoy **INVESTIGANDO** un caso y necesito que me ayudes.

—¿In-investigando?

—Sí, es un caso **MISTERIOSO**. He consultado con un monstruólogo… Pero no perdamos tiempo. Podemos quedar delante de los estudios de Horrywood a **MEDIANOCHE**.

—¡¿A medianoche?! —preguntó Bobo, alarmado. Pero Tenebrosa ya había colgado.

—*Robo*, ¿con quién…

—… estabas…

—… hablando?

Las trillizas Rattenbaum lo RODEARON con aire inquisitivo.

—Con una amiga, Tenebrosa Tenebrax. ¿La conocéis?

Por toda respuesta, las trillizas gritaron muy nerviosas y estallaron en SOLLOZOS histéricos.

—Pe-pero... ¿qué pasa? —preguntó Bobo alarmado.

—No nombres a esa TONTA... ¡Bua!

—A esa ANTIPÁTICA... ¡Buaa!

—A esa INSOPORTABLE... ¡Buaaa!

De pronto, Doña Fifí dijo:

—¿Lo he entendido bien, conde *Robo*? ¿Tiene que marcharse?

—Pues sí. Tengo otro compromiso... debo ir a los estudios de CINE.

—Se llevará consigo a las chicas, supongo.

—¡Siiiii! —exclamaron las trillizas.

A Bobo le tocó resignarse. Fue a casa a cambiarse de ropa y luego se dirigió a los estudios de Horrywood acompañado de las trillizas.

¡Fantástico!

¡Hurra!

¡Siiiii!

INVESTIGACIÓN AL CLARO DE LUNA (LLENA)

—*Aullidos de monstruo*, escena 16, toma primera. ¡CLAC!

—*¡ACCIÓN!* —gritó el director. Había decidido rodar las escenas en que no aparecía Gotelina, a la espera de que la actriz regresara. Al llegar al plató, las trillizas **CORRIERON** hacia Escalofriosky lanzando chillidos de entusiasmo.

—¡¡¡QUEREMOS...

—... QUE NOS DÉ...

—... UN PAPEL!!!

El director arqueó una ceja, pensativo:

—Quizá haya alguna posibilidad de que salgáis en la **PELÍCULA**, pero...

—*Robo*, ¿lo has oído? ¡Vamos a ser actri-ces! ¡Quiero una caravana para mí sola!

—¡Y yo un camerino **DORADO**!

—¡Y yo un equipo de *MAQUILLA-DORES*!

En ese instante, sonaron doce campanadas y Bobo fue en busca de Tenebrosa, dejando a Escalofriosky entre las garras de las trillizas.

—¡Bobito! —lo llamó su amiga—. ¡Estoy aquí! Tenemos que empezar a **INVESTIGAR**.

¡Tenemos... ...muchas ganas... ...de empezar!

—Pero… ¿qué pasa? ¿Y por qué hemos quedado aquí a estas horas de la noche?

—Remolino, el monstruo del foso del Castillo de la Calavera, está **enamorado** de Gotelina, la estrella de Horrywood. Pero ella ha **DESAPARECIDO** y el monstruólogo…

—¿Mo-monstruólogo? —balbuceó Bobo, sin comprender.

—Sí, Míster M.L. El mayor experto en **MONSTRUOS** del valle. Me está mandando pistas para resolver el caso. La idea de venir aquí a medianoche ha sido suya. Me ha enviado este PERGAMINO:

PRIMERA PISTA:
¡ESTUDIOS DE HORRYWOOD,
A MEDIANOCHE!
MÍSTER M.L.

—¿Y yo qué pinto en todo esto?

—Tienes que ayudarme. No puedo investigarlo yo sola. Anda, *¡VAMOS!*

—¿Adónde?

En ese momento, se oyó una marcha fúnebre: era el tono de llamada del móvil de Tenebrosa.

—¡Un MENSAJE de Míster M.L.!

SEGUNDA PISTA:
PARQUE DE LAS PESADILLAS...
MÍSTER M.L.

—¿Qué es el Parque de las **PESADILLAS**?

—preguntó Bobo, muy preocupado.

—Es un lugar muy fantástico. Está en el ala este de los estudios, completamente abandonado. Nadie va por allí…

—¿¡¿Y por qué debemos ir nosotros?!?

—¡Para resolver el caso **MISTERIO-SO**! —dijo Tenebrosa y lo arrastró hasta un sendero muy estrecho.

¿Adón-dónde vamos?

¡A resolver el caso misterioso!

¡MIRA DÓNDE METES LAS PATAS!

Al final del SENDERO, vieron la entrada al Parque de las PESADILLAS, situado en el ala este de los estudios de Horrywood. En cuanto Tenebrosa y Bobo cruzaron el umbral, las pesadas puertas se cerraron tras ellos con un ruido METÁLICO.

Se encontraban en un bosque denso, donde se CRUZABAN varios senderos.

—¿Y ahora hacia adónde vamos? —preguntó Bobo. Se rascó la cabeza, perplejo, y se apoyó en un ÁRBOL.

¡PATAPÚM!

PARQUE DE LAS PESADILLAS
MANTÉN-
GANSE
NO ENTREN
¡FUERA!
¡NO!
PROHIBIDA
LA ENTRADA

El árbol cayó al suelo. Por un momento, Bobo agitó los brazos en el aire, antes de caerse él también.

—Bobito, ¡qué torpe eres! ¡Estás tirando los **DECORADOS**!

—¿Decorados?

—¿No te das cuenta de que no son árboles de verdad? ¡Son cartones **PINTADOS**!

—¡*Por mil tinteros!* —exclamó Bobo y miró una planta—. Todo el bosque es de **MENTIRA**.

—Es el Bosque Oscuro —explicó Tenebrosa—, una atracción del Parque de las Pesadillas... igual que el Lago Negro. ¡Mira allí!

Un poco más lejos, había un lago de aguas oscuras como la **TINTA**.

—Este lago se hizo famoso con el telefilme *Tentáculos tentaculares*.

En ese instante, Bobo tropezó en la orilla y con torpeza **ACTIVÓ** una palanca oculta entre las piedras. El agua empezó a burbujear y del centro del lago emergió un **misterioso tentáculo** que se alargó hasta el escritor cogiéndolo por el tobillo.

¡SOOOOOOOOCOOOOOOORROOOOOO!

gritó desesperadamente el pobre Bobo, suspendido boca **ABAJO** sobre el lago, mientras el monstruoso tentáculo lo balanceaba. De pronto, vio ante él dos ojos verdes espantosos que lo miraban con hostilidad.

—Bobito, no pierdas el tiempo jugando con el Pulpo Gigante. Tenemos que seguir con la investigación.

—¡¡AYÚDAMEEE!!

—Voy a parar el mecanismo —resopló Tenebrosa.

En la otra orilla del lago, estaba el panel de control del pulpo robot. Tenebrosa pulsó una **TECLA**.

—Esperemos que sea ésta… —murmuró Tenebrosa, pero el pulpo empezó a **GIRAR** con más fuerza.

—¡ME MAREEEEO!

—Probaré con ésta —dijo Tenebrosa y pulsó otro **BOTÓN**.

El pulpo se detuvo un instante… y luego comenzó a hacerle **cosquillas** a Bobo con la punta de los tentáculos.

—¡Ja, ja, ja! ¡Ji, ji, ji! ¡Jo, jo, jo!

—rió Bobo.

Tenebrosa suspiró con los brazos en jarras:

—¡Bobito, no tiene gracia! ¡No hacemos más que perder el tiempo!

Impaciente, pulsó la tercera TECLA del panel de control. Por fin, el pulpo se detuvo y soltó de golpe al escritor.

¡PAF!

Bobo tuvo que nadar hasta la orilla.

—¡¿Por qué no me habré quedado en casa?!

La última pista

—Bobito, ¡no puedo estar siempre esperándote! —protestó Tenebrosa, alejándose.

—¡Un momento! —gritó él, ESCURRIÉNDOSE la ropa MOJADA—. ¡No me dejes aquí solo!

Intentó alcanzar a su amiga, pero tropezó con algo y acabó por enésima vez con el morro en la HIERBA.

—Lo mejor será tomar ese camino —propuso Tenebrosa, señalando un estrecho sendero de GRAVA—. ¿Qué opinas, Bobito? ¿Bobito? ¿Dónde te has metido?

—¡UMPF BFRT! —exclamó él, con la boca llena de hierba.

—No me lo puedo creer, ¡te has caído otra vez!

—Sí, pero... **PFUI**... —respondió Bobo, escupiendo un trébol—. He tropezado con una... **LUPA**. La gente lo tira todo por ahí...

—¿Qué? Déjame ver... —dijo la chica. ¡Aquí hay una **NOTA** de Míster M.L.!

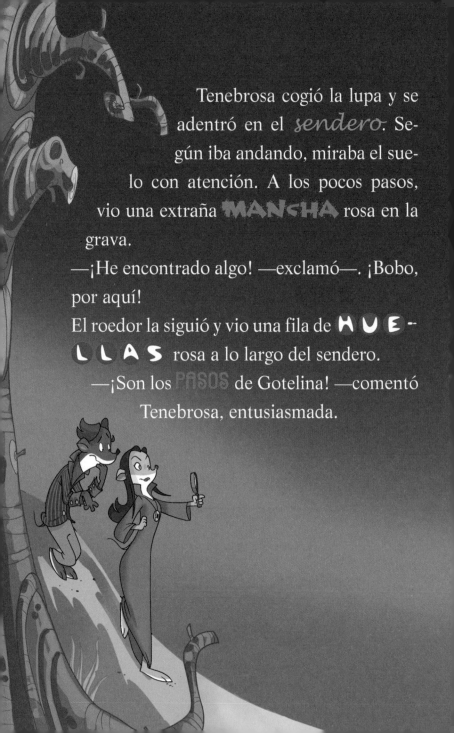

Tenebrosa cogió la lupa y se adentró en el *sendero*. Según iba andando, miraba el suelo con atención. A los pocos pasos, vio una extraña MANCHA rosa en la grava.

—¡He encontrado algo! —exclamó—. ¡Bobo, por aquí!

El roedor la siguió y vio una fila de HUE-LLAS rosa a lo largo del sendero.

—¡Son los PASOS de Gotelina! —comentó Tenebrosa, entusiasmada.

Bobo levantó el morro y vio que el camino desaparecía en la oscuridad.

Aguzó la mirada y distinguió la silueta de un TÉTRICO castillo con una alta torre DÉBILMENTE ILUMINADA.

—Vo-volvamos a casa —suplicó, con un hilo de voz, mientras le castañeteaban los dientes de MIEDO.

Pero Tenebrosa ya corría delante de él.

El sendero terminaba ante un enorme puente levadizo de aspecto PELIGROSO.

Bajo el puente había un foso muy profundo, con el agua tan turbia que no se veía el fondo. Sólo afloraban unos OJITOS amarillos y se oía un ruido seco de mandíbulas.

—¿Qué-qué son? —preguntó Bobo.

—COCODRILOS, supongo —respondió tranquilamente Tenebrosa y cruzó el puente seguida por su tembloroso amigo.

El castillo estaba iluminado únicamente por los rayos de luna que entraban por las estrechas ventanas.

—Sólo está encendida la luz de la torre —reflexionó en voz alta Tenebrosa—. ¡Vamos allí!

Una escalera larga y estrecha conducía hasta arriba. Tenebrosa subió los peldaños de dos en dos. Bobo iba tras ella, jadeando y observaba con PREOCUPACIÓN las aspilleras de la torre que daban al exterior.

—Es-estamos subiendo mucho, ¿no cre-crees? Deberíamos pa-parar aquí…

—Bobito, espero que no tengas **VÉRTIGO**. Cuando lleguemos a lo alto de la Torre de los Murciélagos del Castillo de la Calavera, el panorama te dejará sin aliento.

—Ya… buf… ya estoy sin **ALIENTO**… buf.

Tras una serie interminable de peldaños, llegaron a una pequeña estancia con las paredes de piedra.

—¿Qué-qué hay ahí en me-medio? —balbuceó Bobo—. Pa-parece un a-ataúd.

—Sí, es un **ATAÚD** de cristal —confirmó Tenebrosa—. ¡Vamos a acercarnos!

Bobo observó el ataúd y dio un salto: dos ojos de largas **PESTAÑAS** lo miraban.

Tenebrosa abrió el ataúd y de dentro salió un monstruo completamente rosa, de aspecto **GELATINOSO**.

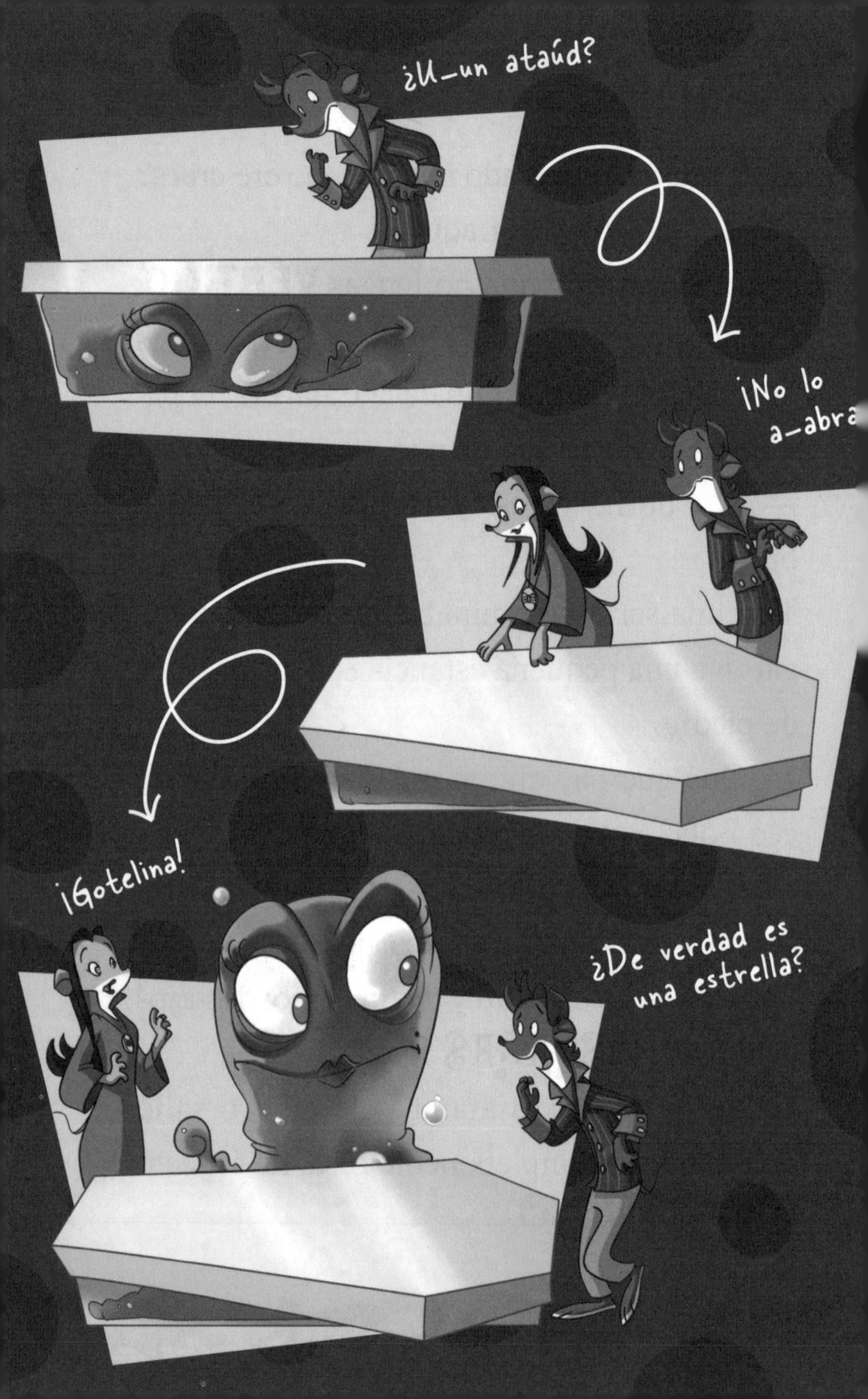

¿U–un ataúd?
¡No lo a–abra
¡Gotelina!
¿De verdad es una estrella?

—¡Gotelina! ¿Eres tú?

—¿Quééé? ¿Ésta es Gotelina? Pero ¿no era una estrella de cine?

—¡Sí! ¡La estrella más **MONSTRUOSA** del valle! ¡Por fin la hemos encontrado!

¡SECUESTRADA!

Mientras Bobo observaba con **ASCO** el barro rosa que caía en el suelo de la habitación, Tenebrosa empezó a hacerle preguntas a Gotelina, utilizando con toda naturalidad el lenguaje de los monstruos.

—¡BLuuuRP BLu BLu BLu BLuu-u-RP! —gorgoteó Gotelina.

—¿¡¿Bluirp?!? —preguntó con interés Tenebrosa.

—BLuuuu... —respondió el monstruo.

Bobo, estupefacto, le preguntó a su amiga:

—Tenebrosa, ¿tú entiendes lo que dice esto... digo esta... o sea «ella»?

—¡Por supuesto! Todos los niños de Lugubria aprenden el idioma MONSTRUÉS desde la más tierna infancia. Es una tradición.

Gotelina se quejó repetidamente.

—¡Oh, pobrecilla! —dijo Tenebrosa—. Dice que la **SECUESTRÓ** el pérfido Doctor Pesadillus.

—¿El doctor… qué?

—El antiguo director del Parque de las Pesadillas. Hace años, era la atracción más famosa de los estudios de Horrywood. Cuando era niña, me gustaba montar en el TIO-VIVO Revuelvetripas. Pero después lo cerraron…

—¡No me sorprende! —exclamó Bobo—. Debía de ser un lugar HORRIBLE.

—Al contrario: era un lugar fascinante. Pero al cabo de unos años, la gente ya no se asustaba y el parque quedó ABANDONADO.

En ese instante, habló Gotelina:

DOCTOR PESADILLUS

QUIÉN ES: experto provocando pesadillas, escalofríos, carne de gallina y chillidos de intensidad variable.

DÓNDE VIVE: oculto en un rincón oscuro y secreto de los estudios de Horrywood. Únicamente sale de noche.

ESTUDIOS: licenciado por la Academia de la Pesadilla con una tesina titulada *Chillidos, gritos y agudos varios*.

AFICIONES: recopilar y clasificar los gritos más espantosos de las películas de terror.

SUEÑOS: devolverle su antiguo esplendor al Parque de las Pesadillas y a sus escalofriantes atracciones, abandonadas desde hace años.

—¡BLuPPPp BLuiRP BLu BLuB!

—Dice que el Doctor Pesadillus sueña con volver a abrir el parque…

—¡BLuP BLuуuP BLu!

—… y quiere obligar a Gotelina a ser la atracción principal.

—¡BLuP…! —gimió ella tristemente, y sus ojazos se llenaron de **LÁGRIMAS**.

—¡Pobrecilla! Su vida es ponerse ante las cámaras, no estar **ENCERRADA** en un parque de atracciones. ¡Tenemos que sacarla de aquí!

Tenebrosa cogió el teléfono y marcó el número de su casa:

—¡Mayordomo! ¡Esto es una *EMERGEN-CIA*! Ven corriendo a la entrada del Parque de las **PESADILLAS**. Y trae el sidecar… el que utilizamos para llevar a Remolino a los **PANTANOS**.

Luego le dijo a Bobo:

—¡Tenemos que salir inmediatamente de aquí! Tú ve **DELANTE** de Gotelina, yo iré detrás.

Mientras bajaban la escalera, una voz retumbó tras ellos.

—¿¡¿ADÓNDE CREÉIS QUE VAIS?!?

Tenebrosa se volvió y vio la silueta espectral del Doctor Pesadillus en la escalera.

—*¡Nos ha descubierto!* —gritó la chica.

Con los nervios, Gotelina chocó con Bobo. Un montón de **LODO ROSA**, del que sobresalían la cabeza y las patas del pobre escritor, rodó escaleras abajo.

Tenebrosa corría tras Gotelina y Bobo:

—*¡RÁPIDO!*

Le dio un puntapié a la bola de barro, que rebotó fuera del castillo y ↶ *RODÓ* ↗ por el sendero que conducía al parque.

El Doctor Pesadillus los seguía y gritaba muy furioso:

—¡Volved aquí!

ESE MONSTRUO ES MÍOOOOOOO,
SÓLO MÍOOOOOO...

De pronto, tropezó con una **mancha** de lodo rosa y cayó al suelo.

PARQUE DE LAS PESADILLAS

En ese justo momento, Mayordomo llegó **A TODO GAS**. Tenebrosa empujó al monstruo rosa hasta el sidecar, y ella se sentó detrás de Mayordomo.

—¡Rápido, al Castillo de la Calavera!

¡¡¡Lo hemos conseguido!!!

Boda en el Castillo de la Calavera

El alba despuntaba por el HORIZONTE e iluminaba el cielo del Valle Misterioso. Una moto se detuvo delante del foso del Castillo de la Calavera. Mayordomo tocó el CLAXON para convocar a la Familia Tenebrax.

—¡TENEBROSA HA VUELTO!

—gritó Nosferatu. Luego, señaló con el ala a Gotelina y preguntó—: ¿¡¿Qué es esa cosa tan... rara?!?

—¡Es GOTELINA! ¡La hemos encontrado! La había raptado el Doctor Pesadillus.

—Qué raro… Gotelina tiene bigotes y cola de roedor —observó Entierratón.

—Ah, ése es Bobo —aclaró Tenebrosa—. Gotelina le ha caído encima y él se ha quedado atrapado dentro de su barro.

—¡PUAJ! —exclamó Bobo, que justo en ese momento consiguió librarse del barro rosa del monstruo.

De repente, el foso BURBUJEÓ, y dos ojos sorprendidos salieron del fango.

Era Remolino, que miraba a Gotelina con amor.

—¡BLUUUB! —dijo Remolino, muy alegre.

—¡BLIRP! —respondió ella. Y parpadeó.

¡Puaj!

La Abuela Cripta suspiró y se llevó las manos al pecho:

—AH, EL AMOR...

—Están hechos el uno para el otro —comentó Entierratón.

—¡Tía! —exclamó Escalofriosa y corrió hacia Tenebrosa—. ¡Mira esto! Acaba de llegar ahora mismo.

Y le tendió un pergamino violeta.

—Es de parte de Míster M.L.

—Bu-bueno, yo ya me puedo ir —dijo Bobo e intentó **ALEJARSE**.

Pero Tenebrosa al ver que se iba lo cogió rápidamente por la solapa.

—No, no, no, Bobito —le dijo muy resuelta—. ¿Adónde crees que vas? Tienes que quedarte al **ENSAYO**.

—¿En-ensayo?

—Sí, el ensayo de la boda. Serás el testigo de Gotelina y Remolino.

¡Enhorabuena!

Ha resuelto el caso de un modo brillante
(gracias a mis pistas, claro está).
Por esta vez, el pérfido Doctor Pesadillus
no ha podido llevar a cabo sus malvados
planes y Gotelina está a salvo. Como ya
habrá adivinado, ella y Remolino están
enamorados desde hace tiempo.
Creo que muy pronto habrá una boda
en el Castillo de la Calavera.
Envíeme las fotos para mi álbum
«Momentos monstruosamente románticos».

La felicito de nuevo,

Míster M.L.
(Mítico Licántropus)

A causa de la impresión que le produjeron las palabras de Tenebrosa, Bobo se DESMA-YÓ. Pero en seguida lo despertó el estridente sonido de su móvil. Era un mensaje de las trillizas Rattenbaum: «*Robo*, ¿dónde te has metido? Te hemos conseguido un papel en la PELÍCULA: ¡tendrás que bajar por un hilo de araña hasta el Pozo sin Fondo! ¿Estás contento?». Al oír estas palabras, Bobo se DESMAYÓ otra vez.

Entre tanto, el Abuelo Ratonquenstein llevó al foso un gigantesco cubo lleno de viejos clavos OXIDADOS:

—Ahora nuestro Remolino parece, por fin, totalmente feliz. ¡Venga, vamos a comprobarlo, muchachos!

Y echó el gigantesco cubo al foso. Remolino devoró los clavos y el cubo, excepto el asa, demasiado limpia para su gusto. La escupió y le dio de lleno a Bobo, que acababa de recobrar el sentido. El escritor se DESMAYÓ por tercera vez.

—¡Prueba superada!

—rio Tenebrosa—. Hemos vivido otra escalofriante aventura. ¡Se la enviaré a *Geronimo Stilton*!

FIN

UNA ESCRITORA...
¡DE MIEDO!

Al terminar de leer, Nosferatu rió:

—¿Te ha gustado la historia? Ya sabes quiénes se **CASAN**, ¿no?

—Pues sí... —respondí yo—. Se casan los dos **MONSTRUOS** del Valle Misterioso: Remolino y Gotelina.

—¡Exacto! —rió el murciélago—. La lápida que has recibido es la **participación** de boda para los invitados... ¡y tú estás entre ellos! Prepárate para el viaje.

—Uf... un matrimonio de monstruos... **¡BRRR!** ¡Se me ponen los bigotes de punta sólo de pensarlo!

—Nada de excusas: ¡el viaje ya está reservado! Pero antes debes publicar este **l** **i** **b** **r** **o**. Y date **PRISA**, porque Tenebrosa ya está terminando otro.

Queridos amigos roedores, estaba claro que en el Valle Misterioso había una escritora... ¡de **MIEDO**! Una escritora superratónica...

¡TENEBROSA TENEBRAX!

ÍNDICE

1. Monte del Yeti Pelado
2. Castillo de la Calavera
3. Árbol de la Discordia
4. Palacio Rattenbaum
5. Humo Vertiginoso
6. Puente del Paso Peligroso
7. Villa Shakespeare
8. Pantano Fangoso
9. Carretera del Gigante
10. Lugubria
11. Academia de las Artes del Miedo
12. Estudios de Horrywood

CASTILLO DE LA CALAVERA

1. Foso lodoso

2. Puente levadizo

3. Portón de entrada

4. Sótano mohoso

5. Portón con vistas al foso

6. Biblioteca polvorienta

7. Dormitorio de los invitados no deseados

8. Sala de las Momias

9. Torreta de vigilancia

10. Escalinata crujiente

11. Salón de banquetes

12. Garaje para los carros fúnebres de época

13. Torre encantada

14. Jardín de plantas carnívoras

15. Cocina fétida

16. Piscina de cocodrilos y pecera de pirañas

17. Habitación de Tenebrosa

18. Torre de las tarántulas

19. Torre de los murciélagos con artilugios antiguos

Geronimo Stilton

**Marca en la casilla correspondiente los títulos
que tienes de todas las colecciones de Geronimo Stilton:**

Colección Geronimo Stilton

Libros especiales de Geronimo Stilton

- ☐ En el Reino de la Fantasía
- ☐ Regreso al Reino de la Fantasía
- ☐ Tercer viaje al Reino de la Fantasía
- ☐ Cuarto viaje al Reino de la Fantasía
- ☐ Quinto viaje al Reino de la Fantasía
- ☐ Sexto viaje al Reino de la Fantasía
- ☐ Séptimo viaje al Reino de la Fantasía
- ☐ Octavo viaje al Reino de la Fantasía
- ☐ Viaje en el Tiempo
- ☐ Viaje en el Tiempo 2
- ☐ Viaje en el Tiempo 3
- ☐ Viaje en el Tiempo 4
- ☐ Viaje en el Tiempo 5
- ☐ La gran invasión de Ratonia
- ☐ El secreto del valor

Grandes historias Geronimo Stilton

- ☐ La isla del tesoro
- ☐ La vuelta al mundo en 80 días
- ☐ Las aventuras de Ulises
- ☐ Mujercitas
- ☐ El libro de la selva
- ☐ Robin Hood
- ☐ La llamada de la selva
- ☐ Las aventuras del rey Arturo
- ☐ Las aventuras de Tom Sawyer
- ☐ Los tres mosqueteros
- ☐ Los mejores cuentos de los Hermanos Grimm
- ☐ Peter Pan
- ☐ Las aventuras de Marco Polo
- ☐ Los viajes de Gulliver
- ☐ El misterio de Frankenstein

Tea Stilton

- ☐ 1. El código del dragón
- ☐ 2. La montaña parlante
- ☐ 3. La ciudad secreta
- ☐ 4. Misterio en París
- ☐ 5. El barco fantasma
- ☐ 6. Aventura en Nueva York
- ☐ 7. El tesoro de hielo
- ☐ 8. Náufragos de las estrellas
- ☐ 9. El secreto del castillo escocés
- ☐ 10. El misterio de la muñeca desaparecida
- ☐ 11. En busca del escarabajo azul
- ☐ 12. La esmeralda del príncipe indio
- ☐ 13. Misterio en el Orient Express
- ☐ 14. Misterio entre bambalinas
- ☐ 15. La leyenda de las flores de fuego
- ☐ 16. Misión flamenco
- ☐ 17. Cinco amigas y un león
- ☐ 18. Tras la pista del tulipán negro

¿Te gustaría ser miembro del CLUB GERONIMO STILTON?

Sólo tienes que entrar en la página web **www.clubgeronimostilton.es** y darte de alta. De este modo, te convertirás en ratosocio/a y podré informarte de todas las novedades y de las promociones que pongamos en marcha.

¡PALABRA DE GERONIMO STILTON!

QUERIDOS AMIGOS ROEDORES, ¡HASTA EL PRÓXIMO LIBRO!

An
Endless
Vista

For the men and women who have labored long to preserve these lands — *pax vobiscum*

An Endless Vista

Colorado's Recreational Lands

by Don Koch

PRUETT PUBLISHING COMPANY
Boulder, Colorado

First Edition
1 2 3 4 5 6 7 8 9

Printed in the United States of America

Library of Congress Cataloging in Publication Data

Koch, Don, 1942–
　An endless vista.

　Bibliography: p.
　Includes index.
　1. Recreation areas—Colorado. 2. Colorado—
Description and travel—1981–　　. I. Title.
GV191.42.C6K63　　917.88′0433　　82-7565
ISBN 0-87108-612-3　　　　AACR2

Front cover photo: Sangre de Cristo view from the South Colony Lakes Road.

Back cover photo: Steamboat Rock in Dinosaur National Monument.

Acknowledgments

Sir Isaac Newton, a scientist rarely given to outbursts of modesty, once remarked that he could not have seen nearly so far were it not that he had been able to stand on the shoulders of his predecessors. Writers, amongst whom modesty is also rare, usually owe a like amount to their predecessors and their contemporaries.

I am particularly indebted to the works of Wallace Stegner, whose sweeping vision of the West, careful scholarship, and finely crafted style remain a model of excellence for those who have followed him. The historical studies of William Goetzmann and Colorado's own Marshall Sprague have also enlarged and sharpened my understanding of how the West was actually won. And no photographer of Western landscapes can fail to acknowledge the debt owed to that master of black and white outdoor photography, Ansel Adams.

My good friend and occasional traveling companion, Glenn Kissinger, who has known and treasured these public recreational lands for so many years, generously contributed a wealth of knowledge, vision, and wisdom regarding nearly every facet of this book. Dr. Lou Campbell, State Cartographer, graciously allowed me to draw freely from his storehouse of map files and cartographic experience. I am grateful for Jody Romano's manuscript typing skills and for the editorial assistance provided by Tom Koch, Norman Koch, Madonna Miller, Leslie Beltrami, Leslie Karnauskas, Jerry Keenan of Pruett Publishing Company, and once again, Glenn and Sue Kissinger.

The regional office staff of the National Park Service and the U.S. Forest Service supplied me with a wealth of information, both printed and verbal. I am especially grateful for the assistance offered by Elsie Cunningham of the Forest Service Regional Office and by the many state and federal field personnel who so cheerfully interrupted other activities to answer my numerous questions. For research assistance, I am indebted to the Denver Public Library and the knowledgeable staff who operate that library's fine Western History Department.

Contents

Allons! the road is before us!
It is safe—I have tried it—my own feet have tried
*   it well—be not detain'd!*
Let the paper remain on the desk unwritten, and the book
*   on the shelf unopen'd!*
Let the tools remain in the workshop! let the money remain
*   unearn'd!*
Let the school stand! mind not the cry of the teacher!
Let the preacher preach in his pulpit! let the lawyer
*   plead in the court, and the judge expound the law.*

Walt Whitman, "Song of the Open Road,"
Leaves of Grass

Introduction

According to an old joke, if the State of Colorado were stretched flat, it would be twice the size of Texas. I believe it.

For more than a decade I have traveled Colorado from one corner to another, living alternately on the front range and on the high plains and visiting the mountains and the plateau lands. I have explored this state on foot and on skis, from the end of a perlon climbing rope, and by passenger car, jeep, motorcycle, boat, and airplane. I have seen Colorado in the desert heat of July on the parched grasslands and in the arctic cold of January on windswept alpine ridges. Yet the more I know of Colorado, the more I learn I have not seen – the more roads I want to travel, the more trails to hike, and the more rivers to run in the early bloom of spring.

I am no glutton for punishment – far from it. I persist in my travels simply because I so much enjoy the sight and sound and smell of outdoor landscapes. It matters little to me whether I have been there before or why I decided to venture outdoors. I like to ski the same trails I have hiked in summers past, seeing how winter snows soften the contours of the land. And I equally enjoy walking through the countryside with a shotgun in hand or stalking scenes to shoot with a camera. A hunter looks at the landscape differently than a photographer, but each learns how to see, understand, and appreciate an environment too rich visually and too complex biologically to unfold many of its secrets on a single visit or to a single-minded visitor.

Nor does it much matter whether my travels take me across the high plains, along the front range, into the Rockies, or through the plateau country. Some travelers consider the plateau lands boring, while others find them beautiful; some men love the grasslands, while others must live among the mountains. Nobody can fault this diversity of preferences. An old Roman proverb expresses it well: in matters of taste, there is no disputing. I, too, prefer certain landscapes, which evoke in me a variety of moods ranging from delight to awe, but these scenes of particular intensity can occur as an afternoon thunderstorm sweeps across the Pawnee Grassland, when the sun rises on the east face of Longs Peak, or in the shimmering summer heat beneath the rim of Hovenweep Canyon.

The grasslands, the front range, the Rockies, and the plateau country, however, all exhibit distinctive characteristics that set them apart from the other regions of Colorado. Recreational lands established within these regions also share common features. These similarities, such as prevailing patterns of vegetation, a shared historical tradition, or related visual elements, seem to me more important than the size of the recreational area, the purpose for which it was established, or the agency empowered to manage it. Accordingly, I have organized the recreational areas included in this book by broad geographical groupings that correspond approximately to the four chief regions of Colorado. Where a case could be made for the inclusion of a recreational area into either of two regions, I have sided consistently with the dictates of reader convenience.

While I hope this book will provide useful travel suggestions, it has not been my intention to create a guidebook or a reference work. Instead, I have prepared the text and photographs as a homage to the stunning diversity of Colorado and to the richness of its recreational lands, which have been for so long a source of enduring satisfaction for millions of travelers. To foster a better understanding of these lands, this book dwells at some length on the natural forces, economic pressures, and political crosscurrents that shaped the development of Colorado. This state and the vast recreational lands carved from it contain a full storehouse of history heavily seasoned with tales of triumph and tragedy – along with a healthy dollop of comedy. I have drawn freely from this stockpile of entertaining anecdotes and serious events in an effort to offer readers a sense of continuity with the past and a familiarity with those who visited these same lands before them. No state that ever hosted so colorful and diverse a cast of characters as Butch Cassidy, Teddy Roosevelt, Bat Masterson, Alferd Packer, and Walt Whitman deserves to have its past forgotten. Most of all, however, my purpose in preparing this book has been to convey by word and picture a shared sense of the excitement, joy, and wonder that these recreational lands of Colorado hold for everyone who seeks them out.

◄ *An overview of Yankee Boy Basin in Uncompahgre National Forest near Ouray.*

The earth never tires,
The earth is rude, silent, incomprehensible at first, Nature
    is rude and incomprehensible at first,
Be not discouraged, keep on, there are divine things well
    envelop'd,
I swear to you there are divine things more beautiful than
    words can tell.

Walt Whitman, "Song of the Open Road,"
Leaves of Grass

About Colorado's Public Recreational Lands

Two hundred years ago, Colorado was a vast landscape of desolation and grandeur. A few intrepid Spanish explorers had visited the southern valleys and trekked across its empty plateau lands, but nomadic Indian bands were the only humans known to live upon this land. In the ten thousand or so years since the last ice age ended, little geological change had occurred, and man had done even less to alter the landscape. Across the semiarid grasslands, enormous herds of bison roamed while bear, wolves, deer, and mountain lions stalked the primeval mountain valleys thick with pine, fir, and aspen.

When immigrants of European stock began to arrive in the middle of the nineteenth century, their purpose was less to settle a new territory than to reap profits from a rich and virgin land. The mountain men and traders sought beaver pelts and buffalo robes. A later generation came West in search of grassland for livestock and mineral deposits rich in gold, silver, and other ores. Land was cheap and the resource base seemed inexhaustible, promoting a frontier ethic of exploitation. Exhausted mining claims, clearcut forests, and overgrazed prairies simply signaled that it was time to move on, seeking out new opportunities.

Contemporary observers of the American West occasionally found fault with this determination to succeed at any cost in a land of new and bold possibilities. James Bryce, an Englishman who saw the American West late in the nineteenth century, wrote:

> ... the unrestfulness, the passion for speculation, the feverish eagerness for quick and showy results, may so soak into the texture of the popular mind as to color it for centuries to come. These are the shadows which to the eye of the traveler seem to fall across the glowing landscape of the West.

This was a minority viewpoint, however, overwhelmed by other, more immediate considerations.

The government in Washington, eager to colonize its trans–Missouri territories and hungry for the mineral wealth and food production needed to fuel the growth of a nation bound for glory, actively stimulated development of the new lands. The Homestead Act of 1862 promoted agricultural development with the offer of nearly-free land. The Mining Law of 1872, which still exists today in amended form, allowed prospectors to stake out mining claims on the public domain and then patent the claims, thereby gaining legal title to the land. The Timber and Stone Act of 1878 authorized the low-cost purchase of quarter sections of public land unfit for cultivation but otherwise valuable for timber or stone. The federal government donated additional holdings both to railway corporations as an inducement to lay track and to the Western territories when they achieved statehood. These last two land-grant categories alone totaled nearly a half million square miles—an area several times larger than the Northeastern United States.

Land, the commodity that the West offered in such abundance, quickly became a driving force of development on the frontier. It was sought after not only for the production of food, fiber, and minerals, but also as a means to attain wealth. D. W. Mitchell, another nineteenth-century English observer of the American scene, wrote:

> Speculation in real estate ... has been the ruling idea and occupation of the Western mind. Clerks, labourers, farmers, storekeepers, merely followed their callings for a living, while they were speculating for their fortunes. ... The people of the West became dealers in land, rather than its cultivators.

As the American frontier era drew to a close, the federal government eventually ceased disposal of its public lands. A century of federal largess had resulted in the devolvement of slightly more than half of the nation's public domain, but so vast had this holding been, once totaling more than one billion acres, that the government found itself with an embarrassment of publicly owned territory. Even today, more than one-third of Colorado (and two-thirds of the state lying west of the Continental Divide) remains in the public domain. Although townsites, homesteads, and mining claims took much of the best land in the West, the remaining territory contained countless billions in mineral wealth, vast timber resources, endless grazing lands, and some of the most magnificent scenery to be found anywhere in North America.

Much of the public domain clearly offered limited recreational potential; it was simply a desolate landscape that stood between a traveler and his destination. But the many natural wonders of the West quickly attracted national attention. William Henry Jackson's photographs, along with the paintings by Moran, Bierstadt, Remington, and Russell, provided the nation with striking visual images of the West. A host of essays, articles, and pamphlets, often filled with more fiction than fact, fed a growing American fascination with the frontier.

There emerged an alliance of Eastern conservationists and Western naturalists, like John Muir in California and Enos Mills in Colorado. Together they often could muster sufficient support in the halls of Congress—depending, of course, on who held office—to enact legislation for the protection of bits and pieces of the Western landscape. A special act of Congress created Yellowstone Park in 1872, and Mesa Verde received national park status in 1906. The Antiquities Act of 1906 enabled the establishment of national monuments on public lands containing features of popular interest and scientific importance. The Forest Reserve Act led to the preservation of woodlands that later became national forests. The National Park Service emerged in 1916 to administer a growing system of park lands. Its mandate included the responsibility to "conserve the scenery and the natural and historic objects and the wildlife therein and to provide for the enjoyment of the same in such manner and by such means as will leave them unimpaired for future generations." Operating chiefly on their own initiative and starting on a large scale with the development of New York's Central Park in 1853, local and state governments also began to establish park and outdoor recreational sites. Denver's extensive network of extraterritorial foothill and mountain parks, including a major ski resort across the Continental Divide, is an innovative example of locally established public recreational areas.

The extensive and diverse network of publicly owned recreational lands in the West hardly emerged in an atmosphere of consensus. Land speculators, timber and mining interests, the railroads, and agricultural associations opposed any laws that might diminish their access to public lands thought to be of significant economic value. This resistance has continued to the present day as resources that were once unknown or of marginal value become ripe for development. The national forests, managed by the U.S. Forest Service, are generally subject to the most intense pressure from competing interest groups that struggle for the right to use these lands for a wide and often conflicting range of activities. Even areas administered by the National Park Service, however, are periodically subjected to development pressure. Dinosaur National Monument in northwestern Colorado is a case in point. Created in 1915 and expanded in 1938, it is a well-established unit of the national park system. In the mid–1950s the proposed construction of the Echo Park Dam endangered its integrity, and again today the proposed Moon Lake electric generating plant and other large-scale energy projects threaten the pristine character of Dinosaur National Monument. At Black Canyon of the Gunnison National Monument, located in west-central Colorado, the construction of several upstream reservoirs has substantially altered the Gunnison River as it flows through the monument.

These pressures for development, however, represent only one side of an enduring struggle to determine how the state's and the nation's public recreational lands shall best be used. Countervailing interests continue to exert their influence. For example, the Colorado Wilderness Act of 1980 created fourteen new wilderness areas and enlarged six already established areas, thereby doubling the amount of designated wilderness land in the state. The act also reserved another one-half million acres for further study as future wilderness. If past events are any portent of the future, the ongoing contest to determine how the public lands shall be managed will continue indefinitely with no single interest group achieving a clearcut, lasting victory. Future generations may someday decide that these lands should be put to other uses or managed in new ways. In the meantime, Colorado's public recreational lands will remain a priceless resource to be enjoyed by us, the present generation, and passed on to future generations.

Springtime view of the Indian Peaks from Red Rock Lake.

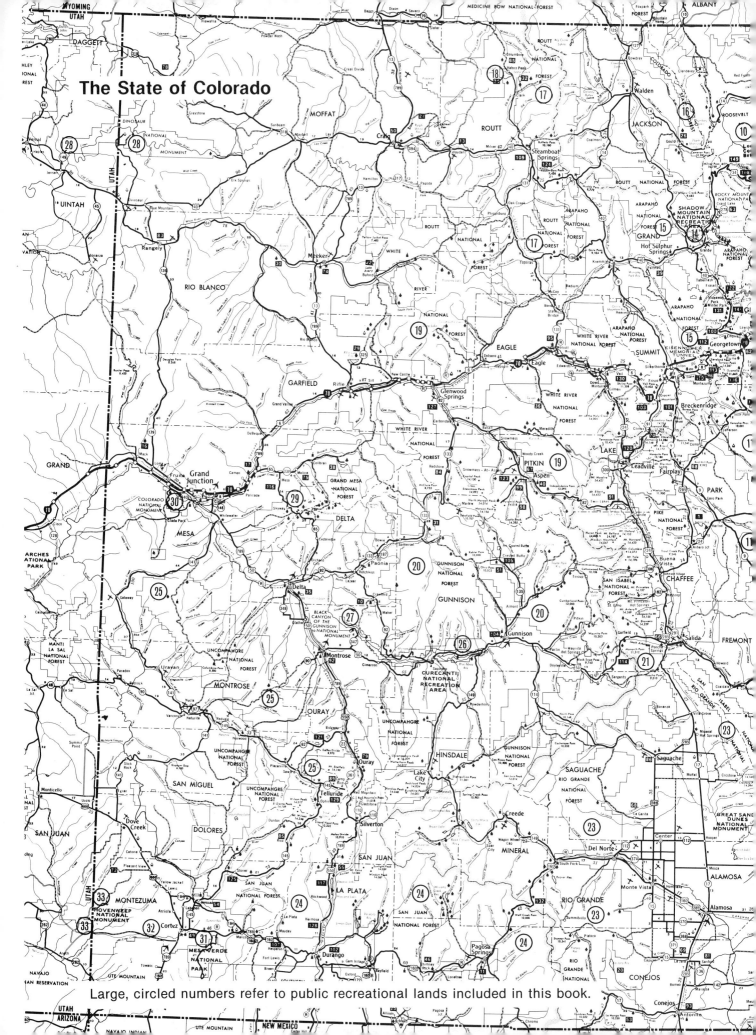

The State of Colorado

Large, circled numbers refer to public recreational lands included in this book.

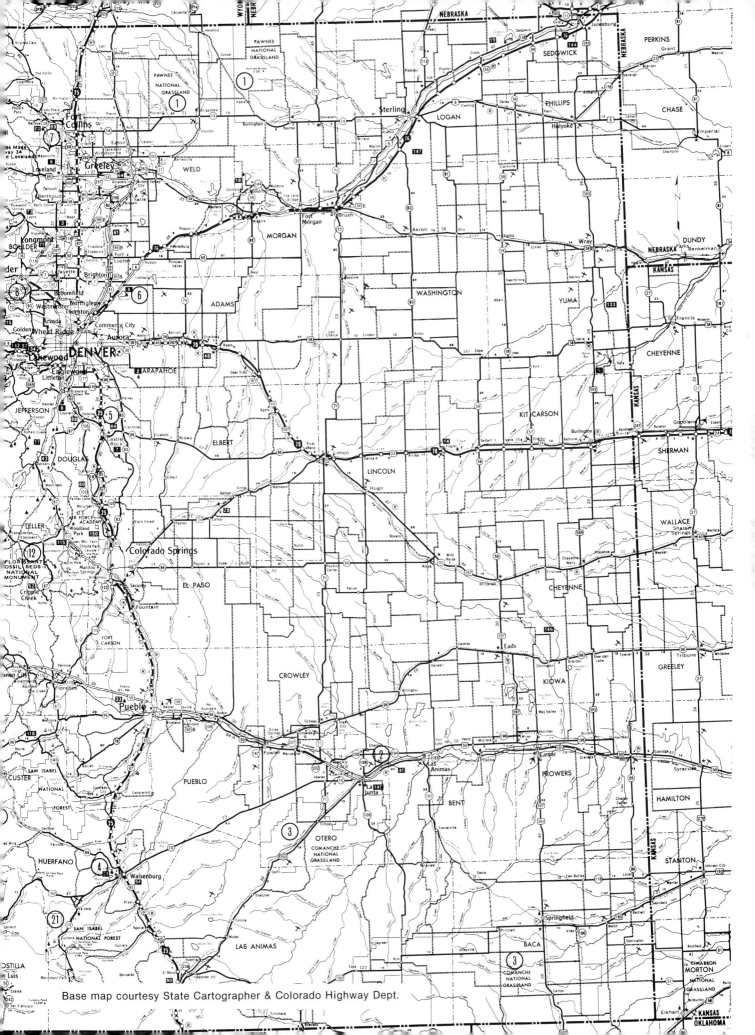

Base map courtesy State Cartographer & Colorado Highway Dept.

Land of the pastoral plains, the grass-fields of the world!

Walt Whitman, "Starting from Paumanok,"
Leaves of Grass

As one traverses the North American continent from east to west, a remarkable transformation occurs at about the 100th meridian of longitude —a line extending along a north-south axis through western Nebraska and Kansas, bisecting the Oklahoma panhandle from the remainder of that state. West of this line the climate, vegetation, and nearly everything else about the land change perceptively. The soils become drier, the sky begins to turn more crisp and blue, dust becomes more prevalent, and trees disappear almost entirely except along waterways. Rainfall, when it occurs, tends to arrive in cloudbursts. These facts of natural history were well known to the early explorers of the American West. Captain Zebulon Pike noted the changes in the land and offered this prognosis on the western plains:

> But from these immense prairies may arise great advantage to the United States; viz: the restriction of our population to some certain limits, and thereby a continuation of the Union. Our citizens being so prone to rambling and extending themselves on the frontiers will, through necessity, be constained to limit their extent on the west to the borders of the Missouri and Mississippi, while they leave the prairies incapable of cultivation to the wandering and uncivilized aborigines of the country.

Thus was born the Great American Desert, a mythic theme that would persist for generations in American thinking about the West. Until the Civil War era, most maps of the United States depicted the entire area between the Rockies and the 100th meridian, more or less, as the Great American Desert. Throughout the latter part of the nineteenth century, a controversy raged between those who believed this area either uncultivatable or suitable for settlement only with severe institutional, cultural, or statutory constraints and those who thought it was a pastoral grassland ripe for development. John Wesley Powell, the explorer of the Colorado River and a visionary planner of the West, stood foremost among the advocates of cautious settlement. A horde of land speculators, politicians, railway men, bankers, and town builders opposed this view, sometimes advocating the curious notion that "rain follows the plow;" in other words, that plowing up virgin sod and subsequent crop production would produce additional moisture.

In the post–Civil War era, the latter viewpoint won out. Railway workers, buffalo hunters, homesteaders, cattlemen, sheep growers, and townsmen sprawled westward across the plains as the U.S. Congress bowed to the pressure of special-interest groups intent upon cheap land and quick profits. Settlement of the semiarid prairies was wrought not by thoughtful planning, but by the forceful application of new technology: the Colt revolver, barbed wire, the Sharps rifle, tempered steel plows, the wind-powered water pump, and repeating carbines. The indigenous culture and native ecosystems of the prairie did not long withstand this onslaught by the products of a modern industrial nation.

The arid prairies soon gave way to permanent human settlement, but at a fearful price. Among the first victims were the plains Indians and the bison— which the early settlers mistakenly called buffalo. It was well known at the time that these two events were closely related. A hunter by the name of Buffalo Jones once wrote of his colleagues: "The buffalo hunters conquered the whole Indian race— not by unerring aim at the red devils themselves— while perchance they circled the camp, or in combat when they often met; but simply by slaying the buffalo and thereby cutting off their source of supplies." On his second expedition to the West, John Frémont hauled a twelve-pound brass cannon from St. Louis. The weapon was brought along to intimidate potentially hostile Indians, but Charles Pruess, Frémont's dour German cartographer, noted in his August 10, 1843 journal entry: "Shoot-

◄ *A summer scene on the grasslands south of La Junta.*

1

ing buffalo with the howitzer is a cruel but amusing sport."

A generation later, the slaughter had reached epidemic proportions. R. W. Snyder, Esq., a Kansas buffalo hunter, penned the following testimonial, dated December 18, 1872, to the Sharps Rifle Company: "The man I sold my old 44 to, killed 119 Buffalo in one day with it. That beats me with my big 50 – as 93 is the most that I have ever killed in one day." The Sharps rifle, an exquisite weapon for shooting at very long range, was reputedly known to the Indians as the gun that "shoots today, kills tomorrow." Analysis of Santa Fe railroad freight records has shown that during the 1870s and the 1880s, three hundred thousand tons of bones were shipped by rail from Kansas alone. That amount is thought to represent the mortal remains of some thirty-one million bison.

The early settlers of the plains often became victims of their own aspirations and delusions. The severe and erratic climate of the high grasslands defeated the majority of those souls initially settling there. Drought, hail, dust storms, insect plagues, and a host of other natural hazards exacted an awful toll on the first several generations of high-plains pioneers. Venal bankers, fraudulent land-company agents, free-lancing confidence men, and the railroad oligopoly contributed to an already long litany of woes. A few settlers, like the Colorado cattle baron John Wesley Iliff, managed to build prosperous rangeland empires. For most prairie settlers, however, the biblical seven lean years did not produce a corresponding number of fat years. The history of the semiarid plains is written in the language of economic downfall: the Depression of 1873, the Big Die-up of 1886, the Panic of 1893, the depressed agricultural markets of the post–World War I era, and the Dust Bowl years following the Great Crash of 1929.

Today few outward signs remind a visitor to the high plains of the century-long struggle between the homesteader and his environment and among the various interest groups – cattlemen and sheepherders, farmers and ranchers, growers and railway agents – who settled the short-grass prairie. Even the character of the land has changed significantly. Where native buffalo and grama grasses once grew,

specially developed hybrid strains of drought-resistant, short-stemmed wheat now thrive. Center-pivot irrigation sprinklers and the magic of modern chemicals yield dense stands of corn where an endless sea of bison once roamed. The irrigated corn, in turn, supports a feeder-cattle industry that otherwise could not exist on the overgrazed prairie, where cactus and other foreign plant species have largely supplanted the native grasses that survived for millennia.

Surely the bison, the native grasses, and the nomadic Indian tribes are unlikely ever to return to the high plains. But several vestiges of this earlier era remain preserved. Bent's Old Fort, meticulously reconstructed by the National Park Service, harks back a century and a half to the era when fur trappers, Spanish traders, buffalo hunters, plains Indians, mountain men, and merchants engaged in a lucrative commerce at remote outposts along the edge of the frontier. On the national grasslands, the sun continues to beat down upon the dry earth as it has done for ages past; massive thunderstorms roll across the land; winter blizzards more fearful than those that descend upon the mountains drive blinding snow over the landscape. Insects, songbirds, and coyotes, all components in a long-established food chain ultimately dependent on the grasses, play out their respective roles. Everywhere above, the sky stretches endlessly across the horizon, dominating the countryside.

Two of the nation's nineteen national grasslands are located in Colorado, one in the northeastern part of the state and the other in the southeastern corner. Together they convey effectively what the high-plains environment is all about: a stark land of extremes, where the eye can see forever and time appears to stand motionless, frozen forever under an everchanging sky and an elemental landscape. It is a world visually and psychologically distinct from the mountains. The landscape is linear and open; the colors are monochromatic. Social life on the plains tends to be extensive rather than intensive, familial rather than fraternal, and depressive rather than manic. This is the forgotten Colorado, a land forsaken by nearly all except the few hearty souls who have settled on these dry plains where nothing comes easily.

1 Pawnee National Grassland

Location: northeastern Colorado
Size: 302 square miles of public grassland
Terrain: grassland with occasional rock outcrops
Scenic Value: considerable
Historical Interest: moderate
Highway Access: US 85, Colorado 14, and Colorado 71
Internal Access: Colorado 14 and 71, an extensive network of improved and secondary dirt roads, and on foot
Maps: U.S. Forest Service (USFS) map of Pawnee National Grassland at 1:125,000; U.S. Geological Survey (USGS) sheets 1, 2, and 3 of Weld County at 1:50,000

When the first generation of European settlers rolled westward along the prairie lands, they found not sandy deserts, but an endless sea of grass. These travelers were the most recent arrivals in a long series of strangers in a strange land. They came, however, with a unique purpose in mind: to establish permanent settlements in a territory where nomadic styles of existence had long predominated.

The European settlers knew of the latter-day plains Indians who, thanks to the Spanish, hunted buffalo (and often each other) from horseback. But they knew nothing of the plains Indians' ancestors, who stalked on foot the prehistoric bison, a more massive and deadly predecessor of the modern-day bison. Nor could they have imagined other extinct species, like the saber-toothed tiger and the hybrid giraffe–camel, that once foraged on these ancient plains. Still earlier, during the last ice age, enormous elephantlike mammoths, standing perhaps twelve feet tall at the shoulder and equipped with long, curving tusks, dominated the Colorado plains, providing food for prehistoric man. The nineteenth-century observers who marveled at the ability of the plains Indians to bring down bison from horseback would have been far more startled to see early man hunting huge mammoths with stone-tipped spears. Archeological evidence strongly suggests that these prehistoric people were adept hunters. In 1932, floodwaters on the South Platte River unearthed the remains of at least a dozen mammoths, along with a number of fluted spear points.

By contemporary standards, the ancestral plains hunting and gathering people were an enduring culture. Aboriginal hunting bands preyed on the mammoths for a period of perhaps ten thousand years, a time span five times longer than the Christian era. But this early human history of the plains would have been inconceivable to the nineteenth-century settlers, who grew to maturity in an age when many still believed, according to the Archbishop James Ussher's chronology, that the act of creation itself had occurred in 4004 B.C.

Indeed, the nineteenth-century settlers came west not to reflect upon the past, but to anticipate a brighter future. A few, like John Wesley Iliff, managed to find it. Iliff arrived at the Pikes Peak gold camps in 1858 but became disenchanted and soon switched to cattle grazing on the public lands. Starting with a small herd of cattle, he obtained contracts to provide beef for the railroad construction crews, and by 1887 his landholdings encompassed a fiefdom stretching from Julesburg to Greeley along the South Platte River.

Few others were so farsighted or fortunate. Many early settlers, taking advantage of the Homestead Act of 1862, staked out their 160-acre claims on the public domain. However, a quarter section was insufficient land for a viable farm or ranch in the semiarid West without the application of irrigation waters. To the west and south of Pawnee National Grassland, along the Platte and its major tributaries, agricultural producers formed ditch companies to construct an extensive network of irrigation canals. To the north, on higher ground farther removed from the major waterways, a homesteader had no choice but to plant his crops and hope for the best.

Symbolic of this hardscrabble existence on the high plains is the town of Keota, a tiny agricultural community located in the eastern management unit of Pawnee National Grassland. In 1920 the population of Keota was 129 persons. By 1940, at the end of the Great Depression, it had declined to thirty-four. The 1980 census of Keota counted only four persons, making it the smallest occupied and incorporated town in Colorado. As the inhabitants of Keota retreated, the grasslands advanced, slowly reclaiming a town that failed. Keota's crumbling buildings and rusted fire hydrants, surrounded by sturdy grasses waving in the summer breeze, offer a picturesque but sad reminder that here the environment has triumphed over man. Just north of Keota is the local cemetery, a plain but fitting prairie resting spot for those who lived their lives in this remote, windswept setting.

About a dozen miles northeast of Keota, in the heart of the national grassland, rises the single most prominent feature in this part of the state. The Pawnee Buttes, looking like lonely sentinels guarding a long-deserted kingdom, rise some three hundred feet above the modern prairie floor. These

Windmill on Pawnee National Grassland.

Rusting fire hydrant in Keota.

two sedimentary landmarks, known in the nineteenth century as White Butte, represent an ancient, higher prairie surface, the remainder of which succumbed to erosion as local storms and torrential spring floods slowly scoured the ground to its present elevation. Improved roads lead to within a mile or so of the Buttes; final access is by way of a rough road across private property.

In addition to these points of interest, which also include the Central Plains Experimental Range on the western edge of the grassland and the nicely shaded Crow Valley Park on Colorado Highway 14, Pawnee National Grassland offers an extensive landscape to wander about by vehicle and on foot, absorbing the high-plains environment and searching out the small details that intensify the grasslands experience.

Pawnee Grassland is a relaxing area through which to drive since the uncrowded roads rarely present any unpleasant surprises and nobody ever gets lost for long because nearly all the routes eventually rejoin a highway. But to grasp and enjoy fully the grassland, pedestrian travel is necessary. Only on foot can a visitor hear the song birds, observe the variety of grasses and the insect life they contain, sense the vastness of the landscape, search the skies for an eagle, and feel the wind, the sun, or the rain on his or her body. The Pawnee Grassland is a composite of little details woven together in a tightly patterned fabric with few dominant features to distract from the patterning. This kind of visual fabric requires close inspection to be appreciated on its own terms.

Spring and fall are the most pleasant times of year to visit the grassland, and the area becomes particularly attractive in the late afternoon, as the low sun angle creates warm, rich colors and long shadows creep across the land. Nevertheless, to understand properly the high plains, a visitor should also experience this countryside in the heat of summer.

Starting out early in the day while the air still holds a bit of morning coolness, the summertime visitor can feel the heat building to its midafternoon zenith, watch the shadows shorten as a harsh glare descends upon the land, then look to the sky as massive thunderheads begin to build, hoping that they will bring relief from the scorching dry heat that has settled upon the land. These dog days, predominant from early July to late August, bring to the grassland an intensity and harshness that best capture the essence of this high and dry, short-grass environment.

2 Bent's Old Fort National Historic Site

Location: southeastern Colorado/east of LaJunta

Size: about 1 square mile

Terrain: river bottomlands

Scenic Value: very high

Historical Interest: unique

Highway Access: US 50, Colorado 109, and Colorado 194

Internal Access: on foot only

Maps: USGS sheet 1 of Otero County at 1:50,000

At the crowning of England's Queen Victoria in 1837, the glory days of the British Empire were close at hand. Across the Atlantic, England's former New World colony had yet to begin earnestly pursuing its goal of Manifest Destiny. Despite expeditions undertaken by Lewis and Clark, Zebulon Pike, and other early explorers, the trans–Missouri West remained an unknown and unsettled wilderness. More than twenty years would lapse before the city of Denver was established on the banks of Cherry Creek. Yet there already existed along the banks of the Arkansas River a comfortable, walled trading post that was extending American commercial interests and political influence across a mountain–plains kingdom larger than England itself.

The trading post belonged to two brothers, Charles and William Bent, and their associate, Ceran St. Vrain. The three men had traveled west from St. Louis in the early days of the Northwest fur trade, when a profitable but competitive market existed for pelts trapped in the upper reaches of the Missouri River basin. After arriving in the Arkansas Valley late in the 1820s, the two Bent brothers and St. Vrain established a mercantile enterprise called Bent, St. Vrain & Company. Three years later they finished construction of a well-fortified trading post beside the Arkansas River.

The site they chose proved ideal for business. It was located on the American side of the river, directly across from territory controlled by Mexico but later claimed by the Republic of Texas. The Mountain Branch of the Santa Fe Trail passed by the fort. Trappers collected their furs in the mountains upstream from the valley, and southern plains Indian tribes inhabited the surrounding valley and grasslands, offering additional opportunities for commerce. The Bent, St. Vrain & Company partners quickly established a triangular trading network with local Indian tribes, with mountain men eager to trade fur pelts for supplies, and with traders exchanging goods of American manufacture for Mexican wares, bullion, and Navaho products.

The Bents and St. Vrain were frontier captains of commerce, profiting as buyers, sellers, and middlemen. The company both employed its own salaried trappers to obtain furs that could be traded for other items, and they exchanged factory goods purchased from the St. Louis wagon trains for furs brought in by self-employed "free trappers" who roamed the high mountain valleys.

The fort did not prosper by commerce alone, however. The partners were widely known as gracious hosts, honest businessmen, and astute diplomats who understood that harmonious relations among their diverse trading partners were a necessary condition for successful commerce and an effective defense against prospective competitors. William Bent, who married the daughter of a powerful Southern Cheyenne medicine man and then, when she died, married her sister, supervised trade with the Indians and mountain men. His older brother Charles, who married a sister of Kit Carson's Mexican wife, oversaw the company's far-flung business operations, which reached from St. Louis to Santa Fe. Ceran St. Vrain traveled widely for the company, conducting business at mercantile outlets and other trade centers.

Evidence of the dominant influence that the trading post exercised throughout its territory remains in the list of persons who visited it. If the Bent brothers had maintained a guest book, it would have read like a who's who of early Western personalities including Jim Bridger, Kit Carson, John Frémont, and the historian Francis Parkman.

The trading center by the Arkansas flourished for nearly fifteen years. By the mid-1840s, however, fashion changes had long since crippled the beaver trade, and the supply of frontier trading posts was exceeding the demand for buffalo robes. Then, in 1846, Colonel and soon to be General Steven Kearney's army marched on Mexico, using the fortified trading post as a field headquarters and supply depot. After Kearney triumphed in a bloodless victory, he appointed Charles Bent governor of the conquered province. The elder Bent was assassinated, however, during an uprising in Taos the next year. St. Vrain departed for New Mexico, and a cholera epidemic swept through the local Indian tribes. As business dwindled, William Bent stayed on, trying to sell his well-fortified post to the government. The negotiations dragged on fruitlessly, and in 1849 Bent loaded his family and goods onto wagons, abandoning the fort that had so well served the territory.

Courtyard of Bent's Old Fort.

Interior view in Bent's Old Fort.

According to various accounts, Bent, in disgust and frustration, burned down the fort or, alternately, local Indians, on whose land it had been built, destroyed it. Bent constructed a new post at a site down the river. Four years later, in 1853, Captain John Gunnison's survey expedition visited the area, noting that there existed two or three log houses that had been occupied as a station by William Bent but which were now vacant and as yet undamaged by Indians. In light of the government's failure to buy the original fort for military purposes, the report of Captain Gunnison's Washington-financed expedition is ironic: "Here, beyond all question, would be one of the most favorable points for a military post which is anywhere presented on the plains."

The Bent brothers and St. Vrain surely would be amused that more than a century later the federal government saw fit to undertake a meticulous reconstruction of their trading post as it existed on the eve of Colonel Kearney's arrival with seventeen hundred troops and a massive supply train. The previous owners could not help but take delight, however, in the quality of reconstruction and attention to detail displayed by the National Park Service. Not only has the Park Service constructed an historically accurate replica of the original structure, it has created an appealing and dramatic piece of architecture in the Spanish adobe style and equipped it with an extensive array of nineteenth-century fixtures and furniture. In addition to the usual uniformed Park Service personnel, the visitor-season staff includes costumed blacksmiths, carpenters, and other artisans representing some of the sixty workers once employed by Bent, St. Vrain & Company. The trade room is stocked with goods; the blacksmith shop rings to the sound of a hammer on red-hot iron; a kitchen helper carries cast-iron utensils; a stable hand tends to the work horses in the corral.

The reconstructed Bent's Fort effectively conveys a style of architecture wholly suited to the time and place in which the original owners built it: high, windowless walls present a formidable exterior to discourage attack; the thick adobe construction material, a mixture of straw and clay, insulates effectively year-round. A central plaza provides protected yet open interior space with direct access to warehouses, trading rooms, workshops, and living quarters. The Park Service's reconstruction effort has produced a life-sized model that honestly recreates a sense of the past.

As a concession to the modern era, a prerecorded tape message describes the history of Bent's Fort, and modern restrooms are hidden at the end of a narrow arcade. Otherwise, no dioramas, informational signboards, slide shows, or book stands detract from the atmosphere. Mercifully, the Fort site remains largely in a pristine state, with no gasoline stations, ranch homes, or power lines to deteriorate the view. When Frémont's second expedition camped at Bent's Fort in early July of 1844, his cartographer, who rarely found anything in the West to his liking, complained bitterly of the mosquitos. A visit to the Fort in the same month of the year nearly 140 years later will confirm that some things never change—civilizations may rise and fall, but the insect population endures.

Bent's Old Fort is located on Colorado Highway 194, about eight miles northeast of LaJunta. Visitors who wish to see the countryside surrounding the Fort have two choices: they can take a short hike from the Fort to the Arkansas River, enjoying the lush vegetation along the river banks, or they can drive a dozen or so miles south of LaJunta on Colorado 109 or US 550 to the interconnecting back roads of Commanche National Grassland. The bison and the prairie wagons are long since gone, of course, but the grasslands remain largely unchanged from the days when the Bent brothers traveled this route between their all-purpose frontier trading post and the exotic marketplaces in Taos and Santa Fe.

3 Commanche National Grassland

Location: southeastern Colorado

Size: 655 square miles of public grassland

Terrain: grassland with occasional rock outcrops and arroyos

Scenic Value: considerable

Historical Interest: substantial

Highway Access: US 50, US 350, US 287, and
US 160

Internal Access: US 35, US 160, US 287, Colorado 109, and an extensive network of improved and secondary roads

Maps: USFS map of Commanche National
Grassland at 1:125,000
USGS sheets 2 and 3 of Otero County, sheet
7 of Las Animas County, and sheets 1, 3, and
4 of Baca County at 1:50,000

For many millennia a state of equilibrium existed on the high plains. The soils absorbed moisture that fell to the ground while grasses and other vegetation used the water to form a protective cover over the soil, evapotranspirating some of their moisture back into the atmosphere. The grasses, nurtured by water and minerals trapped in the soil, supported a host of vegetarians from rabbits to bison. The carnivores fed upon the vegetarians and upon each other, and the omnivores sustained themselves on both flora and fauna. Even man, the ultimate predator, initially did little to change this balance of nature—less because prehistoric and early peoples did not wish to intervene than because the means to do so had not yet become available.

When the means did become known, change occurred rapidly, altering the character of a fragile land. Where water could be applied to the soil, as occurred along most of the lower Arkansas Valley, agriculture and commerce flourished. On the tablelands above the valley, however, no feasible method of irrigation existed, and the landscape offered no natural respite from the wind, the heat, and the cold. There the cruel environment failed to support crop cultivation or intensive grazing on a long-term basis.

This drama of a harsh, fragile land defeating those who sought to change it is particularly evident at Commanche National Grassland. The environment here tends to be hotter, drier, and more desolate than along the lands north of the Platte River. Thin vegetation and more parched soils enhance the likelihood of erosion. The sun beats down unmercifully, making the struggle for existence dif-

ficult. South of the Arkansas River in a dry summer the climate is truly arid, supporting a desert grassland that seems on the verge of dying out completely.

Yet this is an enigmatic land, supporting contrasts. Fresh vegetation sprouts from a roadway while the adjacent prairie grasses wither. Calves frolic in a pasture near the skeletal remains of a decomposed steer. A jackrabbit bounds across a cemetery near Timpas. The distant Spanish Peaks hover above the horizon in the morning light, reminding the grasslands visitor and resident that the world is not altogether flat. The visual impact of these contrasts, which elsewhere might not be so striking, is heightened by the character of the grassland: the dark, somber colors of later summer, the remoteness of the location, the lack of topographic relief, and the immense blue sky above. Together, these features generate a sense of isolation in a brightly illuminated landscape of minutely detailed patterns that are repeated endlessly across the horizon. Any irregular elements stand out in sharp contrast, like mismatched tiles on a parqueted floor.

Although the Commanche National Grassland lies well removed from any major population centers and was only sparsely settled, it remains an area of significant historical interest. These grasslands sit astride a famous path of commerce and migration. Starting in the early 1820s, trade routes developed between the United States and the Spanish Southwest that lay beyond the boundaries of the Louisiana Purchase. Among the best known of these routes was the Santa Fe Trail. Starting in Independence, Missouri, it led through Kansas and up the Arkansas River to the vicinity of LaJunta; from there it traveled across the high plains and over Raton Pass to Taos and the Rio Grande Valley of New Mexico.

To avoid the Raton Pass crossing, many later travelers took the Cimarron Cutoff, detouring through what is now southwestern Kansas and the Oklahoma panhandle. This southern route across the "Cimarron Desert" traversed a portion of the Cimmaron National Grassland in Kansas, passing a dozen or so miles below the southern portion of Commanche National Grassland. The Mountain Branch, as the original route was often called, descended from the Arkansas River and cut through what is now the northern unit of Commanche National Grassland, bisecting it approximately along the present-day route of US Highway 350. On Colorado 71, close to its intersection with US 350, the Daughters of the American Revolution have placed an inconspicuous stone marker commemorating the main route of the Santa Fe Trail.

The two units of Commanche National Grassland

An abandoned homestead fence on Commanche National Grassland.

Prairie rattler by the roadside, Commanche National Grassland.

are separated by one-half hour of driving time, and the southern unit encompasses a sprawling jurisdiction some seventy miles long. To visit both units requires a full day of energetic traveling. The northern unit, adjacent to US Highway 50, is the more compact, accessible, and historically interesting of the two units; US 350 and Colorado 109 both cut through it. The part of the unit along David Canyon Road and to the south and east of Timpas offers the most varied and interesting terrain. This northern unit lies only a short distance from Bent's Old Fort, affording visitors an opportunity to observe the high-plains backcountry that made the fort a favorite resting place for trappers, traders, hunters, and commercial travelers trekking between St. Louis and Santa Fe. The southern unit of Commanche National Grassland is readily accessible from US 160 east of Trinidad, Colorado; it offers the high-plains traveler a grasslands experience similar to the northern unit. The southeastern portion of the southern unit provides the most varied and interesting terrain within the unit; here the prairie tablelands give way to a distinctly Southwestern landscape of arroyos and small canyons.

Visitors to either of the Commanche Grassland units should be prepared to travel at their own risk on lightly trafficked back roads rarely visited by Forest Service personnel or anyone else and periodically subject to washouts, deep mud, and arbitrary private landowner closures. Foot travel is also necessary in the Commanche National Grassland if a visitor wishes to appreciate the environment, and at no time of the year is the grassland experience more intense than under a brilliant midsummer sky. However, two cautions are in order. First, even short-distance walking should be done while properly attired to avoid danger from the broken glass, rusted nails, cactus spines, barbed wire, and occasional rattlesnakes that are found on the grassland. Second, midday summer temperatures on the Commanche National Grassland often soar to desert levels far in excess of 100 degrees. The heat begins building rapidly by midmorning, and extreme temperatures can persist through early evening. This intense dry heat rapidly saps body strength and deteriorates mental judgment, producing disorientation and dizziness. Midday hiking, if done at all under hot-weather conditions, requires a hat, sturdy boots, deeply tinted sunglasses, ample liquids, and desert hiking experience.

View of the Spanish Peaks from Lathrop State Park. ➤

4 Lathrop State Park

Location: west of Walsenburg
Size: about 2 square miles
Terrain: grassland with piñon–juniper uplands
Scenic Value: considerable
Historical Interest: slight
Highway Access: from US 160
Internal Access: by all-weather road, foot trail, and boat
Maps: Colorado Division of Parks and Outdoor Recreation sketch map
USGS sheet 2 of Huerfano County at 1:50,000

Lathrop State Park, located a few miles west of Walsenburg, offers a wide variety of recreational amenities in a typical south-central Colorado setting of high-plains grassland and piñon–juniper uplands rising to wooded ridges. The park's appeal derives from the opportunity to pursue various recreational activities in a transitional landscape where the grasslands rise up to meet the mountains. To the east the plains stretch gently downward across eastern Colorado. The Sangre de Cristo Mountains rise to the west, and beyond them lie the San Luis Valley and the San Juan Mountains.

The most dramatic vista that Lathrop State Park offers is a striking view of the Spanish Peaks, located about twenty miles south in San Isabel National Forest. From the easy hiking trail that ascends the rock outcroppings at the north edge of the park (a two-mile circle trip) visitors can enjoy views of East and West Spanish peaks and, weather conditions permitting, Pikes Peak far to the north, along with several other lesser peaks.

The west side of Lathrop Park offers a wholly different environment. This portion of the park includes a wildlife management area in a grasslands setting, where migratory waterfowl abound in season. In addition, the park supports a population of coyotes, rabbits, occasional deer, and other smaller mammals, along with a variety of birds. Since rattlesnakes also inhabit Lathrop Park, visitors should exercise caution while hiking in the grass or near rocks. Fishing is popular year round at the two lakes in the park, both of which are stocked with rainbow trout and channel catfish.

In addition to hiking, sightseeing, bird watching, and fishing, Lathrop State Park offers picnicking, camping, swimming, waterskiing, sailing, and both small-game and waterfowl hunting. Camping facilities include ninety-eight units complete with showers, flush toilets, and a laundry; the city of Walsenburg provides a golf course adjacent to the park. Horseshoe Lake, in the western portion of the park, is closed to water-contact sports such as swimming and waterskiing.

Visitors to the park, which was established in 1962 and named after the first director of the Colorado Division of Parks and Outdoor Recreation, should consider visiting other attractions in the area. These include the southern extension of San Isabel National Forest (home of the Spanish Peaks), Great Sand Dunes National Monument, and the Wet Mountain Valley. To travel through the Wet Mountain Valley, take Colorado Highway 69 north from Walsenburg to Westcliffe or continue on to Cotopaxi, located on US 50 beside the Arkansas River. One particularly scenic side trip in the Wet Mountain Valley includes a journey, starting at Gardner, along the lovely upper Huerfano River to Red Wing, returning to US 160 by way of the Pass Creek Pass road. The Pass Creek route, however, is not well suited to trailers or passenger cars with limited ground clearance.

See, vast trackless spaces,
As in a dream they change, they swiftly fill,
Countless masses debouch upon them,
They are now covered with the foremost people, arts,
    institutions, known

Walt Whitman, "Starting from Paumanok,"
Leaves of Grass

II. The Front Range

On a clear day, travelers entering Colorado from the east encounter a sight that has stirred the imagination for generations. On the horizon a low ridgeline appears, barely visible from the rolling prairie crests. Then the ridgeline grows gradually in height and breadth until it becomes a snow-capped mountain range soaring two miles above the prairie and stretching from one end of the horizon to the other. Something stirs in the memory, recalling to the traveler's mind that long-forgotten image of purple mountain majesties above the fruited plain. Here, indeed, they exist in a setting of appropriately epic grandeur. No chamber of commerce could arrange a better introduction to Colorado.

Among geologists, these snowcapped mountains visible from the plains are called the Colorado Front Range. The most easterly spur of the Rockies, they extend in a narrow band about thirty miles wide from the Wyoming border south to the vicinity of Cañon City. On their western edge, the Front Range peaks gradually give way to other ranges, but along their eastern flank, they rise abruptly from the plains with only a thin belt of rolling hills and hogback ridges separating them from the grasslands below.

Both this series of mountain ridges and the adjoining high plains are often referred to as the front range. In this less technical usage, the front range encompasses a fifty- to sixty-mile-wide mountain–plains zone straddling the 105th meridian of longitude from north of Fort Collins to south of Pueblo. Economically and politically, this narrow region is the heartland of Colorado; it houses about eighty percent of the state's population, most of its industry, the chief financial centers, the seat of government, and the core of Colorado's transportation and communication networks. Despite the steady growth of urban sprawl, the front range still includes many landscapes of haunting beauty and sites of extraordinary geological interest. Spectacular rock formations, lovely canyons, steep-walled gorges, and other scenic attractions occur throughout this mountain–plains borderland.

Though natural beauty has long been a characteristic of the front range, only in recent times did the region emerge as the state's dominant commercial and population center. The exploration and settlement of Colorado originally occurred from the south, as Spanish explorers and traders pushed up the Rio Grande into the San Luis Valley. Spanish settlers founded San Luis, Colorado's oldest still-functioning community, nearly a decade before Denver existed. This nation's bloodless victory in the Mexican War of 1846 ended Spanish dreams of a Rocky Mountain empire, but one other event proved crucial to the future development of the front range. In the summer of 1858, prospectors found placer gold in Dry Creek and soon established townsites nearby on both banks of Cherry Creek at its confluence with the South Platte River. Thus Denver was born, the name of the infant town being chosen to honor the governor of Kansas Territory, General James Denver. The following year brought additional gold finds above Boulder Creek, in Fountain Creek, and along Clear Creek. Communities quickly sprang up at Boulder, Gold Hill, Pueblo, Black Hawk, and Central City, and the Pikes Peak Gold Rush got under way in earnest. As miners discovered rich lodes of ore, the mountain and plains towns competed fiercely for the glory and profits that soon accumulated. Ultimately, better access, lower transportation costs, and more growing room allowed the flatland communities to prevail. With diversified economies based on mining, agriculture, and local industry, they could survive the severe economic fluctuations that destroyed those mountain towns solely dependent for their existence on gold or silver.

The advent of World War II brought renewed

◄ *Front Range view from the high plains.*

growth to the front range as defense contractors and military installations located in the area. In the postwar period, growth continued – first at a slow pace, then at an accelerating rate. Aerospace and high-technology firms, followed by the energy industry, fueled an expanding economy. The growth of tourism and a general population drift from the frost-belt states to the sun-belt region provided further economic stimulus. A steel, glass, and concrete canyon of skyscrapers sprang up in downtown Denver, and the population soared in Fort Collins, Boulder, the Denver suburbs, and Colorado Springs.

As the population expanded along the front range, so too have air quality, water quality, and other environmental problems multiplied. Longtime residents recall, wistfully, the days when the thin, dry air of the region made it a haven for persons afflicted with respiratory problems. Ironically, a still earlier generation could recall the era when front range ore smelters, open incinerators, and coal-burning furnaces belched pollutants into the thin atmosphere.

The problems that occurred then and now stem from the special physical setting of the front range, which is not naturally well suited to support large urban populations. Situated in a rain shadow on the leeward side of the Rockies, the region rarely receives ample moisture. Natural stream flows are insufficient to satisfy water demand along the front range, requiring the costly diversion of water from the western slope to the east side of the Rockies. What little moisture the front range does get often arrives in the form of cloudbursts which can swell streams, already filled with spring runoff, to raging torrents. Starting with Auraria and Denver, built along the banks of Cherry Creek and the South Platte River, front range towns sprang up in the shallow river valley floodplains. And starting with a disastrous flood on Cherry Creek in 1864, front range communities have continued to pay a high price for building in floodplains that look deceptively harmless until an upstream cloudburst occurs.

Because of its proximity to the mountains and because of the prevailing weather patterns, the front range is highly susceptible to seasonal atmospheric inversions that trap airborn pollutants in the shallow urban basins, causing smog. The thin air, which contains significantly less oxygen than at sea level, exacerbates the effect of elevated pollution levels on the population. Even the front range soils present an obstacle to urban settlement. They contain high concentrations of a swelling-prone clay, called bentonite, which can fracture foundations and crack the walls of buildings improperly constructed on it. To this list of woes must be added the addi-

tional hazards presented by high winds that occasionally sweep along the front range, and by abnormally high levels of radiation in some front range soils and water supplies as the result of naturally occurring radioactive elements in the ground.

The presence of natural hazards, however, has never long deterred man from building cities where he pleased – whether it be along the flood-prone valleys of Mesopotamia, in the shadow of Mount Vesuvius, or astride the San Andreas Fault. The dictates of commerce have always taken precedence over proximity to natural hazards in the history of city building. The front range is no exception to this rule. It lies close to a treasure trove of mineral wealth and includes productive agricultural lands. Shallow valleys and gently rolling plains offer good transportation access to the east, the north, and the south. Mountain rivers afford natural gateways leading deep into the Rockies. Moreover, despite occasional extremes, the climate tends to be dry and mild with an abundance of sunshine.

The front range offers an additional attraction for recreational enthusiasts – it lies within a transitional zone that includes both plains and mountains. Ecologists call the border area within this kind of region an ecotone or tension zone. Typically it supports a greater number of plant and animal species than exist in either of the adjoining zones. The more tolerant species from each of the bordering areas can inhabit it, and an ecotone sometimes supports additional species not well adapted to any neighboring communities. Front range landforms exhibit these same characteristics. Prairie grasslands extend to the edge of the mountain province and even spill over into some foothills valleys, as at Lory State Park. In addition, the front range includes its own unique landforms, most notably the hogback ridges and sandstone formations that rise so dramatically at Red Rocks Park, Roxborough Park, the Garden of the Gods, and various other locations.

Mountain rivers flowing down to the plains have carved magnificent rock canyons looming above the grasslands. These steep-walled canyons, which dominate the mouth of the Cache la Poudre River, Boulder Creek, South Boulder Creek, Clear Creek, and a number of other streams, serve both as mountain gateways and as intensively used recreational sites for activities ranging from technical rock climbing to fishing and picnicking. Then, too, the grassland portion of the front range includes additional attractions, such as the splendid canyon setting at Castlewood Canyon State Park.

At present, however, the future of the front range hangs in the balance. Will it be graded and paved to make way for an undifferentiated strip city sprawling more than 100 miles across the prairie and foothills, swamping the landscape under a sea of mansard roofs and glass-slab architecture? Will urban enclaves of instant-chalet architecture overrun our mountain valleys? Or will we manage to concentrate front range growth in clustered, energy-efficient patterns, preserving intact for future generations a countryside that continues to delight the eye and please the senses? The growth of urban areas is not necessarily incompatible with the preservation of natural beauty – but neither is it inevitable that this beauty will be preserved.

Roadside grass beside Barr Lake State Park.

5 Castlewood Canyon State Park

Location: south of Denver/east of Castle Rock

Size: about 80 acres

Terrain: steeply cut canyon surrounded by a rolling valley

Scenic Value: very high

Historical Interest: slight

Highway Access: Colorado 86 from Colorado 83 or Interstate 25

Internal Access: Castlewood Canyon Road and on foot

Maps: USGS sheet 2 of Douglas County at 1:50,000

Castlewood Canyon is one of the best-kept secrets in the Denver metropolitan area. A vest-pocket park only eighty acres in size, it is located in eastern Douglas County halfway between Castle Rock and Franktown. No highway signs point out the location, and it is situated in a deeply eroded canyon that cannot be seen from neighboring roads.

What Castlewood Canyon State Park lacks in size or fame is readily compensated for in scenic beauty. The surrounding countryside is a gently rolling valley with occasional rock outcrops and a fine view of Pikes Peak to the southwest. Within this setting is a steeply cut canyon that contains an ecosystem unique to the area. At the bottom of the canyon, Cherry Creek meanders downstream and the sides

18

View of Castlewood Canyon, looking north.

Cherry Creek in Castlewood Canyon State Park.

of the canyon are lush with pine, scrub oak, and other species of vegetation not commonly found on the prairie tablelands. Above the vegetation rise dramatic rock walls punctuated by an occasional tree jutting skyward.

When I first visited the park early one summer morning a few years ago, the setting was highlighted by a crisp blue sky, a few cumulus clouds building in the distance, and a hawk drifting about overhead in lazy spirals. The busy skyscrapers of downtown Denver are only thirty miles distant, and the malignant sprawl of Douglas County subdivisions has crept to within ten minutes' driving time of Castlewood Canyon. But the park is so secluded and bucolic that it seems set in a remote landscape far removed from any urban intrusions and the canyon walls provide a sense of visual confinement, effectively closing out images of the exterior world.

At the south end of Castlewood Canyon is the Castlewood Canyon Dam, on private land at a point where the canyon broadens into a valley. This masonry structure, constructed for irrigation purposes in 1890, ruptured nearly a half century ago, causing one million dollars' worth of property damage and killing two people. The jagged remains of the dam are a scenic but grim reminder that ultimately all engineering solutions fail. This dam, built in a time predating the civilian construction programs of the U.S. Army Corps of Engineers, will also remind visitors that there was once a day when dams were attractive structures, blending into and enhancing the natural beauty of their settings.

The other principal attraction of Castlewood Canyon Park is a waterfall created at a point where Cherry Creek plummets some forty feet into a small pool. Here, close to the deepest point in the canyon, the sense of solitude, broken only by the sound of falling water and the chirp of insects, is at its most intense.

A short trail beginning at the roadside and traveling south provides scenic views of the falls. Several steep, rough trails descend the embankment, providing access for hikers who wish to visit the creek either above or below the falls. Hiking should be done with caution, however, for the Colorado Division of Parks and Outdoor Recreation warns that the abundant wildlife in the area includes prairie rattlesnakes, whose skin coloring camouflages all too well with such canyon settings.

To visit Castlewood Canyon State Park, take Interstate 25 or Colorado Highway 83 (Parker Road) to Colorado 86. Turn south on Castlewood Canyon Road about one-quarter mile west of Colorado 83 and proceed three miles to the park entrance. Interstate 25 is the quickest access route to Castlewood Canyon, but Colorado 83, starting either in Denver or Colorado Springs, provides a more scenic though sometimes traffic-clogged route to Castlewood Park. Visitors to the area may also wish to see the Cherry Creek Recreation Area, located about fifteen miles to the north on Colorado 83. This popular recreational site surrounds another stretch of Cherry Creek, impounded behind an earthen dam and spread across a shallow valley at the edge of suburban Denver.

6 Barr Lake State Park

Location: northeast of Denver

Size: 4 square miles

Terrain: high-plains reservoir and grassland

Scenic Value: moderate

Historical Interest: modest

Highway Access: Interstate 25

Internal Access: gravel road, on foot, and by boat

Maps: USGS sheet 1 of Adams County at 1:50,000
Colorado Division of Parks and Outdoor Recreation sketch map, unscaled

Barr Lake State Park, located on the Adams County prairie about thirty miles from downtown Denver, is a high-plains grassland surrounding a large reservoir that supports an extensive population of common and exotic birds.

Barr Lake's location is hardly conducive to a genuine wilderness experience. Commercial airliners rumble overhead on their way to and from Stapleton International Airport, and the mainline Burlington Northern railroad tracks, which carry a heavy volume of freight traffic, parallel the park along its northeast boundary. Yet the resident and migratory birds inhabiting the park seem undisturbed by these intrusions, and the park's location is otherwise ideal. Lying on the outskirts of Denver, it is readily accessible from anywhere in Colorado's largest metropolitan area. The setting is semiarid grassland with tall, straw-colored grasses blowing in the wind and sunflowers scattered about the landscape. Thick stands of cottonwood grow adjacent to the lake, and lush riparian vegetation blankets the shoreline. In addition, Barr Lake is located close enough to the Front Range that visitors can enjoy watching Longs Peak, the Indian Peaks, and other Front Range landmarks shimmering along the western horizon. On clear mornings, the sight of these snowcapped peaks in the distance serves as a reminder that a very different world lies close at hand.

The motivation for the construction of Barr Lake was not recreational, but agricultural, to which the several irrigation ditches running through the park attest. Because the lake is still used to supply local irrigation needs, the water level fluctuates dramatically during the course of the year. In fact, at low-water level the reservoir separates into two pools divided by a land mass that emerges in the middle of the lake. In late summer this variation in water level creates acres of dense, colorful vegetation as aquatic plants spring up along the wetlands left by the receding shoreline.

A shoreline view of Barr Lake State Park.

Despite the multiple purposes served by Barr Lake, its history as a popular resort area dates back to Colorado's early days of statehood. The lake was once an elite sportsman's playground with a reputation for some of the finest fishing in the West. Industrial pollution dramatically deteriorated water quality for a number of years, but since the passage of federal water pollution legislation, the quality of the reservoir and its ability to support fish and birds have improved. Starting in 1977, the Colorado Division of Parks and Outdoor Recreation gained responsibility for administration of the reservoir and a surrounding area of about one square mile as a public park.

The management emphasis at Barr Lake decidedly favors conservation values and nonmotorized forms of recreation. Vehicular traffic is limited to several short roads on the east side of the park. However, an extensive network of paths for hiking, bicycling, and horseback use encircle the reservoir and branch out along the many irrigation canals in the area. Powerboats are prohibited altogether from Barr Lake, while sailboats and hand-propelled craft may not be operated in the south end of the lake. Pets must remain on a leash in the north end of the park, and they are prohibited in the wildlife refuge.

These strict efforts to minimize human intrusions on the south side of Barr Lake were undertaken in order to build and maintain a wildlife refuge for waterfowl and other birds. The area presently supports a bird population that includes owls, eagles, falcons, geese, and gulls, along with such locally exotic species as white pelicans, great blue herons, egrets, grebes, and cormorants. Observation blinds are available on the south side of the park for bird watching. Though many bird species populate the reservoir on a full-time basis, autumn, when the migratory season is under way, remains the best time of year to watch the great flocks of birds that travel the Central Flyway.

Waterfowl hunting is permitted at Barr Lake on a controlled basis at the hunting blinds located on the north edge of the park. The state also permits fishing on the north side of the reservoir, which game officials stock with trout, perch, bass, and other species. Barr Lake offers no camping facilities, and the picnicking facilities are limited. The intensive management practices in evidence at Barr Lake State Park effectively preclude many forms of outdoor recreation. Trail-bike enthusiasts, water-skiers, and snowmobilers clearly are not welcome here. However, the restriction of uses has created a specialty park unique in the variety of wildlife it supports in such close proximity to a major metropolitan area.

Wildlife refuge area at Barr Lake State Park.

21

7 Lory State Park

Location: north-central Colorado/west of Fort Collins

Size: about 4 square miles

Terrain: enclosed valley surrounded by foothills

Scenic value: considerable

Historical Interest: slight

Highway Access: US 287

Internal Access: gravel road and foot trails

Maps: USGS sheet 4 of Larimer County at 1:50,000

Colorado Division of Parks and Outdoor Recreation sketch map at about 1:25,000

Lory State Park preserves for public use a lovely plains–foothills transitional environment on the west end of Horsetooth Reservoir, just outside of Fort Collins. Once private ranchland, the park was purchased by the State of Colorado in 1967 and named in honor of Dr. Charles A. Lory, who served as president of Colorado State University from 1909 to 1940.

At the core of the park is a U-shaped valley carpeted with rich prairie grasses and bisected by a well-graded gravel road. Gently scalloped sandstone formations, known as hogbacks, border the eastern edge of this valley, and beyond these ridges lie Horsetooth Reservoir and the fertile farming lands of eastern Larimer County. The west side of the valley is formed by steep rock walls lightly covered by broken stands of timber and cut by small canyons giving access to the higher, more rugged western edge of Lory State Park. Scrub oak grows beside the rock formations at the edge of Horsetooth Reservoir, knee-high grasses interspaced with prickly-pear cactus predominate in the valley, while at the higher elevations in the park, ponderosa pine and other mountain flora occur. The variety of terrain within Lory Park supports a diversity of wildlife including deer, bear, grouse, turkey, rabbits, prairie rattlers, and, according to the Division of Parks and Outdoor Recreation, bobcats and an occasional mountain lion.

The special charm of Lory State Park derives, however, not from any single feature but from its secluded location in an area offering such a wide

Grassland and hogback ridges in Lory State Park.

variety of attractive views. The nicely sheltered valley of the park provides a central vantage point, situated well above the eastern Colorado plains but walled in by the foothills bordering it on the west. Between the valley and the flatlands rise the undulating, sculptured formations of the hogbacks, which recede toward the horizon like a wave frozen in time. Adding to the visual effect is an unusual variety of textures: the distant patterning of life on the plains, the fine detail of prairie grass reaching into the distance, and the sharply carved rock formations jutting upward in angular contrast to the remainder of the landscape. The sum of these elements, seen in the soft light of midmorning or later afternoon, leaves the traveler with a strong sense of having visited a unique terrain harmoniously formed from the separate pieces of a huge jigsaw puzzle.

The remote location of Lory State Park enhances the secluded character of the area. Bordered on the east and west by manmade and natural obstacles, and on the south by a roadless private ranching valley, the park is reachable only from the north.

Starting from US Highway 287 at La Porte, the route travels west on Colorado 28 to the Belleview store. From there it is a three-mile trip to the park entrance. In this short journey, the countryside changes in distinct steps from rich, irrigated cropland to rolling foothills and narrow valleys.

In addition to sightseeing, Lory State Park offers backcountry camping (by permit only at designated sites), horseback riding, hunting, twenty-two miles of designated hiking trails, and some interesting technical rock climbing on Arthur's Rock, located two miles from the southern end of the road. Picnicking facilities include both individual sites and a group picnic area, available on a reservation basis, that can accommodate up to 150 people.

Visitors to the park may wish to combine their trip with an excursion to the several other recreational sites in the area. Directly east of Lory Park is Horsetooth Reservoir, a popular water-sports area. West of the park, by way of US Highway 287 and Colorado 14, is the scenic Poudre River, a lovely free-flowing river that descends from Cameron Pass.

8 Eldorado Canyon State Park

Location: south of Boulder
Size: about 320 acres
Terrain: steep-walled canyon
Scenic Value: very high
Historical Interest: moderate
Highway Access: Colorado 93 and Colorado 170
Internal Access: gravel road and on foot
Maps: USGS single sheet of Boulder County at 1:50,000

South Boulder Creek, descending from its headwaters high in the Front Range, has carved a steep canyon through the rock walls that rise above the foothills of Boulder County. At the very mouth of the canyon, where the stone is brightly hued, a series of massive rock formations tower above the town of Eldorado Springs. This dramatic setting, coupled with mineral springs in the area, long ago established Eldorado Springs as a resort community that once enjoyed a national reputation.

The sheer rock formations surrounding the canyon entrance have also made the area a nationally recognized center for technical rock climbers wishing to pit their skill against some of the most demanding rock walls in North America. For many decades Eldorado Canyon remained a local preserve for Colorado climbers. Then, late in the 1950s Layton Kor arrived in Colorado, having conquered a variety of hair-raising climbs on the massive rock formations in the Yosemite Valley. Kor, whose climbing abilities were legendary in the rarefied world of technical rock climbing, pioneered a string of first ascents on Redgarden Wall, the Bastille, and other lesser-known formations in Eldorado Canyon. Other California climbers followed Kor's example, and the Colorado climbing community joined the effort to ascend sheer routes that a decade or so earlier were thought unclimbable.

Although most of the major challenges that the canyon walls offer have been conquered at least once, the area remains a climbing paradise filled with easily accessible, high-quality rock fractured in challenging patterns. As morning sunlight filters

Rock formations in Eldorado Canyon State Park.

through the canyon, visitors can watch a strange breed of sports enthusiasts arriving to practice their craft. They come dressed in the standard uniform of the sport: battered climbing boots, shorts, and ragged T-shirts, with fifty-meter coils of rope slung over the shoulder, and equipment bandoliers strung with a bewildering variety of climbing hardware. Technical climbing is principally a participant sport; one that has been described as producing long periods of boredom interrupted by brief moments of terror. It also makes an interesting spectator sport, however, as roped climbing teams ascend a sunlit rock wall and bouldering aficianados practice their low-level acrobatic moves on the rocks that jut up from the roadside.

In addition to the joys of technical climbing, Eldorado Canyon State Park offers fishing, hiking, and picnicking opportunities. In late spring and early summer the canyon is at its most scenic, with a profusion of wildflowers and the creek tumbling down small waterfalls. Eldorado Canyon can also prove attractive in the wintertime. When gentle snow is falling, a softness descends on the land-scape, blotting out extraneous detail and blurring the angular rock walls. An eerie silence pervades this cathedral setting, the mood broken only by the distant ring of a piton entering rock as a solitary climbing party practices a winter ascent.

Although Eldorado Canyon is open year round, the State of Colorado has not gained access to the roadway leading west from the park; consequently, travelers must exit the site by the same route they entered. There is, however, no shortage of other recreational opportunities in the area. During the summer season, visitors can enjoy the mineral springs pool at Eldorado Springs. Directly to the north lies Boulder Mountain Park. This lovely local parkland provides extensive hiking opportunities beneath the flatirons, along with a variety of well-known technical climbing routes on the dramatic rock formations between Boulder and Eldorado Springs. Additional recreational attractions in the area include Flagstaff Mountain, located directly west of Boulder, and Boulder Canyon, which stretches between Boulder and Nederland along Colorado Highway 119.

Winter in Eldorado Canyon State Park.

9 Golden Gate Canyon State Park

Location: west of Golden

Size: about 14 square miles

Terrain: rolling meadows and wooded ridges

Scenic Value: moderate

Historical Interest: slight

Highway Access: Colorado 93, Colorado 72, and Colorado 119

Internal Access: paved and secondary roads and foot trails

Maps: USGS sheet 1 of Jefferson County and single sheet of Gilpin County at 1:50,000, Colorado Division of Parks and Outdoor Recreation sketch map at about 1:28,000

Golden Gate Canyon State Park occupies a slice of pretty, rolling countryside between Central City and Golden. The park features no dramatic canyons, awesome waterfalls, or sheer cliffs. Instead, it offers visitors a readily accessible and well-managed mountain park for camping, picnicking, hiking, fishing, horseback riding, hunting, and winter sports. Several small, friendly streams traverse the park, which includes one 10,000-foot peak (Tremont Mountain), a high ridgeline, several attractive meadows, and one of the best mountain vistas anywhere in the area.

From Golden, travelers can reach the park by Colorado Highway 93, turning west on Jefferson County Road 70. This winding route enters the park along Ralston Creek, leading to the visitor center and the south side of Golden Gate Park. About a mile west of the visitor center, the road forks. The main branch of the route exits the park by way of Golden Gate Canyon Road to Colorado 119, several miles north of Central City. The north branch, called Mt. Base Road, ascends a steep 19 percent grade (trailers are prohibited) along the west side of Promontory Ridge to the Reverends Ridge Campground and an exit route west to Colorado 119. A well-maintained gravel road continues to Panorama Point and several camping sites before exiting the north side of Golden Gate Park to Jefferson County Road 2. From here the route joins Colorado 72, ending at Colorado 93 several miles north of the Ralston Creek road into the south side of the park.

Promontory Point, located in the northwest corner of Golden Gate Canyon State Park, is the single most interesting site reachable by auto. Here, at a sprawling pavillion constructed by the Division of Parks and Outdoor Recreation, an imposing mountain panorama reaches across the western horizon. The mountain landscape extends from north of Longs Peak through the Indian Peaks and south to Grays and Torreys peaks. An illustrated signboard points out the names and locations of the various major peaks visible from Promontory Point.

No roads traverse the interior of Golden Gate Canyon State Park, in order to preserve the area in as pristine a state as possible. The interior is accessible by the forty miles of well-marked hiking and

Mountain landscape seen from the west side of Golden Gate Canyon State Park.

horseback trails available for public use. The park provides five different types of camping facilities for visitor use. The Reverends Ridge Campground offers 106 sites, complete with laundry and shower facilities. Aspen Meadow Campground, at the north edge of the park, includes twenty-two sites in a less highly developed setting. Primitive camping in the park's interior is available by permits issued at the main visitor center. The Rifleman Phillips Group Camping Area is set aside on a reservation basis for camping groups. In addition, Rimrock Loop at Aspen Meadows Campground provides camping facilities for horseback-riding groups and is also available on a reservation basis.

10 Roosevelt National Forest

Location: northern Colorado/east of the Continental Divide

Size: 1,232 square miles

Terrain: mountain peaks and river valleys

Scenic Value: very high

Historical Interest: considerable

Highway Access: primary access by US 34, US 36, Colorado 7, Colorado 14, Colorado 72, and Colorado 119

Internal Access: paved highways, improved and primitive dirt roads, and foot trails

Maps: USFS map of Roosevelt National Forest at 1:125,000
Various USGS sheets of Larimer, Boulder, and Gilpin counties at 1:50,000
USFS Indian Peaks Wilderness map at 1:63,000
USFS Boulder District Winter Sports Trails map at 1:32,000

For eons, rainwater and snowmelt originating high in the Rockies have tumbled down to the foothills and spilled onto the plains, forming a wide, shallow floodplain through which the South Platte River runs. In earlier ages, but quite recently by the standards of geological time, melting glaciers and a more humid climate than we know today in Colorado created raging torrents of water coursing down these mountain valleys. The action of water and erosion material, aided at higher elevations by glaciers, cut wide subalpine valleys and deep foothill canyons, flowing vast quantities of sand and aggregate onto the plains. Alluvial deposits stretching far beyond the recent floodplain boundaries of the Front Range streams give eloquent testimony to the magnitude of these older rivers.

Today these same streams continue to flow their water and sediment onto the plains. From Denver north to the Wyoming border, a series of streams drain into the South Platte: Coal Creek, Boulder Creek, St. Vrain Creek, the Little Thompson River, the Big Thompson River, and the Cache la Poudre River. In the springtime, following periods of rapid snowmelt and as the result of cloudbursts, these normally scenic mountain streams can quickly become raging torrents that sweep away nearly anything in their path.

Roosevelt National Forest, located in northern Colorado on the east side of the Continental Divide, is a patchwork federal forestland encompassing several dozen of these mountain waterways. Originally part of Medicine Bow Forest Reserve, it became Colorado National Forest in 1910. President Herbert Hoover renamed it in 1932 to honor Theo-

dore Roosevelt, the outdoorsman–president who maintained a particular love for the Colorado mountains and who wrote extensively about the West. Modern-day Roosevelt National Forest reaches from south of Boulder to north of Fort Collins, spanning the distance between the foothills and the Continental Divide. Established in a period when extensive human settlement already had occurred along much of the Front Range, Roosevelt Forest is

A winter scene by the East Portal of the Moffat Tunnel.

interspersed with numerous private holdings and a number of patented mining claims.

Early settlement in the area of Roosevelt National Forest began in the southern portion, along the canyons and ridges extending west from Boulder, where prospectors discovered surface deposits of gold in December 1858. This early discovery of gold occurred along the northeastern edge of what is known as the Colorado mineral belt, a band of highly mineralized rock starting in the western portion of Boulder County and extending southwesterly to the San Juan country around Telluride, Silverton, and Ouray. Most of the major ore discoveries in Colorado have occurred in this mineral belt, the major exceptions being the gold deposits at Cripple Creek, the silver ores around Silvercliffe and Westcliffe, and the uranium deposits of western Colorado near Uravan and Nucla. The history of precious-metal mining in Colorado tends to follow this northeast–southwest axis, starting in the Denver and Boulder area and then progressing through Central City to Breckenridge, Leadville, and Fairplay, the Aspen area, and the San Juans.

The early placer gold unearthed near Gold Hill, west of Boulder, soon resulted in additional discoveries around Ward, Nederland, Sunshine, and Magnolia. In 1869, prospectors discovered silver deposits at Caribou, high in the mountains above Nederland. By the end of the century, these mining towns had fallen into hard times and seemed destined for oblivion, but the discovery of tungsten ores in the Nederland area around 1900 again brought boom times to western Boulder County. From the start of the twentieth century to the end of World War I, Boulder County remained the nation's principal supplier of tungsten ore.

Mining products are themselves of little practical value without the transportation system necessary to haul in men and equipment and to transport the ore to a marketplace where it can be sold. Consequently, rail and wagon transportation routes, which are still used today, developed apace with mining activity in the southern end of Roosevelt National Forest.

The best known of these historic routes through the area was built by John Quincy Adams Rollins, a nineteenth-century entrepreneur who risked forty thousand dollars on a wagon road from north of Central City across Boulder Pass (known later as Rollins or Corona Pass) to Middle Park. The Denver, Northwestern and Pacific railroad converted the crossing into a railroad route, later adding the Moffat Tunnel to avoid the high, snowswept alpine crossing. Subsequently, the route was reconstructed for automobiles and now offers summer travelers access to lovely high-mountain countryside in that portion of Roosevelt and Arapaho national forests. The Forest Service provides an informative self-guiding auto-tour booklet with authoritative explanations of the historic and natural points of interest along the way, but the road is no longer a through route due to a rockfall in the tunnel near the summit. Visitors to the Rollins Pass area can also travel to the east portal of the Moffat Tunnel and explore the vast network of roads and trails around Eldora, Tolland, and Caribou.

Less well known than the Rollins Pass road is the railway network that once ran through the now heavily used recreational lands west of Boulder. The Colorado and Northwestern railroad, a subsidiary of the Union Pacific, constructed a narrow-gauge line from Boulder Canyon and Four Mile Canyon to Salina and Sunset. Starting in 1898, the Colorado and Northwestern Railway Company continued the route to Gold Hill, down to Left Hand Canyon, and on to Ward. Then, shortly after the turn of the century, the C&NW extended its tracks west from Sunset to Nederland and up Middle Boulder Creek to Eldora. Few remains of the railway can be seen today. Nevertheless, travelers intent on following the best-known portion of the route, chronicled in Forrest Crossen's book, *The Switzerland Trail,* can retrace this segment by taking the road from Salina to Sunset and then continuing toward Sugarloaf Mountain and west to the Peak to Peak Highway (Colorado Highway 72).

West of the Peak to Peak route is the Indian Peaks Wilderness. The designation of wilderness areas was authorized by the Wilderness Act of 1964, which defines a wilderness as "an area where the earth and its community of life are untrammeled by man, where man himself is a visitor who does not remain. . . ." Congress established the Indian Peaks Wilderness in 1978 from segments of Roosevelt and Arapaho national forests. This area, long thought by some people to merit inclusion within the boundaries of an expanded Rocky Mountain National Park, spans both sides of the Continental Divide for 120 square miles. Included within the wilderness are vast expanses of tundra and almost fifty alpine lakes topped by a range of imposing peaks. It is an intensively used recreational area, attracting a heavy volume of summertime hikers and winter travelers.

The Peak to Peak Highway from Nederland on Colorado 72 to Colorado 7 and Estes Park ranks among the most scenic all-weather highways in the Front Range, and it remains the most dramatic entrance route to Estes Park. When combined with a trip along the Big Thompson Canyon or a side excursion up the paved road to Brainard Lake, at the edge of the Indian Peaks Wilderness, it provides a comfortable day-long circle tour of the Front Range high country. I have enjoyed traveling the route for more than a decade now, with frequent side trips to explore the spiderweb of dirt roads branching from the main route.

When traveling the canyon portions of Roosevelt National Forest, travelers should bear in mind that flash flooding is an everpresent spring and summer-

Poudre Falls on the Cache la Poudre River.

time danger. The signs warning visitors to seek high ground in the event of flood were placed in the canyons following the Big Thompson disaster of 1976, when a flash flood in the canyon claimed more than 100 lives and caused many million dollars' worth of property damage. The ten Colorado canyons posing the greatest risk of catastrophic flooding, such as Boulder and Big Thompson, are concentrated along the front range from Fort Collins south.

The most scenic—and also one of the most flood-prone—Colorado canyons east of the Continental Divide traverses the northern portion of Roosevelt National Forest. This idyllic mountain river, twisting and tumbling downhill from its alpine headwaters north of Rocky Mountain National Park to Fort Collins, goes by a romantic name—Cache la Poudre. The name, uncommon in a territory not settled by the French, has an appropriately exotic story behind it. In 1836 a trapping party organized by the Hudson's Bay Fur Company was traveling from St. Louis to Green River, Wyoming. After camping beside the river one evening, they awoke in the morning to discover that a heavy snowfall blocked the route. In order to lighten the load of their wagons, the party cached provisions and gunpowder before moving onward; hence the French name meaning "hide the powder."

Whether this tale is true or not, it has provided a lovely name, nowadays commonly shortened to the Poudre, for the last of the free-flowing rivers along the front range. The territory adjacent to the Poudre contains no known significant mineral deposits and offers no broad valleys to support a large range-cattle industry or to cultivate row crops. Hence the area has experienced little human development to infringe on its natural beauty, and the Colorado Wilderness Act of 1980 designated a fifteen-square-mile segment as the Cache la Poudre Wilderness.

Starting at the mouth of the river and winding past the Narrows, a visitor can travel for dozens of miles beside a cascading river that offers a near-perfect picture of what a mountain stream should look like. Springtime, when the river reaches peak flow, is the most dramatic season to take the route (Colorado Highway 14) from Fort Collins to Cameron Pass, but it can prove beautiful in the autumn and be especially attractive after an early-season snowfall. Travelers who have seen the majestic Uncompahgre River stained bright yellow from mining drainages or who have viewed industrial pollution along stretches of the South Platte River should especially appreciate the Poudre—and help ensure that it remains forever in its relatively pristine state.

The Narrows on the Cache la Poudre River.

11 Pike National Forest

Location: central Colorado/Platte and Arkansas river basins

Size: 1,729 square miles

Terrain: mountain peaks and valleys

Scenic Value: very high

Historical Interest: high

Highway Access: Interstate 25, US 24, and US 285

Internal Access: paved highways, improved and primitive dirt roads, and foot trails

Maps: USFS map of Pike National Forest at 1:125,000
Various USGS sheets of Douglas, Jefferson, El Paso, Teller, Park, and Clear Creek counties at 1:50,000

On July 15, 1806, Lieutenant Zebulon Pike and his command of twenty-three men set out from St. Louis for the West. According to Pike's formal orders, his mission included locating the Red River, which the government in Washington took to be the boundary between the newly purchased Louisiana Territory and the Spanish Empire in the New World. Pike's actual mission, given him by the governor of the Louisiana Territory, more likely was to establish favorable contact with the Indian inhabitants of the southwestern portion of the territory, to scout out the terrain, and to spy on the Spanish. Nearly four months after starting out, Pike and his expedition reached Colorado by way of the Arkansas River. On November 15, Pike obtained his first view of the mountains. In his journal entry for that day he wrote:

> At two o'clock in the afternoon I thought I could distinguish a mountain to our right, which appeared like a small blue cloud; viewed it with the spy glass, and was still more confirmed in my conjecture. . . . When our small party arrived on the hill they with one accord gave three *cheers* to the *Mexican Mountains.*

Later the same month, Pike spent four days attempting to climb the highest ridge (known to him as Grand Peak) in the mountain chain he had first observed several weeks earlier. Insufficient knowledge of the terrain, inadequate equipment, and winter weather conditions defeated his attempt to scale the mountain we now call Pikes Peak. A successful assault on the summit would occur about a dozen years later when Stephen Long's expedition passed through the area. Much ink has been consumed in speculating on which peak Pike actually climbed in his attempt, and many theories on the subject abound, since insufficient evidence exists to prove any of them wrong – or right.

For the better part of the next month, Captain Pike and his followers explored to the north and west of the Colorado Springs area. Finally, in January 1807, the expedition crossed into the San Luis Valley and headed down the Rio Grande, where they were captured by Spanish soldiers and escorted to the interior of Mexico, not to be released from their involuntary-guest status until the spring of the following year.

Pike National Forest was created in 1907 from the Pikes Peak, Plum Creek, and South Platte timberland reserves. It is now an intensively used year-round forest playground, stretching west from the Colorado Springs suburbs and the outskirts of the Denver metropolitan area to the headwaters of the South Platte River. Encompassed within the forest is much of the territory that Captain Pike visited in the weeks following his unsuccessful climbing venture.

Ute Pass, located a short distance west of Colorado Springs, is the traditional gateway into the area. This attractive and historic route, which has received extensive use since prehistoric times, is also the path that the Colorado Midland Railway took from Colorado Springs to Aspen. The other famous gateway into Pike National Forest is the route from Denver up the South Platte River (now US Highway 285) to the top of Kenosha Pass and across the broad expanse of South Park to the rich mining districts that once reached from Montezuma through Breckenridge, Leadville, and beyond. It was this same route that the Denver, South Park and Pacific railroad followed from Morrison, on the outskirts of Denver, along the wall of the South Platte canyon, reaching the summit of Kenosha Pass on May 19, 1879. From there the narrow-gauge railroad tracks (only three feet wide, rather than the standard gauge's four feet and eight inches) descended across the South Park grasslands and entered the Arkansas Valley by way of Trout Creek Pass (now US 24), opening the way for the route's sturdy little locomotives to reach Gunnison. From South Park, another branch of the ambitious Denver, South Park and Pacific railroad cut north along the Breckenridge Pass wagon road, renamed Boreas Pass by the railroad men, to Breckenridge and eventually on to Leadville. The Boreas Pass route from Como to Breckenridge, now reconstructed as an automobile road, travels through an area rich in history.

To the east of Breckenridge, the discovery of rich ore deposits along both flanks of the Continental Divide brought a succession of mining booms to the northwest rim of the area encompassed by Pike

Mount Bierstadt and the Sawtooth from the Guanella Pass road.

National Forest. Thousands of fortune seekers swarmed up Handcart Gulch, Hall Valley, and nearly every other likely drainageway in search of the surest route to instant riches. They left in their wake an abandoned kingdom of mine buildings, ghost towns, and narrow, twisting roadways, the remains of which are still very much in evidence throughout the northern corner of Pike National Forest.

Probably the best-known point of interest in Pike National Forest is Pikes Peak. Well over one-quarter million visitors a year reach the summit that Zebulon Pike thought was unattainable, traveling there by auto road, cog railroad, on foot, and on horseback. The Pikes Peak auto road begins by US Highway 24 at Cascade; the cog railroad terminal is located in Manitou Springs. Every Fourth of July, the nationally famous Pikes Peak Hill Climb automobile race takes place on the upper portion of the road to the top of Pikes Peak. Also in the same portion of Pike National Forest is the well-known—and often heavily used—Rampart Range Road connect-

ing Sedalia and the Garden of the Gods area of Colorado Springs. This winding but well-graded dirt road travels through an attractive pine forest and affords several excellent plains vistas (especially from the rock outlook called Devil's Head), along with a progressively impressive view of Pikes Peak, when traveling the road south toward Colorado Springs.

The winding streamside roads along Buffalo Creek, Tarryall Creek, Elevenmile Canyon, Trail Creek, and the South Fork of the South Platte River are also popular and highly scenic byways through the eastern portion of the national forest. These routes are particularly delightful to travel during off-season periods, when the higher mountain routes are snowbound and before the summer tourist season begins in earnest.

The northern and western portions of Pike National Forest offer somewhat more remote and less frequently traveled mountain landscapes. The backcountry roads over Webster, Georgia, and Mosquito passes provide access to some of the most

34

A wintertime scene on the South Platte River near Deckers.

spectacular Colorado scenery east of the Continental Divide. The less primitive roads over Boreas, Weston, and Guanella passes offer additional high-country access for hiking, fishing, hunting, tour skiing, and just plain sightseeing. Near the summit of the Guanella Pass road, which is open to passenger cars year round, visitors can stop to admire one of the nicest wintertime views in the area: Mt. Bierstadt and the Sawtooth rising in snowcapped splendor from the Abyss Lake Scenic Area. The Pike National Forest side of the Guanella Pass road also leads to a downhill skiing area at Geneva Basin and a variety of cross-country skiing routes above and below timberline.

In the eastern portion of the rugged and little-visited Tarryall Mountain Range is the Lost Creek Scenic Area. The scenic area, about twenty-five square miles in size, offers a quality backcountry experience in an area of dramatic rock formations unexcelled elsewhere in this part of the state. The Colorado Wilderness Act of 1980 incorporated the scenic area into a newly designated 165-square-mile Lost Creek Wilderness. Another particularly dramatic area within Pike National Forest is located near Colorado Highway 9 as it approaches the summit of Hoosier Pass. To the west of the highway, at the northern end of the Mosquito range, three massive peaks rise above the valley: Mount Bross, Mount Lincoln, and Mount Democrat, all fourteeners. Beneath them is the Bristlecone Pine Scenic Area. These mountains and the surrounding high valleys, a site of extensive mining a century ago, can be reached by four access roads, the most easily negotiable of which is the route from Alma up Buckskin Creek. Just south is the historic and famous four-wheel-drive road to the summit of Mosquito Pass.

One additional feature of Pike National Forest deserving special mention is the series of reservoirs within and adjacent to it. Chatfield, Cheesman, Elevenmile Canyon, Tarryall, and Antero reservoirs are the largest of these bodies of water and the most popular of the water-based recreational sites stretching through Pike National Forest, but several dozen smaller lakes and reservoirs dot the landscape. It is in this area, near South Fork, that the Denver Water Board hopes to build the Two Forks Dam, which would inundate many miles of canyon country along the South Platte River.

12 Florissant Fossil Beds National Monument

Location: west of Colorado Springs

Size: 9 square miles

Terrain: subalpine meadowlands and forested ridges

Scenic Value: modest

Historical Interest: exceptional paleontological interest

Highway Access: from US 24 at the community of Florissant

Internal Access: by all-weather road and on foot

Maps: USFS map of Pike National Forest at 1:125,000
USGS single sheet of Teller County at 1:50,000

At first appearance, the site of Florissant Fossil Beds National Monument is unremarkable: rolling grasslands bordered by pine- and fir-covered ridges, with a distant view of Pikes Peak to the east. In a state noted for its dramatic landscapes, this quiet setting would seem to merit no special attention.

However, picture the same location in the Oligocene period, about thirty-five million years ago. Sprawling across the valley was a lake formed when flows of lava from a nearby volcanic field dammed an upstream drainage now called Grape Creek. The climate of the area then was subtropical, producing warm, moist weather in which more than a thousand insect species flourished. The elevation of the lake was about 3,000 feet, nearly a mile lower than the valley floor today. In place of the present flora was dense vegetation including palm trees, birch, oak, magnolia, and huge sequoia trees reaching perhaps 300 feet above the forest floor. Birds, fish, and smaller mammals inhabited the valley, but no human being would every gaze upon this scene. By the time man arrived, the forces of geology had reshaped the valley.

Considerable volcanic activity occurred during this ancient period, raining debris upon the area and causing mudflows of ash and water that swept through the forest surrounding the lake. Some of the trees killed by mudflows turned to stone, while plant and animal specimens were buried by the settling ash and washed into the lake, where they became fossilized as the accumulating ash compacted to form layers of shale. Eventually the lake filled in with debris, and grassy, rolling meadows emerged where the water had stood. But beneath the surface of this later fill, a rich geological record, a natural lithograph in stone, lay undisturbed and protected from the elements.

For at least the past eight thousand years, the area around the former lake has been the site of human activity. Early Indian peoples left evidence of their visits, and the Utes periodically inhabited the surrounding countryside until the early twentieth century. Shortly after the close of the Civil War, European settlers moved into the valley, constructing homesteads and grazing cattle where the waters of prehistoric Lake Florissant once supported a semitropical environment. One of the early settlers, Judge James Castello, founded the town of Florissant, which he named after the St. Louis, Missouri community where he grew up.

In 1874 Dr. A. C. Peale, a U.S. Geological Survey scientist, discovered fossil impressions in the lakebed shale. Since then, scientists have removed over eighty thousand specimens from their resting places. The site proved to be one of the richest fossil beds in the world, including more than 1,100 insect species, 140 different types of plants, and the petrified remains of several giant sequoia trees. The present monument museum building was constructed in 1924 and served as the headquarters for the Henderson Petrified Forest, which was later renamed the Pike Petrified Forest. This earlier facility remained in operation until the 1960s. Florissant Fossil Beds National Monument was established by Congress on August 20, 1969, and in 1974 the Park Service purchased the headquarters building and renovated it for use as a museum and administrative offices.

Visitors to Florissant Fossil Beds National Monument should try to visit the three central attractions offered by the monument. First on the list is a visit to the museum, where interpretive materials explain the geology of the area and where many of the finely detailed fossils are on display. The second feature is a short nature trail, less than one-half-mile long, that leads to the site of several fossilized sequoias and other subjects of interest. The third site of special interest is the renovated Hornbeck Homestead, located a short distance north of the monument headquarters building and adjacent to the main road.

At the homestead site, visitors can take a self-guided tour of the main house and outbuildings situated amidst the waving grasslands that once beckoned invitingly to so many pioneer homesteaders in search of free land and an unhampered life-style. The carefully restored homestead is surely more immaculate than a working frontier homestead would have been, but an afternoon visit to the site, with gathering storm clouds in the distance and a brisk wind blowing through the grass, effectively conveys a sense of what life on the frontier was like a century ago.

Fossilized Sequoia tree trunks at Florissant Fossil Beds National Monument.

An old wagon on the Hornbeck Homestead at Florissant Fossil Beds National Monument.

Land of sierras and peaks!

Walt Whitman, "Starting from Paumanok,"
Leaves of Grass

III. The Rockies

At least three times before the dawn of man, the land along the backbone of Colorado thrust upward, creating a succession of mountain ranges. Twice, erosion wore these mountains down to rolling plains. Then, primordial seas washed across the land and retreated, leaving in their wake deposits of sand and mud that compressed into rock and heaved upward as mountains reformed. After the most recent period of upheaval some seventy million years ago, when the earth once more rose up and volcanos spewed forth their lava and ash, erosion again took charge. Glaciers repeatedly advanced and receded, carving massive cirques in the rock and sweeping vast quantities of debris seaward through deepening mountain canyons. As the climate became more arid and mild, high lakes filled in with sediment, becoming mountain meadows, stream flows diminished, and the rate of erosion slowed.

Thus in broad-brush outline have the Rocky Mountains evolved in Colorado over a two-billion-year time span. So immense is this time period that if it were reduced to a single day, then the most recent geological era of mountain building and erosion, during which the modern Colorado Rockies were formed, would occupy only the past hour. Man's first known appearance in the region, as measured by this same shortened time scale, took place within the last second. And settlers of European ancestry have inhabited the Southern Rockies for a still briefer period of time.

During the past century, white settlers have brought more change to Colorado than did their predecessors in the previous ten thousand years — and still larger-scale changes seem likely to occur in the future. Yet it is important not to overestimate the magnitude of these events. Man may hollow out entire mountains, dam the once free-flowing rivers, and build sprawling towns across the valley floor. Measured, however, against the scale of natural forces working through geological periods of time, these activities seem trivial and transitory. If the past record of geological activity is a portent for the future, it is unlikely that any change wrought by man upon the mountain landscape will have a lasting impact. When another generation of mountain ranges rises up in place of the present Rockies, a new taxonomy will most likely be needed to classify the creatures that inhabit this future land.

The present and many future generations of man, however, will continue to live with the Rocky Mountains in their present form. The part of the Rockies that traverses Colorado is known as the Southern Rocky Mountain Province, and it consists largely of high, broad granite formations oriented along a north–south axis and flanked by softer, angled sedimentary rocks. At various locations throughout the province, most notably within the San Juan Range in southwestern Colorado, volcanic rock contributes significantly to the present-day configuration of the Rockies.

Although Colorado lies close to the southern end of the Rockies, it includes the very highest portion of the entire mountain system. At several other locations in the Rocky Mountain chain, even the tallest peaks reach an elevation of two miles or less above sea level. In Colorado, valley floors occasionally reach that elevation, and the tallest peaks soar thousands of feet higher. More than one thousand Colorado peaks rise above 10,000 feet, and fifty-four of the sixty-eight peaks in the contiguous United States that reach above 14,000 feet are in Colorado. Thirteen of the remaining "fourteeners," as they are called, occur in California; the remaining tall peak is Mount Ranier in Washington.

Because the elevation of many Colorado mountain valleys and parks is so high, the peaks rising above them seem lower than they actually are. To the west of the Arkansas Valley is the Sawatch Range, which includes the largest concentration of fourteeners found anywhere in the North American Rockies. Yet because the valley floor is nearly two miles high at its northern extremity, the neighboring mountains, which include Colorado's two tallest peaks, rise less than a mile above eye-level. Farther south in the valley, where the elevation drops several thousand feet, the Collegiate Group fourteeners soar nearly 7,000 feet above the valley, although their actual height is slightly less than the two peaks dominating the head of the valley. Similarly, the large Front Range peaks such as Longs Peak and Pikes Peak seem particularly impressive since they rise almost 10,000 feet above the plains.

The Colorado Rockies are imposing not only because of their sheer size, but on the basis of their extent and diversity, as well. The various spurs and branches of the Rockies sprawl across Colorado in a bewildering pattern of ridges, valleys, and peaks. Some fifty separate mountain ranges and groupings have been named in Colorado, and even a generalized classification includes about a dozen different ranges. Some of these, like the Front Range, are massive granite formations. Others, like the Elk Range, are capped with colorful sedimentary rock. Still others, like the San Juans, were formed principally of volcanic rock with some exposed granite uplifts, as in the Needle Mountain district. Colorado's mountainous terrain varies from rolling hills to massive flat-topped peaks, conical mountains, steeply angled rock slabs, jagged ridges, and soaring symmetrical peaks. On the east the Rockies rise abruptly from the high plains, while on the west they give way irregularly to the mesa and canyon country of the plateau province.

In the center of the Colorado Rockies lie three open basins, known as North Park, Middle Park, and South Park. Here, respectively, the headwaters of the North Platte, the Colorado, and the South Platte rivers arise. These rivers, in turn, flow through broad valleys and steep-walled canyons on their way toward the sea. The Southern Colorado Rockies include two adjacent valleys, each framed by mountain ranges and traversed by major rivers. The Rio Grande, originating high in the San Juans, flows across the broad expanse of the San Luis Valley. The Arkansas River crosses the scenic Wet Mountain Valley before plunging into the Royal Gorge.

Because temperature, precipitation, and wind vary with elevation, the abrupt changes in relief common to the Colorado Rockies produce a variety of climates. A day hike or a short automobile ride can be the equivalent of a journey several thousand miles to the north, from dry sage-covered hills to cold, moist tundra country 2,000 feet above the level where trees can survive. Nowhere is this pas-

sage through steeply layered life zones more evident than on the automobile roads to the tops of Pikes Peak and Mount Evans. In a single day's journey, travelers can sometimes experience the passage of three distinct seasons between the edge of the plains and the alpine zone above timberline.

In this alpine zone the environment is unremittingly harsh, and life remains a constant struggle against the elements. Only lichen, moss, short grasses, and a few low shrubs survive at this altitude, but in the summer the alpine tundra is often awash in a sea of small wildflowers that carpet the ground. Beyond the tundra, rock, snow, and ice predominate in this world of high ridges, glacially carved cirques, and panoramic views. It is the favored world of the true mountaineers, their just reward for having struggled upward from the valley floor and forests below.

Twisted, dwarf fir and spruce trees usually demarcate the timberline. Below this level exists a subalpine zone characterized by lodgepole pine and Englemann spruce mixed with stands of aspen. Known as an upper montane forest, this transitional zone tends to occur in Colorado at elevations between 10,000 and 11,500 feet. The montane zone, where ponderosa pine and Douglas fir predominate, occurs at a lower elevation. There, better soils, less wind, and warmer temperatures provide a more favorable environment to support the luxuriant growth of trees, shrubs, and grasses. The rich vegetation in turn provides ample wildlife habitat in the forests and well-watered meadows. Particularly when they provide the foreground setting for a sweeping alpine view, montane forests represent the conventional image of the Rocky Mountain woodlands.

Despite this popular picture of the Colorado mountains, Colorado's western mountain valleys and the boundary between the mountains and the plateau land lie within lower and much drier life zones. In transitional areas the vegetation includes piñon, juniper, and scrub oak; lower in the sonoran zone sage, greasewood, yucca, and cacti predominate. Where rivers travel through the dryland country, cottonwoods, poplars, and willows often grow across the road from desert vegetation. Tightly compressed life zones and contrasting landforms characterize the Colorado Rockies more than picture-postcard mountain views.

The Indians who first traveled these mountains understood well the different life zones, wintering in the valleys and hunting game in the summer high country. Early white trappers, traders, and miners, pushing westward beyond the plains, traveled these same valley routes whenever possible. Unlike the Indians, they held little if anything in the mountains sacred. Yet they, too, learned of the mountains; those that failed to do so soon perished or went broke.

This first wave of European immigrants to the West included a tough and amibitous breed of men willing to try almost anything, despite the risk of failure. Looking always for more gold and silver, they stripped out the streambeds, deforested hillsides, and tunneled through mountains. Pushing first roads, then railways across the top of the Rockies at elevations beyond where any paved roads or steel rails travel today, they constructed a spectacular though precarious frontier civilization in the high country. Much of their handiwork has vanished, the victim of fickle marketplaces and a harsh mountain environment. Yet much also remains in the form of deserted mines and mills, historic railways where steam power still holds sway, and fabled mining towns transformed into booming resort communities.

The attraction of the Colorado Rockies stems both from the beauty and variety of the landscape and from the cultural imprints of the past still contained within it. Ample wilderness exists for those visitors who prefer their mountain experiences to be as free as possible from the signs of human impact on the environment. There also exist spacious tracts of mountain landscape, much of it preserved as national forests, where the evidence of man's action, both contemporary and past, remains highly visible. For many visitors, these points of intersection between man and nature, whether they be a ghost town or ski area, epitomize the mountain recreational experience.

This diversity of available choices in a land of endless variety is the hallmark of the Colorado Rockies. It is also the reason for their enduring attraction, and more than sufficient reason that they be saved for the benefit and entertainment of future generations. Geographically and symbolically, they are the heartland of Colorado.

13 Rocky Mountain National Park

Location: northern Colorado

Size: 412 square miles

Terrain: lush valleys, dramatic vistas, and high peaks

Scenic Value: exceptional

Historical Interest: moderate

Highway Access: US 34, US 36, US 40, Colorado 72, and Colorado 7

Internal Access: paved roads, improved gravel roads, and foot trails

Maps: USGS map of Rocky Mountain National Park at 1:50,000
USGS sheets 3 and 4 of Larimer County, single sheet of Boulder County, and sheets 2 and 4 of Grand County at 1:50,000
National Park Service vicinity maps, road guides, and trail guides for Trail Ridge Road, Bear Lake, Horseshoe Park, Wild Basin, Moraine Park, Lulu City, and Holzwarth Homestead

Rocky Mountain National Park is the centerpiece of Colorado's public recreational lands, a special place long known to contain some of the most remarkable scenery found anywhere in the Rockies. Generations of painters, poets, and photographers have discovered here an enduring source of inspiration. No visual image or printed word, however, can convey effectively what it feels like to see the early morning sun rise on the sheer east face of Longs Peak or to hear the afternoon thunderstorms rolling through the Never Summer Mountains.

The tribal peoples who hunted game in this splendid landscape since the end of the last ice age may have known these experiences, but they left us no record of their impressions. The first Europeans to have seen the area, even from a distance, were Spanish explorers and traders of the later eighteenth century; they were followed by Zebulon Pike's expedition of 1806 and Stephen Long's exploration of the front range in 1820. Just as Pike never climbed the mountain bearing his name, neither Long nor any members of his party scaled the peak that was named in his honor. The first recorded ascent of Longs Peak, which is the highest mountain in Rocky Mountain National Park, did not occur until 1868, when a survey party led by the explorer and scientist John Wesley Powell reached the summit.

By the time Captain Powell climbed Longs Peak, mountain men had been trapping beaver and other furbearing animals in the area for decades, and the park's first settler had already arrived and de-parted. His name was Joel Estes and he arrived in 1859. When the Estes family left seven years later, they departed no wealthier than they had begun, but perhaps they were enriched spiritually by the experience. In the years following Estes's departure, much of the land in the area belonged to a European nobleman, the Earl of Dunraven, who found the countryside so much to his liking that he decided to buy it. At one time his landholdings in the Estes Park area, much of it fraudulently obtained, amounted to nearly twenty-five square miles. Among the Earl's friends who shared his enthusiasm for the area was the Western landscape painter, Albert Bierstadt. Though Bierstadt lacked the means to buy entire landscapes, he was gifted with a special talent for portraying them in a haunting, romantic style that evoked a strong sense of atmosphere. One of his best-known canvasses, called simply "Estes Park, Colorado," hangs in the Western History Room of the Denver Public Library. Painted in 1877, it conveys an idealized sense of the beauty and majesty of Estes Park in the days before gas stations, fast-food outlets, and utility lines cluttered the landscape beneath Rocky Mountain National Park.

Bierstadt's massive paintings may have contributed to the popularity of the area. A more material inducement occurred late in the 1870s with the discovery of gold, silver, and lead in the mountains west of the Continental Divide. Towns quickly sprang up at Lulu City and Gaskill, both located within the present national park boundaries. Lulu City, named for a daughter of the town's founder, is the more famous of the two sites. It received its supplies by way of Thunder (then Lulu) Pass and La Poudre Pass, at the northwest corner of the park, and quickly could boast of several lumber mills, a hotel, a post office, and a couple hundred residents. The ore deposits, however, proved less extensive than hoped, shipping costs were high, and, fortunately for the future of the picturesque area, both sites were soon abandoned.

A late but very influential person to arrive on the scene was Enos Mills, who came to Estes Park in 1885. He built a cabin there, prospected for a while at Cripple Creek and in Alaska, learned to love the land around Estes Park, and developed a close friendship with John Muir, the conservationist who helped establish Yosemite National Park in California. Mills became a Longs Peak guide, reportedly climbing the mountain 297 times. He found the spare time to campaign vigorously for the establishment of a national park to preserve the mountain lands he knew so well. Mills's pamphlets, articles, and personal persuasion triumphed on September 4, 1915, when Rocky Mountain National Park was

Horseshoe Park and the Mummy Range in late spring from Trail Ridge Road. ➤

dedicated. Neither the original nor the present boundaries encompass a national park of the scope that Mills first envisioned. Yet the addition of Routt, Arapaho, and Roosevelt national forests, the Colorado State Forest, the Arapaho National Recreation Area, and several recently designated wildernesses have built piecemeal a transmountain recreational preserve that balances the often-conflicting desires of competing public land-interest groups.

In fact, the integrity of Rocky Mountain National Park is less threatened by external development interests than by those very people who strive to enjoy it. Over the years, the Park Service has worked diligently to protect and improve the land it manages in Rocky Mountain National Park. It has purchased many of the private inholdings, reintroduced elk and otter to the park, installed a reservation system to prevent overcrowding of fragile camping sites, begun a shuttlebus service at Bear Lake, and prohibited snowmobiles on the east side of the park. Even so, the park suffers from intensive use that damages delicate tundra, drives wildlife from its natural habitat, and causes excessive soil erosion. The problem is less one of too many people for not enough park land, than a maldistribution of the population. Not one in a hundred park visitors will walk to the Mummy Range, hike through the Never Summer Mountains, or climb the fine rock formations along the Twin Owls Trail. These areas comprise somewhat more than one-half of Rocky Mountain National Park, and they represent a *de facto* wilderness for those few who bother to explore off the beaten track.

In no small measure, the geography and road network of Rocky Mountain National Park determine where the majority of visitors go. The park spans a forty-mile stretch of the Continental Divide. It is

bordered on the north by the Mummy Range, on the northwest by the Never Summer Mountains, on the west by the North Fork of the Colorado River, on the east by Estes Park and Colorado Highway 7, and on its southern boundary by an arbitrarily drawn line separating it from Arapaho and Roosevelt national forests. Within this park area are seventy-one peaks over 12,000 feet high; more than 150 bird species; over 300 miles of trails; a downhill skiing area; the highest continuous, paved automobile road in the country; and, on a very busy summer day, more than thirty thousand visitors.

The single most popular route through the park is US Highway 34, a magnificent summertime route (closed at higher elevations in winter) along Trail Ridge Road. It travels from Estes Park through the lower meadows and upper valleys to an eleven-mile stretch above timberline, crossing the Continental Divide at Milner Pass and descending along the North Fork of the Colorado River to the triple lakes of Arapahoe National Recreation Area. For first-time visitors with only a day to spend in the park, this splendid semicircular excursion offers the maximum sightseeing pleasure in the minimum possible time. It is a dramatic and memorable trip, especially in spring or fall, even for persons who have traveled the route many times previously.

Day travelers to Rocky Mountain National Park not intending to undertake this circuit journey have another option available on the east side of the park. Trail Ridge Road is the modern, paved route to the top of the Continental Divide, giving spectacular views from the high ridgeline it follows. The original Fall River Road, opened to traffic in September 1918, travels from Horseshoe Park up a lovely streamside route, joining Trail Ridge Road at the summit of Fall River Pass. The Park Service has preserved this older highway as a graveled one-way route uphill. For visitors intending to stay on the east side of the park, the trip up the Fall River Road and back down Trail Ridge Road provides a more varied experience than is available solely from traveling the paved highway. The Trail Ridge route provides a dramatic alpine journey, but Fall River Road, which is set in a moist subalpine forest, offers travelers an opportunity to experience the forest details and observe the changing vegetation patterns that occur with increased elevation. Addi-

Forest Canyon seen from near the top of Trail Ridge Road

tionally, the Fall River Road is sheltered from the howling winds that often whip over Trail Ridge and, since the traffic moves more slowly and in a single direction, some motorists find the route less threatening to negotiate than the paved highway. However, trailers and large motorized vans are prohibited from the Fall River Road due to the narrow, winding switchbacks.

Another popular tourist site on the east side of the park is Bear Lake, which can be reached by automobile or by the free shuttlebus system starting at Glacier Basin. The paved road to Bear Lake travels into a high mountain basin from which trails branch out deep into the park. The Park Service provides a self-guided nature trail around the lake, and from the parking lot it is only a three-mile round trip on foot past Dream Lake to Emerald Lake, nestled at the foot of Hallett Peak and Flattop Mountain. From Glacier Gorge Junction, additional popular hiking trails lead to Mills Lake and the Loch, both of which are picture-postcard settings.

The most dramatic hiking and climbing area in the park is located in the southwest corner in the vicinity of Longs Peak and Wild Basin. Except for short access roads, no roads penetrate this area—all travel is on foot, horseback, skis, or snowshoes.

Longs Peak is, beyond question, the single most impressive and best-known feature in Rocky Mountain National Park. Like the centerpiece of a jeweled crown, it sits surrounded by four ridges radiating out to an equal number of 13,000-foot peaks: Mount Meeker, Pagoda Mountain, Storm Peak, and Mount Lady Washington. It is a massive, rugged mountain with only one walk-up route and a towering east face that presents some of the most difficult and varied big-wall rock climbing in North America.

Although perhaps eclipsed in fame by Pikes Peak, Longs Peak is a more imposing formation that has captured man's imagination for centuries. Indians familiar with Longs Peak and Mount Meeker called them *Nesotaieux,* "The Two Guides," and the French fur trappers and traders in turn gave them the name *Les Deux Oreilles,* "The Two Ears." Even fiction writers have found a fascination with Longs Peak. Jules Verne's *From the Earth to the Moon,* published in 1866, envisioned a nearly three-hundred-foot telescope on the summit of Longs Peak to observe the progress of a lunar spacecraft. More recently, Longs Peak was a dominant feature of the Western landscape in James Michener's epic story *Centennial.*

Since John Wesley Powell's first recorded ascent in 1868, Longs Peak has exerted an almost mystical attraction on American and European climbers. In 1960 two California climbers managed to ascend the sheerest part of the east face, known as the Diamond and long thought to be unclimbable. Seven years later Layton Kor and Wayne Gross pioneered a winter ascent of the Diamond, and it was climbed solo in 1970. Despite these record first ascents, the Diamond still remains a supremely challenging technical ascent which many skilled climbers fail to complete.

For nearly fifty years the standard route up Longs Peak was via the Cable Route, where a set of fixed steel cables provided assistance over a short, steep pitch. The Park Service removed the cables in 1973; thus most climbers take the longer but less steep Keyhole Route. To date, more than one hundred thousand people have climbed Longs Peak, including the technical routes, with only slightly more than two dozen fatalities. Most experienced and acclimated hikers can comfortably make the eighteen-mile trip to Longs Peak summit and back in good weather. However, the upper portion of the Keyhole Route is quite exposed and should not be attempted with snow or ice on it except by properly trained and equipped climbers.

Day hikers who simply want to explore this imposing mountain can hike the Longs Peak trail, either descending from above timberline to Chasm Lake for an awesome view of the east face or continuing through the aptly named Boulderfield to Chasm View, which provides an equally awesome topside view of Chasm Lake and the east face. Once at Chasm View, casual hikers may be tempted to continue up the north face to the summit. The cable route, however, is quite exposed for a stretch, prone to loose rock and even in midsummer it can be coated with *verglas,* a thin coating of very slippery ice. It is a route best left to experienced climbers.

Several days is the minimum period necessary to explore even the fringes of Rocky Mountain National Park. Despite more than one hundred miles of automobile routes, it is not principally a roadside park. Instead, it should be explored by leg power, preferably on several return visits during different seasons of the year. But wherever visitors go, they should tread lightly and remember that man is little more than a guest here, that the various Park Service rules exist for good reason, and that this land, which lay here for eons of time before the dawn of human civilization, should be allowed to change in accordance with the forces of nature, not the whims of man.

14 Arapahoe National Recreation Area

Location: northern Colorado

Size: 53 square miles

Terrain: mountain reservoirs in a high river valley

Historical Interest: moderate

Scenic Value: very high

External Access: from US 34

Internal Access: paved and dirt roads, foot trails, and boat

Maps: USFS map of Arapaho National Forest at 1:125,000
USFS sketch map of Arapaho National Recreation Area at 1:63,000
USGS sheets 2 and 4 of Grand County at 1:50,000

View of Shadow Mountain from the west side of Shadow Mountain Lake.

The headwaters of the Colorado River lie in a magnificent mountain valley sculptured by glacial action and surrounded on three sides by the meandering course of the Continental Divide. Where the valley begins to open onto a wide grassland (once called Old Park and now known as Middle Park) is Grand Lake, the largest naturally occurring body of water in Colorado. Long a favorite Indian hunting and camping ground, it is an area where the Ute and Arapaho battled before white settlers arrived.

For decades the only white men who knew this valley were a few fur trappers, explorers, and government surveyors. With the discovery of precious ores in the upper portions of the valley around 1880, settlers streamed into the area, constructing mining camps high in the forestlands and a supply town next to Grand Lake. For a few years the community of Grand Lake Village was a rough-and-tumble boom town where one of Colorado's most famous shoot-outs occurred. The encounter, apparently caused by political rivalries compounded by personal animosity, involved the three county commissioners, the county clerk, the sheriff, and an undersheriff. When the smoke had cleared from the gun battle, two of the county commissioners were dead; the other commissioner and the county clerk lay fatally wounded. The sheriff died shortly thereafter in Georgetown of a gunshot wound inflicted under mysterious circumstances, and rumors of a violent death followed in the wake of the other lawman's departure.

Indian battles and wild-west gunfights are now a distant memory in the Grand Lake area, but the twentieth century brought renewed political strife. As water resource development replaced mining as the principal economic attraction of the upper Colorado River Valley, eastern-slope agricultural and urban interests developed a complex plan to divert water from the Colorado River into the South Platte basin. Following extensive controversy, the U.S. Congress enacted legislation in 1937 to undertake the Colorado–Big Thompson Project. This massive diversion scheme required the construction of two dams on the Colorado River, creating reservoirs that would carry their waters into Grand Lake. From Grand Lake the diverted water would flow through a tunnel under the Continental Divide to Estes Park; from there the Big Thompson River would transport the water into the South Platte Valley. A portion of the electricity generated at hydroelectric stations along the route would be used to pump water from the lower reservoir into the upper body of water created by the project. A decade later, following the construction of Shadow Mountain Lake and Lake Granby and the expenditure of some fifty million dollars, water began flowing through the system.

In order to capitalize on the considerable recreational potential of two reservoirs located on the edge of Rocky Mountain National Park and Roosevelt National Forest, Congress created the Shadow Mountain National Recreation Area. Originally, the National Park Service administered the area. In

1978 Congress authorized the creation of Arapaho National Recreation Area, which includes a larger area than its predecessor, and management responsibility shifted to the Forest Service. The expanded boundaries of Arapaho National Recreation Area include two major reservoirs (Shadow Mountain Lake and Lake Granby), along with Willow Creek Reservoir, Meadow Creek Reservoir, and Monarch Lake. Grand Lake, although it borders on the national recreation area, lies outside the boundary. The enlarged southern portion of the recreation area adjoins the Indian Peaks Wilderness.

Together these six bodies of water and the adjoining public lands represent one of the state's premier outdoor recreational units. The significance of the area results from its size, the diversity of recreational opportunities available on a year-round basis, the natural beauty of the setting, and the ease of access to neighboring recreational sites.

Winter sports, principally cross-country skiing and snowmobiling, are an increasingly popular activity at Arapaho National Recreation Area. The area remains, however, primarily a summertime water-sports and camping area with sufficient facilities to support comfortably a large user population. Nearly four hundred campsites, including one group-camping facility, are available at five different sites, in addition to several dozen square miles devoted to dispersed (nonmotorized) camping. The boating facilities include eleven marinas and six publicly owned boat-launching ramps in addition to a host of private docks. Rental boats are available at most of the marinas. Sailboating, powerboating, and waterskiing are particularly popular on Shadow Mountain Lake and Lake Granby. Boating activities on Willow Creek and Meadow Creek reservoirs are restricted to small powercraft; Monarch Lake is closed to motorboats.

A winter scene in Arapaho National Recreation Area near the edge of Lake Granby.

15 Arapaho National Forest

Location: north-central Colorado Rockies

Size: 1,602 square miles

Terrain: mountain peaks and valleys

Scenic Value: very high

Historical Interest: very high

External Access: from Interstate 70, US 40, US 285, and other state and local roads

Internal Access: paved highways, improved and primitive dirt roads, and foot trails

Maps: USFS map of Arapaho National Forest at 1:125,000

Various USGS sheets of Grand, Summit, Clear Creek, and Gilpin counties at 1:50,000

Once a favorite Arapaho Indian summer hunting ground, Arapaho National Forest has enjoyed a rich historical past. Mountain men and fur traders traveled these lands a century and a half ago, followed by explorers like John Frémont, whose second expedition traversed the Blue River Valley past the site of present-day Breckenridge in 1844. F. V. Hayden's famous Western surveys crisscrossed the area in the course of their travels. A succession of gold and silver booms in Central City, Idaho Springs, Montezuma, Breckenridge, and hundreds of other sites brought an instant frontier civilization to the mountain lands lying on both sides of the Continental Divide. Wagon roads and railway routes rapidly replaced the foot trails that had long been the sole mode of transportation through the high forests.

By the time President Theodore Roosevelt established Arapaho National Forest in 1908, the golden era of the nineteenth-century mining towns had ended. Yet mining activity still continues on a significant scale in Arapaho National Forest, most notably at the huge Henderson molybdenite mine and mill that spans the Continental Divide between Berthoud Pass and the Blue River Valley. Starting before World War II, water interests began the development of large-scale storage and diversion projects such as the Colorado–Big Thompson in the upper Colorado River Valley. In the 1960s the Denver Board of Water Commissioners constructed a 3,200-acre storage facility, called Dillon Reservoir, on the Blue River to provide additional water for the Denver metropolitan area. To the north of Dillon Reservoir are Green Mountain Reservoir and the Williams Fork Reservoir.

More than anywhere else in Colorado, Arapaho National Forest is the heartland of the state's downhill skiing industry. A combination of good snow conditions and ready access to the populous front range gives Arapaho National Forest a competitive edge in attracting Colorado skiers. Loveland Basin and Loveland Valley, located just east of the Continental Divide, and Arapaho Basin, a few miles to the west, have long provided challenging downhill runs. Because Loveland Basin and Arapaho Basin sit at a higher elevation than any other downhill skiing areas in the nation, they offer more reliable snow conditions and a longer season than many of Colorado's more famous ski resorts. Winter Park, owned and operated by the City and County of Denver, provides a quality skiing experience on a wide variety of terrain; it also is in Arapaho National Forest, along with two smaller ski areas, Berthoud Pass and Ski Idlewild. Arapaho National Forest now supports three more downhill skiing facilities with national reputations: Breckenridge, Copper Mountain, and Keystone. Three other ski areas, Eldora, Vail, and Steamboat Springs, are located only a short distance from the borders of Arapaho National Forest, thus placing it squarely at the center of the nation's greatest concentration of downhill skiing terrain. If this were not sufficient to support the forest's position as a premier winter-sports haven, the countryside around Winter Park, Berthoud Pass, Keystone, Guanella Pass, Breckenridge, and Shrine Pass includes many of Colorado's most popular cross-country ski trails.

Arapaho National Forest encompasses a considerable expanse of alpine terrain, and it lies close to the rich northeastern edge of Colorado's mineral belt, where intensive mining development occurred throughout the second half of the nineteenth-century. A number of the nineteenth-century transportation routes have become all-weather highways, and many other of these historic routes continue to exist as backcountry roads and hiking trails. Consequently, the sprawling high-country terrain within Arapaho National Forest ranks among the most accessible in Colorado, offering hikers and motorists alike a nearly endless maze of routes to explore. Above Central City, Idaho Springs, Montezuma, Georgetown, and Breckenridge is a network of ghost towns, mining sites, and historic backcountry roads equalled elsewhere in Colorado only in the San Juan country and in the mountains above the upper Arkansas River.

Despite the expanse of high country in Arapaho National Forest, the area includes only four of Colorado's fifty-four peaks reaching over 14,000 feet in elevation, but all four of them rank among the more readily accessible of Colorado's big peaks. Quandry Peak, at an elevation of 14,264 feet, is located three miles west of Colorado Highway 9, between Breckenridge and the summit of Hoosier

Summit Lake and distant peaks from the top of Mount Evans.

Pass. A dirt road leads from Colorado 9 up Monte Cristo Creek. It is a short though steep hike from the road to the summit of Quandry and a fine overview of the upper Blue River Valley. Grays Peak and Torreys Peak once ranked among the major tourist attractions in the state. These two peaks, the ninth and eleventh highest in Colorado, are located near Interstate 70 at the head of an imposing box canyon called Stevens Gulch; from where the road ends, it is a short and scenic hike to the foot of these dramatic twin peaks.

The other 14,000-foot peak in Arapaho National Forest is the best known of the group by virtue of the paved road that ascends to the summit. Mount Evans, which dominates the ridgeline of mountains rising west of Denver, was named in honor of Colorado's second territorial governor and long-time railroad promoter. Although the road to the top of Mount Evans is short on guardrails, and though the upper portion of the route is severely frost heaved, this highest paved automobile road in the nation offers travelers who would not otherwise visit the summit of a large mountain the opportunity to drive to the top of Colorado's fourteenth-highest peak. Starting in Idaho Springs at an elevation below 8,000 feet, the road (Colorado 103 to Colorado 5) climbs 7,000 vertical feet, traveling past subalpine and alpine lakes on its scenic route to the stone summithouse. Even for travelers who have climbed to the top of large mountains, the auto trip up Mount Evans's flanks can be a rewarding excur-

sion. The view from the roadside is marvelous and Mount Evans supports a sizable herd of bighorn sheep, along with a bristlecone pine forest located near timberline in the Mount Gothic Natural Area. Careful observers will note that some of the tundra on Mount Evans is not the alpine variety normally found above timberline in Colorado, but the water-saturated arctic tundra rarely encountered below the Arctic Circle.

Visitors wishing to seek a quieter, nonmotorized experience can select from among three wilderness areas in Arapaho National Forest. The best known and most heavily used of these areas is the Indian Peaks Wilderness, located along both sides of the Continental Divide to the south of Rocky Mountain National Park. The Eagles Nest Wilderness, which spills over into the White River National Forest, is located high in the Gore Range on the southwestern border of Arapaho National Forest, and surrounding Mount Evans is the recently created 115-square-mile Mount Evans Wilderness. Several hundred additional square miles of little-used forestlands are available in the Williams Fork Mountains, located southeast of Kremmling, and in the Vasquez Mountains and the Fraser Experimental Forest, situated west of Winter Park and Berthoud Pass.

The Winter Park area, nestled high in the Fraser River Valley, offers a wide range of summer and winter recreational opportunities. In addition to downhill skiing at Berthoud Pass, Winter Park, and Ski Idlewild, the area offers a wide variety of cross-

A December scene near Winter Park, looking toward Berthoud Pass.

Detail view of an uprooted bristlecone pine in the Mount Gothic Natural Area on Mount Evans.

country skiing terrain at Second Creek, Jim Creek, around Devils Thumb (with its forty miles of nordic trails), and many other locations. Experienced nordic skiers can travel a strenuous but spectacular route from Winter Park over the Continental Divide to East Portal, on South Boulder Creek near the base of the Rollins Pass road. Summertime visitors not inclined toward vigorous hiking can travel from Winter Park over the Continental Divide along the lengthy but spectacular Rollins Pass route originally constructed by John Quincy Adams Rollins.

From the Winter Park area it is a short journey to the northeastern corner of Arapaho National For-

est. Here, by the headwaters of the Colorado River, are the Never Summer Mountains, the west side of Rocky Mountain National Park, and the water-sports facilities at Arapaho National Recreation Area. To the west of the national park, Arapaho National Forest forms an irregular arc encompassing the woodlands that rise above the high, rolling grasslands of Middle Park. This little-visited section of Arapaho National Forest includes portions of the Rabbit Ears Range and the Park Range, both of which offer many hundreds of additional miles of backcountry roads and hiking trails for travelers who like to explore off the beaten track.

16 Colorado State Forest

Location: north-central Colorado

Size: 113 square miles

Terrain: mountainous

Scenic Value: considerable

Historical Interest: modest

Highway Access: Colorado 14

Internal Access: Colorado 14, improved and primitive dirt roads, and foot trails

Maps: USFS map of Roosevelt National Forest at 1:125,000
USFS map of Routt National Forest at 1:125,000
USGS sheets 2 and 4 of Jackson County at 1:50,000
Colorado Division of Parks and Outdoor Recreation sketch map at about 1:100,000

North of the lovely valley where the Colorado River originates lie the Medicine Bow Mountains. These mountains, known sometimes as the Rawah Range, an Indian word for wilderness, border the broad basin called North Park. Carved from the west side of this little-known range and from the very northern edge of the Never Summer Mountains is a 72,000-acre forest preserve owned by the State of Colorado and designated as the Colorado State Forest. Management of the land is entrusted to the Colorado Board of Land Commissioners, an obscure but powerful state agency that oversees Colorado's landholdings. The land is leased in turn to the Colorado Division of Parks and Outdoor Recreation, which supervises recreational activities in the State Forest.

Because it is bordered by two national forests (Roosevelt and Routt), by a designated wilderness area (Rawah Wilderness), and by Rocky Mountain National Park, Colorado State Forest is not well known. Judged solely on the basis of aesthetic values, Colorado State Forest offers less magnificent scenery than is available to experienced hikers willing to explore deep in the Rawah Wilderness or the remote northwestern corner of the national park. However, because the State Forest is more readily accessible than these other two areas, it provides visitors an opportunity to travel through a large expanse of little-seen yet very pretty countryside.

Most of the best scenery, the easiest access, and the areas of greatest historical interest are concentrated in the southern portion of Colorado State Forest. This area first attracted widespread attention in the 1870s when prospectors found precious ore deposits in the vicinity. Mining towns quickly sprang up at Lulu City, located within the present boundaries of Rocky Mountain National Park, and at Teller City in North Park. A wagon road was constructed north from Lulu City over the Continental Divide, and in 1870 General Robert Cameron discovered another crossing between the Never Summer Mountains and the Medicine Bow Mountains, providing a link between the valley of the Cache la Poudre and North Park. A toll road was established along this route in 1882 to provide freight and passenger service for the boom towns and mining camps that had sprung up in the area. Colorado Highway 14 approximately follows the old stage route over Cameron Pass and into the southern portion of Colorado State Forest.

As Colorado Highway 14 winds down through Colorado State Forest from the summit of Cameron Pass, it provides excellent views of the Medicine Bow Mountains to the north and the Never Summer Mountains to the south. At lower elevations the road opens onto the flat expanse of North Park, which stretches out in the distance. Farther down the highway, about two miles beyond the Aspen Campground cutoff, a side road enters the state forest and travels along the North Fork of the Michigan River. This well-graded gravel road passes by North Michigan Reservoir, which is the largest body of water in the state forest and a scenic vantage point for viewing the Medicine Bow Mountains that rise in the background. The only backcountry route in the forest suitable for passenger cars, this access road continues to the Brockman Lumber Camp, an abandoned lumbering site operated by the five Brockman brothers between 1949 and 1972.

From the lumber camp, four-wheel-drive routes branch off to the north and south. The northern routes end at trailheads leading to Ruby Jewel Lake, Kelly Lake, and Clear Lake, all of which are situated high in the Medicine Bow Mountains below alpine peaks. The most accessible of these lakes is Ruby Jewel, located below 12,951-foot Clark Peak on the border of the Rawah Wilderness. The southern routes travel past a cutoff back to Colorado Highway 14 and through areas of past timber cutting to the summit of Montgomery Pass, a windswept, narrow saddle just above timberline that affords a fine alpine view to the south and a stunning view of North Michigan Reservoir, North Park, and the distant peaks along the Continental Divide. Hikers can reach Montgomery Pass by means of a short trail starting on Colorado 14 at Montgomery Creek a mile or so east of the Cameron Pass summit.

North Michigan Lake in Colorado State Forest.

The northern portion of Colorado State Forest includes several additional hiking trails and a considerable number of four-wheel-drive routes, the most notable of which are the primitive roads to Ute Pass and Coon Peak. Because these routes cross little-used forestland, travelers should be prepared to cope by themselves with whatever problems arise. The southern tip of Colorado State Forest, on the south side of Colorado Highway 14, includes an access road leading to a scenic campsite and several trailheads that give access to Lake Agnes, the Nokhu Crags, Snow Lake, and the rarely visited Thunder Pass trail into Rocky Mountain National Park.

The Nokhu Crags, which reach far above the timberline, are the most dominant feature in this portion of Colorado State Forest. But the highest peak in the Never Summer Mountains, Mount Richthofen, is located only a mile distant on the border of Rocky Mountain National Park. The peak, which is a popular objective for climbers, was named by one of the nineteenth-century survey parties for a German geographer and geologist, Baron Fredrick von Richthofen, who had participated in the early surveying of California and who later mapped many of the high peaks of inner China. Experienced hikers can combine a visit to the Lake Agnes area with a climb of the Crags and Mount Richthofen.

17 Routt National Forest

Location: northern Colorado

Size: 1,760 square miles

Terrain: forested mountain ridges and valleys

Scenic Value: high

Historical Interest: moderate

External Access: US 40, Colorado 14, Colorado 125, Colorado 127, and Colorado 134

Internal Access: paved highways, improved and primitive dirt roads, and foot trails

Maps: USFS map of Routt National Forest at 1:125,000
Various USGS sheets of Jackson, Routt, Rio Blanco, and Moffat counties at 1:50,000

North Park is a high, wide, and windswept valley surrounded on three sides by mountain ranges: the Park Range to the west, the Rabbit Ears Range and the Never Summer Mountains to the south, and the Medicine Bow Mountains on the east. The several dozen streams coursing down from the mountains onto the dry valley floor form the headwaters of the North Platte River. Above these headwaters the ridgeline of the Continental Divide dips down in a variety of low crossing points, making North Park long a favorite route for explorers and mountain men.

In the early days of the trans–Mississippi fur trade, Ceran St. Vrain, one of the founders of Bent's Fort, along with other 1820s fur traders, traveled through North Park in search of beaver pelts. John Frémont, on his second expedition, crossed into North Park in June 1844 by way of the North Platte River and traveled south into Middle Park over a shallow crossing of the Continental Divide now known as Muddy Pass (the present-day route of US Highway 40).

As he followed the North Platte River up the "remarkable mountain cove" known to his expedition as New Park, Frémont could observe close at hand the Park Range peaks that form the western border of the basin, and the Rabbit Ears Range and Never Summer Mountains to the south. These three mountain groups, together with the Elkhead Mountains and the portion of the Medicine Bow Mountains not included within the Colorado State Forest, constitute Routt National Forest—a sprawling woodland preserve that reaches from the edge of Rocky Mountain National Park to the plateau country of northwestern Colorado. First established by Theodore Roosevelt as the Park Range Forest Reserve, the present national forest is named in honor of John L. Routt, a Kentuckian who had fought with

General Grant and who rose to become Colorado's last territorial governor and the first state governor in 1876.

Except for a few 12,000-foot peaks in the Mount Zirkel Wilderness and the Never Summer Mountains, Routt National Forest is not a land of soaring peaks, nor does it contain many stunning rock formations or cascading mountain rivers. Instead, it is a landscape of forested ridges, quiet streams, and scenic valleys rising above the North Platte and Yampa rivers. Wildlife is abundant and the area has long been a favorite location for fishing and hunting. With the development of a major downhill skiing facility at Steamboat Springs, cross-country skiers and other winter-sports enthusiasts are now taking increased advantage of the ample snowfall and attractive terrain available throughout the area.

Traditionally the north-central Colorado area has seen little mining activity, and the principal mineral resource, coal, is generally found at lower elevations, outside the boundaries of Routt National Forest. Consequently, the forest is almost wholly without the mining scars that predominate in other areas of Colorado, and it also lacks the extensive backcountry road network found in Colorado national forests where widespread mining activity has occurred. Nowhere is this roadless quality more evident in Routt National Forest than along the Park Range, directly east of Steamboat Springs. In this central unit of the forest, spanning both sides of the Continental Divide for a distance of more than fifty miles, only one road crosses the Park Range between the Wyoming border and US Highway 40 over Rabbit Ears Pass. That road, the backcountry route over Buffalo Pass between Steamboat Springs and Walden, is closed during the winter months and negotiable by passenger cars only under optimal conditions.

However, an extensive array of hiking trails covers the area, and many subalpine lakes exist on both sides of the Divide. The central portion of the area has been designated the Mount Zirkel Wilderness. One of the original five Colorado wilderness areas created in 1964, Mount Zirkel was expanded by the Colorado Wilderness Act of 1980 to nearly twice its original size, gaining more than 100 square miles of additional territory. The wilderness area, centered around 12,180-foot Mount Zirkel, is most easily reached from the west by taking US Highway 40 a short distance west of Steamboat Springs and traveling north on Routt County Road 129 to Clark, then bearing northeast on an improved Forest Service road. This scenic route travels past three Forest Service campgrounds, ending at the site of Slavonia, an isolated nineteenth-century mining camp near the confluence of Gilpin and Gold creeks.

A meadow near the summit of Troublesome Pass in Routt National Forest.

Fall aspen hear Hahns Peak.

From Slavonia, hiking trails reach into the Mount Zirkel Wilderness, and several side roads branch farther into Routt National Forest from various points along the Slavonia road.

Several miles farther up Routt County Road 129, as the valley narrows, there are additional features of interest. At the head of the valley lies Steamboat Lake (see Steamboat Lake State Park) and, above it, Hahns Peak. This symmetrically shaped formation, which dominates the Elk River valley below, was the site of the only significant mining activity in the area. Joseph Hahn discovered gold here in the early 1860s. Several years later, large-scale mining efforts began in the Hahns Peak area and by 1874, gold ore yields had reached the level of five million dollars a year. For three decades Hahns Peak was a sufficiently prominent community to be the county seat of Routt County, a distinction that Steamboat Springs did not gain until 1912.

Today, recreational activities have taken the place of mining as the principal endeavor in the Hahns Peak area. From the Hahns Peak community on the east side of Steamboat Lake, a primitive road branches into the national forest, one fork traveling toward the mountain and the other winding along a circuitous route to the Mount Zirkel Wilderness boundary. Routt County Road 129 continues past Steamboat Lake, exiting the national forest on the Little Snake River; from there it continues to Savory, Wyoming, located about a dozen miles from the forest border. Several side roads branch off from this main route, giving access to the Hahns Peak Lake Campground, Big Red Park, and many dozens of additional square miles of little-used forestlands along the Wyoming border.

This brief armchair tour of the Hahns Peak area could be repeated in the remote Elkhead Mountains extension of the forest, located to the west of Steamboat Lake; in the southeast corner of the forest below picturesquely named Mounts Cirrus, Cumulus, Nimbus, and Stratus in the Never Summer Mountains; or in the Routt National Forest unit west of Yampa, where trails thirty miles and longer in length lead into the Flat Tops Wilderness. For mountain travelers wanting to escape the crowds that flock to Colorado's better known and more accessible outdoor recreational sites, Routt National Forest offers an abundance of little-used but lovely countryside to explore.

18 Steamboat Lake State Park

Location: northern Colorado/north of Steamboat Springs

Size: about 2 square miles

Terrain: mountain valley reservoir

Scenic Value: high

Historical Interest: modest

External Access: Routt County Road 129 and US 40

Internal Access: gravel roads, by foot and by boat

Maps: USFS map of Routt National Forest at 1:125,000
USGS sheet 2 of Routt County at 1:50,000
Colorado Division of Parks and Outdoor Recreation sketch map, unscaled

North of Steamboat Springs there lies a splendid mountain valley some two dozen miles long reaching from the Yampa River to the foot of Hahns Peak. It begins as picturesque ranching land, with cattle grazing quietly amid the neatly stacked bales of hay and thick stands of cottonwood growing by the banks of the Elk River. As the valley floor rises, the cottonwoods give way to aspen, and a broad, lush meadow dominated by the symmetrical shape of Hahns Peak replaces the nicely manicured fields in the lower valley.

In the summertime it is a deceptively idyllic land, pastoral in its lower portions with a classic mountain setting at the head of the valley. But harsh winter storms sweep through the area, bringing bitter weather and deep snows. Joseph Hahn, who discovered gold below the peak that bears his name, died here of starvation and exposure in the spring of 1865 as he and a companion struggled out after wintering by their claim.

Today, cross-country skiing, ice fishing, and snowmobiling have replaced mining as the dominant winter activity in the upper valley. And the creation of the two man-made lakes below Hahns Peak has greatly expanded year-round recreational activities throughout the Elk River valley. Steamboat Lake, covering nearly two square miles, was completed in 1967, and Lester Creek Reservoir, now called Pearl Lake in honor of a local resident, was first filled several years earlier. Steamboat

View of Hahns Peak from the south.

Afternoon storm clouds gathering beyond the shore of Steamboat Lake.

Lake State Park encompasses both of these reservoirs.

The two bodies of water at Steamboat Lake State Park offer different recreational opportunities. Steamboat Lake, the larger of the reservoirs, sits on the open valley floor commanding an excellent view of the rugged peaks along the Continental Divide. The lake is stocked with rainbow trout and open to waterskiing, along with other water sports, and the concession operator rents a variety of boats during the summer season. Pearl Lake is a small reservoir surrounded by woods and nestled in a narrow valley. Powerboats may operate in Pearl Lake only at wakeless speed, and fishing for the cutthroat trout that dwell there is by lure and fly only. It is a secluded, sheltered lake populated by waterfowl and ideally suited for the use of hand-powered boats.

Both Steamboat Lake and Pearl Lake support marshes, and the various coves at Steamboat Lake produce scenic wetlands. These shoreline ecosystems, which are accessible by foot and from small boats, produce vegetation not normally found at higher elevations, and they support a variety of wildlife. The waterfowl inhabiting the park area (mostly on a migratory basis) include ducks, geese, teal, cranes, and other species. Deer, elk, coyote, bear, fox, beaver, and other smaller mammals live in the upper valley surrounding the park.

Steamboat Lake and Pearl Lake both provide camping and picnicking facilities, with a total of 240 campsites at the two lakes. The location of these camping facilities in a high valley almost totally surrounded by woodlands makes Steamboat Lake State Park an excellent base camp for exploring the extensive network of roads and trails extending through Routt National Forest and into Wyoming's Medicine Bow National Forest. At Glen Eden, on Routt County Road 129 about six miles from Steamboat Lake, an improved Forest Service road follows Elk Creek past several additional campgrounds, providing access to a variety of more primitive roads and foot trails leading into the Mount Zirkel Wilderness. Additional, little-used national forest lands are available in the Elkhead Mountains west of Steamboat Lake and north of Hahns Peak.

19 White River National Forest

Location: west-central Colorado

Size: 3,064 square miles

Terrain: scenic river valleys, high peaks, and mountain wilderness

Scenic Value: high to exceptional

Historical Interest: very high

External Access: Interstate 70, US 24, Colorado 13, Colorado 82, Colorado 131, and Colorado 133

Internal Access: paved highways, improved and primitive dirt roads, and foot trails

Maps: USFS map of White River National Forest at 1:125,000
Various USGS sheets of Eagle, Pitkin, Gunnison, Garfield, and Rio Blanco counties at 1:50,000

Today the principal industry of the White River National Forest is not mining, ranching, or timber cutting, but tourism. The visitors who flock here both in summer and winter support a thriving local economy and provide the forest with a widely known reputation as one of the premier mountain reserves in North America.

The reason for the international popularity of the White River National Forest area in both summer and winter is twofold. First, White River encompasses some of the most spectacular mountain scenery anywhere in the nation; the contours of the landscape are as varied as they are rugged and beautiful. Second, high-quality snow and nicely shaped mountainsides provide downhill skiing opportunities equal to the best winter resorts in Europe. Other ski areas in North America offer longer seasons, more vertical drop, higher mountains, deeper powder, or more challenging individual runs. But nowhere else on the continent is there as much high-quality skiing in so compact and picturesque an area as the White River National Forest. The Eagle–Vail section of the forest offers three separate ski mountains at Vail Village, Lionshead, and Beaver Creek. Aspen provides four individual ski areas at Aspen Mountain, Aspen Highlands, Buttermilk, and Snowmass. Still more major ski areas are in the planning stages, such as Little Annie at Aspen and Adams Rib on scenic East Brush Creek behind Eagle.

The emergence of the White River Forest as an internationally known winter-sports paradise occurred only in the past several decades. At the end of World War II, Aspen was a sleepy mountain town. Where the instant-chalet architecture of Vail now sprawls down Gore Creek there lay virgin meadows and lovely subalpine forestlands. Among the veterans returning home after the war were former members of the famed 10th Mountain Division, who had received their mountain warfare training at Camp Hale, near Leadville. A number of these veterans settled in Colorado and played an instrumental role in the growth of Aspen and in the state's emergence as the skiing capitol of the nation.

The boom-town growth in population and wealth among the White River resort communities repeats the history of the area in the past century, which has alternated between periods of explosive growth and rapid decline. The first population boom that occurred in the mountains west of Leadville brought to the area settlement patterns and life styles that persist to the present day. Through the Civil War era, the Ute Indians occupied the scenic valleys and wooded hillsides that lay on the far side of the Arkansas River, beyond the Continental Divide. With the discovery of rich silver deposits by the Roaring Fork River and its upper tributaries, the hapless Utes found their territory invaded by prospectors, miners, and footloose fortune seekers, who founded a community called Ute City at the head of the Roaring Fork Valley. Additional ore discoveries multiplied the population, which peaked at more than ten thousand persons in the late 1880s — far exceeding the current Aspen area permanent population. By 1890 Aspen had become a major Colorado mining city, with its two railroads, three newspapers, municipal electric lighting system, and ornate opera house all supported by the endless cargo of ore streaming out of the local mines.

To the west of Aspen, Glenwood Springs became a regional transportation center and resort town. In the majestic Crystal River Valley, additional mining activity, principally for coal and high-grade marble, led to the establishment of Redstone, Marble, and Crystal. The Yule Creek marble quarry closed several decades ago, but coal mining still occurs on a large scale above Redstone.

Mining, ranching, and the recreation industry have been the three economic cornerstones of the White River Forest area for over a century. Despite the current dominance of tourism, all three activities remain in evidence today: the sweet aroma of freshly cut alfalfa drifting down the ranching valleys of Pitkin County, the steep ski runs of Ajax Mountain so visible from downtown Aspen, the enormous blocks of marble lying beside the road along Yule Creek, heavily laden coal trucks traveling down the Crystal River to Carbondale, and cattle grazing in their high summer pastures among the pine and fir trees on public domain lands.

Yet the White River National Forest is also a land

View of the Crystal River Valley from Lead King Basin.

of true wilderness, where the imprint of human civilization remains barely visible. North of Glenwood Springs is a remote, detached unit of the White River National Forest. Several improved roads enter the area, providing motorized access to Sweetwater Lake, Heart Lake, Meadow Creek Lake, and Anderson Lake. But the core of the area is designated as the Flat Tops Wilderness, a plateau eroded by wide canyons that form dramatic rock escarpments and natural amphitheaters where they join the headlands. North of Vail is the Eagles Nest Wilderness, stretching across the White River and Arapaho national forests in an area where urban water interests and environmental groups have long battled for control. Directly east of Aspen, in another area contested by water diverters and conservationists, is the Hunter–Fryingpan Wilderness, a dramatic mountain preserve bounded on the east by the 13,000-foot-high ridgeline of the Continental Divide and encompassing the upper drainage of the Roaring Fork and Fryingpan rivers. South of the Hunter–Fryingpan Wilderness is the western end of the newly designated Collegiate Peaks Wilderness.

But the centerpiece of the White River wilderness area – and, indeed, the centerpiece of the entire national forest – is located southwest of Aspen, high in the Elk Mountains. Here, in the recently enlarged Maroon Bells–Snowmass Wilderness, an area mercifully spared from past mining activity, exists some of the most beautiful mountain scenery in the West. It is a land of steep valleys, pristine meadows awash with wildflowers, high alpine lakes, and, dominating everything else, a profusion of beautifully hued peaks reaching a half mile above timberline. The heart of the Sawatch Range, to the east of Aspen, contains a higher proportion of Colorado's fabled fourteeners. In mountaineering circles, however, most of these mountains in the main branch of the Sawatch Range are known as big ant hills, massive but inelegant formations that any flatlander with enough determination can climb in good weather. The Elk Range peaks, on the other hand, more nearly approach the Alps in grandeur and ruggedness. Of the six fourteeners in the Elk Range, local mountaineers classify only one as a "walk-up" mountain. The remainder require varying but additional levels of skill and experience.

Typical of the Elk Range peaks in this regard are the Maroon Bells. The Mona Lisa of Colorado mountains, their image is so well known that it has become nearly a cliche. This most photographed, painted, and sketched of all Colorado mountain settings, a scene of spectacular beauty, is also a notoriously dangerous place for climbing enthusiasts, too

many of whom have lost their lives or suffered serious injury trying to scale the steep, rotten rock of the Maroon Bells. The crowd of visitors traveling the paved road from Aspen up Maroon Creek to see the Bells has become so great in recent years that the Forest Service now prohibits automobile use in Maroon Valley during the morning and afternoon hours from Memorial Day to Labor Day. Bus service is available, however, from the Aspen Highlands Ski Area for visitors wishing to travel up Maroon Creek. A paved road up Castle Creek remains open to passenger-car traffic except during the winter months; this route leads to the scenic remains of Ashcroft, a nineteenth-century mining community, and provides a stunning view of the high peaks on the eastern border of the Maroon Bells–Snowmass Wilderness. Several difficult but spectacular four-wheel-drive routes continue from upper Castle Creek over the top of the Elk Range and descend into Gunnison National Forest.

A number of other areas in this portion of White River National Forest deserve special mention. First among them is the Crystal River Valley. The drive through this lovely area starts at Carbondale, where Colorado Highway 133 branches off from Colorado 82. At Redstone, once a utopian company mining town, the countryside becomes outstanding, and it continues to delight the eye along the side road that begins by the foot of McClure Pass and travels to Marble (where most passenger cars must stop), Crystal, and then ascends a treacherously steep, rough route through the Crystal River canyon to the top of Schofield Pass and down to Crested Butte in Gunnison National Forest.

The second area of special interest is the Fryingpan River basin. Starting at Basalt on Colorado Highway 82, a long, scenic road follows the route of the old Colorado Midland railroad to Ruedi Reservoir and the abandoned ghost towns that sprang up to serve the railway. The route continues over scenic Hagerman Pass, a four-wheel-drive route near the summit, with a half dozen major side roads of good quality branching deep into White River National Forest. The longest of these side roads begins at Thomasville and crosses a low divide at Crooked Creek Pass, then descends into a lush valley to Swan Lake, and follows West Brush Creek to the town of Eagle and Interstate 70. A particularly interesting side road from this route travels along East Brush Creek, starting about two miles inside the forest boundary. The East Brush Creek route traverses private property earmarked as the site of a proposed ski area on Adam Mountain and ends at the former mining town of Fulford, which once supported a population of several hundred people.

Both the upper Fryingpan basin and the Brush Creek area offer uncommonly attractive scenery in a relatively little-known and lightly used portion of White River National Forest—although development of the sprawling Adams Rib ski project, if approved by the U.S. Forest Service, will substantially diminish the appeal of the East Brush Creek area. The final area of special interest lies along the upper Eagle River, on the opposite side of the Sawatch Range from Brush Creek and the Fryingpan. This area, accessible by an all-weather highway (US 24) between Interstate 70 at Downds Junction and Tennessee Pass, travels through a steep canyon past Gilman, passes by the mining town of

Redcliff, then opens onto a wide valley that ends dramatically at the Continental Divide.

It was in this valley, at Camp Hale, that the 10th Mountain Division did its training during World War II. The concrete bunker foundations are still very much in evidence, and two large stone markers at the summit of Tennessee Pass commemorate the achievements and losses of the nation's only World War II mountaineering division. The Forest Service has designated the training site as the Camp Hale Recreation Area; a sign along the road provides background information.

At Redcliff, a well-known side road travels east along Turkey Creek to Shrine Pass, ending at the

An alpine view near the border of the Maroon Bells–Snowmass Wilderness.

Vail Pass exit on Interstate 70. The route, which provides several excellent views of Mount of the Holy Cross, offers a popular cross-country skiing and snowmobiling trip in the winter and it is a lovely warm-weather recreational area.

Several miles to the south, on US Highway 24 at the Blodgett Campground, an improved gravel road ascends Homestake Creek to the Homestake Reservoir, and a side road notoriously difficult even for the most sturdy four-wheel-drive vehicles travels to the site of Holy Cross City, a nineteenth-century mining town that once included a hotel, a school, and several stores. Mount of the Holy Cross, the peak made famous by William Henry Jackson's photograph taken in 1873 and by subsequent paintings by the English painter Thomas Moran, was designated a national monument in 1929. But claims that the famous snow-filled arms of the cross were deteriorating—along with a declining interest in the monument—caused its demotion in 1950 from national monument to national forest status. The Colorado Wilderness Act of 1980, however, provided the mountain with a measure of renewed protection by including it within the newly created 200-square-mile Holy Cross Wilderness Area.

Pearl Mountain and other Elk Range peaks rising above the headwaters of Castle Creek.

20 Gunnison National Forest

Location: west-central Colorado/Gunnison
   River basin

Size: 2,598 square miles

Terrain: alpine peaks and mountain valleys

Scenic Value: very high to exceptional

Historical Interest: very high

External Access: US 50, US 24, and US 285

Internal Access: paved highways, improved and
   primitive dirt roads, and foot trails

Maps: USFS map of Gunnison National Forest
   at 1:125,000
   Various USGS sheets of Gunnison,
   Saguache, Hinsdale, and Delta counties at
   1:50,000

Good fortune rarely seemed to accompany Captain John W. Gunnison on his Western expeditions. While attempting to hunt bison from horseback on his first trip west, Gunnison accidently shot his horse in the head, narrowly escaping serious injury. On his final expedition, in 1853, Gunnison set out from Fort Leavenworth, Kansas in search of a transcontinental railroad route along the thirty-eighth parallel. Captain Gunnison's survey party was one of four authorized by Congress that year to settle upon a suitable rail route. Jefferson Davis, then secretary of war, commanded all four survey expeditions; Gunnison's path approximately paralleled the route of Frémont's expedition of 1848–1849, which had come to grief in the Cochetopa Hills near the Continental Divide (see Rio Grande National Forest).

Windswept trees at the summit of Old Monarch Pass.

ison traveled west from Fort
L   Bent's Fort, crossed the Continen-
ta   hetopa Pass, traveled down the
C   ) the Green River, and passed
th   ch Mountains in eastern Utah.
O   3, Gunnison wrote his wife that
h   through countryside in which
the   Indian bands were at war.
Eight days later, a Paiute war party killed Gunnison
and nearly all the other members of his expedition.

Gunnison National Forest, named in honor of a
brave and experienced army explorer, includes a
small part of the route traveled by Captain Gunnison and his ill-fated command. Today, Cochetopa
Pass is a backroad gateway into the southeastern
section of the forest. In its entirety, Gunnison National Forest forms an irregular crescent bordered
on the north by the Elk Range and on the east and
the south by the Continental Divide. At the center
of this crescent is the city of Gunnison and the
broad valley of the Gunnison River. The national
forest lands encompass most of the high alpine and
subalpine drainages that flow into the Gunnison
River.

The first European settlers of the area came not
to the lowlands of the Gunnison River, but to the
high mountain valleys above. The discovery of rich
mineral deposits in the later decades of the nineteenth century lured hordes of fortune seekers up
the Arkansas River Valley, across the Continental
Divide, and into the high, remote valleys of a virgin
mountain land.

Trails hardly suitable for a mule team widened
into wagon roads and later became railroad grades
as prospectors, miners, wagonmasters, and an
array of less savory characters streamed into the
area. Overnight, towns sprang up in the dense
forests, the mere rumor of gold being sufficient to
attract a footloose element always searching for the
instant wealth that lay just over the next hill. High
up in the western flank of the Sawatch Range,
major communities emerged at Tincup, Pitkin, and
White Pine. To the north, Crested Butte, Gothic,
Irwin, Ruby, Pittsburg, and a dozen lesser towns
sprang up beneath the tall peaks of the Elk and
Ruby ranges. By 1881 the Denver and Rio Grande
Railway had arrived in Gunnison and soon would
reach to the rich coal trade in Crested Butte. Two
years later the Denver, South Park and Pacific was
providing freight and passenger service by way of
the Alpine Tunnel to Pitkin and Gunnison.

Exhausted ore deposits, excessive transportation
costs, and declining market prices for gold and silver dramatically depopulated the towns and mining
camps of the area by the close of the nineteenth

century. Once-thriving communities like Gothic
and Irwin became ghost towns. A few other communities, like Crested Butte and Gunnison, survived until an era when tourism and outdoor recreation replaced mining as the economic mainstay of
the region. Much of the contemporary appeal of the
Gunnison area derives from this century-old mining
heritage, which remains preserved in the mine
sites, ore mills, community buildings, and con-
necting road network.

Summertime visitors to Gunnison National Forest
can travel by automobile over Cottonwood Pass,
once a wagon and stagecoach route, to Taylor Park
and Taylor Park Reservoir. From there, routes continue south to Tincup and then over Cumberland
Pass both to Brittle Silver Basin and the Alpine
Tunnel portal, which is one of the most spectacular
drives in the area, and to Pitkin, now a thriving
summer resort community. From Pitkin, where the
Denver, South Park and Pacific narrow-gauge
trains used to stop on their way between Gunnison
and the Alpine Tunnel, Forest Service secondary
roads travel over Waunita Pass to the former resort
community of Waunita Springs and east over the
low crossing at Black Sage Pass—a once heavily
traveled stagecoach route—to White Pine, or south
to Sargents on US Highway 50. From Sargents,
additional routes lead back over the Continental
Divide by way of modern Monarch Pass, old
Monarch Pass, and along the historic railroad crossing, now a backcountry road, at Marshall Pass. Particularly in autumn, when the aspen are in full color,
this interconnecting network of roads through the
eastern side of Gunnison National Forest provides
some of the best scenic tours in all of Colorado.

In the northern part of Gunnison National Forest,
an equally extensive series of improved gravel
roads, backcountry roads, and trails winds through
the open meadows of Taylor Park and ascends the
forested foothills and high country of the Elk
Range. From Almont, on Colorado Highway 135,
good Forest Service roads follow all of the major
drainages of the area, opening up a large expanse of
territory for fishing, camping, picnicking, or sightseeing. From Crested Butte, equally good roads
travel west over Kebler Pass to the North Fork of
the Gunnison River, or north along a beautiful route
to Gothic, once a boom town of eight thousand persons and today the home of the Rocky Mountain
Biological Laboratory. Beyond Gothic and the lush,
majestic valley surrounding it, a primitive road extends along the nineteenth-century stagecoach
route past scenic Emerald Lake to Schofield Pass.
Additional roads extend northwest from Crested
Butte into the little-traveled Ruby Range and high

into the Elk Range. Farther to the west, a nearly endless network of hiking trails crosses through the West Elk Wilderness area, which the Colorado Wilderness Act of 1980 doubled in size. This act also carved a new 106-square-mile Ragged Mountains Wilderness in the alpine countryside north of the West Elk Wilderness.

In the southeastern corner of Gunnison National Forest, the landscape is less dramatic but more varied, the handiwork of human history less evident, and the visitors fewer in number. From US Highway 50, a winding paved road that extends down Cochetopa Canyon branches east to travel over Cochetopa Pass and connects with a dirt road past Old Agency. Old Agency, now the site of a Forest Service work camp, was originally called the Los Piños Indian Agency; it served as the administrative center for the Southern Ute Indian bands displaced from the San Luis Valley in 1868 and was a well-known stopping point for road-weary nineteenth-century travelers making their way by horse and stagecoach down the long route to Lake City and beyond.

Beyond Old Agency, the dirt road continues through little-used countryside, travels over Los Piños Pass, and descends along the Powderhorn Primitive Area and the Cebolla Game Management Area, both of which are located just beyond the forest boundary. This route then travels beside Mill Creek, a popular fishing stream, and exits the forest just west of Slumgullion Pass, at the site of the huge Slumgullion earth flow. Slumgullion slide, which began flowing some seven hundred years ago, is a slow-moving natural earth flow now about four miles long and more than a quarter mile wide. In relatively recent times the slide blocked the Lake Fork of the Gunnison River, forming the body of water known as Lake San Cristobal. This lake, located just beyond the forest boundary, is the second-largest naturally formed body of water in Colorado.

In addition to the points of interest and other features already mentioned, Gunnison National Forest offers excellent fishing on Taylor Park Reservoir and its tributaries, along with a diverse range of camping facilities in twenty-seven designated campgrounds that provide nearly four hundred camping units. The campsites range in elevation from as low as 6,800 feet to the alpine site at Crystal Lake, situated above timberline at 11,700 feet.

The special attraction of Gunnison National Forest lies in the diversity of passive and active recreational opportunities it affords in a setting of unusual physical beauty and high historical interest. It is not the largest, the best known, the most spectacular, nor the most frequently visited of Colorado's national forests, but it offers an abundance of the diversified pleasures that make Colorado's public recreational lands a year-round national attraction.

An old church in Tincup, converted to other uses.

21 San Isabel National Forest

Location: south-central Colorado

Size: 1,736 square miles

Terrain: alpine peaks and rugged mountain lands

Scenic Value: very high to exceptional

Historical Interest: moderate to high

Highway Access: US 50, US 24, US 160, Colorado 12, Colorado 17, and Colorado 82

Internal Access: paved highways, improved and primitive dirt roads, and foot trails

Maps: USFS map of San Isabel National Forest at 1:125,000
Various USGS sheets of Lake, Chaffee, Fremont, Custer, Huerfano, and Pueblo counties at 1:50,000
USFS map of Leadville district ski trails at 1:24,000

San Isabel National Forest is a sprawling landscape of high alpine peaks and rugged, mountainous scenes rising above the upper Arkansas River Valley and the Wet Mountain Valley. Unlike other Colorado national forests, San Isabel encompasses no broad valleys, and few significant rivers flow through it. Instead, it offers the single largest concentration of 14,000-foot peaks found anywhere in Colorado – or for that matter, anywhere in the contiguous United States. In fact, about half of Colorado's fourteeners are located in or adjacent to San Isabel National Forest.

Impressive statistics do not themselves guarantee beauty, nor does the number of large mountains in an area ensure dramatic vistas. If that were the case, an armchair traveler could judge the beauty of the land simply by reading topographic maps. The appeal of San Isabel National Forest lies in the arrangement of this imposing mountain landscape in three distinct groupings: the Sawatch Range, the Sangre de Cristo Mountains, and the Spanish Peaks.

The Sawatch Range forms the western edge of the upper Arkansas Valley and is the highest and most massive ridgeline in Colorado. From Salida to

The Sawatch Range from the Mosquito Pass road east of Leadville.

Leadville, a distance of some sixty miles, this towering rock wall rises above the valley floor in an unbroken line that includes more than a dozen four-teeners. Mount Elbert and Mount Massive, Colorado's two highest peaks and among the easiest of the large mountains to climb, form a portion of the Sawatch Range. At the center of the range is the Collegiate group, a particularly impressive row of large peaks that the early surveyors and mountain climbers named in honor of Harvard, Yale, Princeton, Columbia, and Oxford universities. The sight of these snowcapped peaks reaching across the western horizon from US Highway 24 ranks among the best scenic views in Colorado, and the Colorado Wilderness Act of 1980 designated a 250-square-mile portion of this area as the Collegiate Peaks Wilderness.

The east side of the Sawatch Range, however, offers much more than sweeping highway vistas. This section of San Isabel National Forest is a hiking, camping, fishing, and climbing preserve with endless sightseeing opportunities. At the north end of the range is Turquoise Reservoir and Twin Lakes Reservoir, both parts of the Fryingpan–Arkansas water diversion project. Turquoise Reservoir is accessible by a circumferential roadway, and

on the south side of the reservoir an unmarked backcountry road leads along the historic route of the Colorado Midland Railway to the top of Hagerman Pass and then down the Fryingpan valley to Ruedi Reservoir and the town of Basalt. The road to Twin Lakes Reservoir (Colorado Highway 82) crosses Independence Pass (open only in summertime) and descends along the beautiful Roaring Fork River to Aspen. West of Buena Vista, a well-graded gravel road (Colorado 306) winds through the heart of the Collegiate group, between Mount Yale and Mount Princeton, following the nineteenth-century wagon road over Cottonwood Pass to Taylor Park and the Gunnison country in Gunnison National Forest.

About a half dozen miles to the south, Colorado Highway 162 skirts the chalk-colored cliffs of Mount Princeton to the resort community of Mount Princeton Hot Springs and the scenic ghost town of St. Elmo. From there the road, still passable by automobile, ascends to the site of Romley and Hancock following the route of the old Denver, South Park and Pacific railroad. From Romley, hikers and four-wheel-drive enthusiasts can travel to the closed east portal of the Alpine Tunnel or up Han-

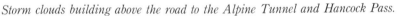

Storm clouds building above the road to the Alpine Tunnel and Hancock Pass.

cock Pass to the imposing Brittle Silver Basin above the headwaters of Quartz Creek. At the southern end of this San Isabel National Forest unit is the Monarch Pass road and the less frequently traveled backcountry road over Marshall Pass, where the narrow-gauge trains of the Denver and Rio Grande Railway Company once steamed.

An abandoned house in St. Elmo.

At the northern end of San Isabel National Forest is Leadville, surrounded by private land and Bureau of Land Management holdings. Here, starting in 1878 and lasting for more than a decade, a mining boom of immense proportions took place, producing nearly 100 million dollars' worth of silver and some of the great legends of Colorado history. Pop-

ular tourist attractions include the historic district of downtown Leadville, where the Taylor Opera House and other boom-day monuments still stand. The scarred flanks of the Mosquito Range, where mining fortunes were once made and lost weekly, rise a short distance east of town. About a half-dozen miles south of Leadville on US Highway 24 is the start of the scenic Weston Pass backcountry road, once a traffic-jammed stage and wagon route over the Mosquito Range to Fairplay.

The central portion of San Isabel National Forest includes the eastern side of the Sangre de Cristo Mountains and the little-known Wet Mountains. Between these two ranges is the Wet Mountain Valley, a land rich in local history and blessed with a majestic view of the high and rugged Sangre de Cristos. In the winter of 1806–07, Lieutenant Zebulon Pike wandered through the Wet Mountain Valley, struggling to find the Sangre de Cristo crossing that eventually took him into the San Luis Valley and to house arrest by the Mexican government. On the east side of the Wet Mountains, in an area long contested by the Ute and Arapaho Indians, trappers and merchants established a series of trading posts and small adobe communities during the 1830s and 1840s. John Frémont passed through one of these communities, called Hardscrabble, in December 1848 on his disastrous fourth expedition West in search of a transcontinental railway route.

The first European settlement of the Wet Mountain Valley occurred in 1870 when some three hundred members of the German Colonization Society arrived there hoping to found a utopian community. They established a town called Colfax in honor of Schuyler Colfax, then vice-president of the United States. Internal rivalries, inept leadership, the short growing season, and outside hostility brought this early frontier agricultural cooperative to as swift an ending as Vice-President Colfax, whose political career was ruined by his involvement in the Crédit Mobilier scandal. Little evidence of the German Colonization Society remains, but its memory continues in place names such as Colfax Lane, a gravel road that travels from Colorado Highway 69 beside a fine view of Humboldt Peak, and Colony Lane, a road south of Westcliffe that leads up South Colony Creek toward two rugged fourteeners, Crestone Peak and Crestone Needle.

Today the Wet Mountain Valley and surrounding national forest lands remain a little-visited but spectacular corner of Colorado. The Sangre de Cristos still rise majestically above the placid valley, and the Wet Mountains offer some of the best scenery in the state. The trip from Wetmore (on Colorado Highway 67 south of Florence) to Hardscrabble

Divide, Westcliffe, and down the valley to Gardner provides stunning views and solitary travel far from the crowds that cluster about the better-known recreational areas. Specific attractions in the area include Lake Isabel, located on Colorado 165 west of Rye; the Lake Hermit area, west of Westcliffe; south Colony Lakes, located at the foot of the Crestones; and the charming upper Huerfano River Valley, from Gardner to the forest lands above Sharpsdale.

The southernmost unit of San Isabel National Forest lies on the east side of the Sangre de Cristos and south of the town of La Veta. This area includes some lovely Spanish-style ranching country and one of the best-known landmarks in the Southwest—the Spanish Peaks. These two volcanic mounds, which tower more than 7,000 feet above the plains, served as a guidepost for generations of Indian, Spanish, Mexican, and American travelers. Known to the Indians as "Wahatoya" (several other spellings exist), or breasts of the earth, they are readily visible seventy-five miles to the east along the Santa Fe Trail as it ascends from the Arkansas River toward Raton Pass.

Although the Spanish Peaks lie near the Sangre de Cristo Mountains, the two mountain groups are geologically distinct. The twin peaks represent the remains of ancient volcanoes where molten rock intruded the seams of softer sedimentary formations. As erosion deteriorated the softer stone, the harder igneous rock remained, giving the East and West Spanish peaks their distinctive form. These igneous intrusions are most evident in the massive spiked ridges, or dikes, that radiate out from the peaks. The dikes, which are as much as one hundred feet high and up to fourteen miles long, have formed along other mountain flanks, but nowhere else in the world are they known to exist in such size and abundance.

The Spanish Peaks are accessible by two roads and several hiking trails. Colorado Highway 12, between La Veta and Trinidad, passes through this portion of San Isabel National Forest about a half dozen miles west of the peaks. It is a lovely winding route with exciting views of the Spanish Peaks, the Culebra Range directly to the west, and the more distant Sangre de Cristos. The other route, an unpaved secondary road starting at the summit of Cucharas Pass, travels to the south of the Spanish Peaks, affording close-up views of the rarely seen back side of the twin formations. After traversing Apishapa (an Indian name for stinking spring) Pass, the road travels under a dramatic masonry arch constructed by the Civilian Conservation Corps through one of the dikes, and eventually terminates at the town of Aguilar by Interstate 25.

22 Great Sand Dunes National Monument

Location: San Luis Valley/northeast of Alamosa

Size: 61 square miles

Terrain: high-desert sand dunes bounded by alpine peaks

Scenic Value: unique

Historical Interest: considerable

Highway Access: from US 160 and Colorado 17

Internal Access: by foot and one four-wheel-drive route

Maps: USFS map of Rio Grande National Forest at 1:125,000
USGS sheet 5 of Saguache County and sheet 1 of Alamosa County at 1:50,000
USGS composite map of Great Sand Dunes National Monument at 1:24,000

By late January of 1807, Zebulon Pike's expedition had crossed the Colorado plains, explored the area around Pikes Peak, wandered along the front range, and crossed through the South Platte and upper Arkansas valleys into the Wet Mountain Valley. Without adequate winter clothing or provisions, Pike's men struggled southward in the shadow of the Sangre de Cristos—near starvation, demoralized, suffering from frostbite, and quite obviously lost in their search for the Red River.

On January 27 an advance party of the expedition marched through snow in some places three feet deep along a crossing of the Sangre de Cristos that descended to a small creek running west, which Pike said in his journals they "hailed with fervency as the waters of the Red River." The next day Pike and his men followed the creek downstream, discovering at the foot of the mountain ridge a series of "sand hills" about fifteen miles long and five miles wide. In his journal entry of January 28, 1807, Pike reported of these hills: "Their appearance was exactly that of a sea in a storm (except as to color) not the least sign of vegetation existing thereon." After camping for the night, Pike climbed one of the highest sand hills, from which he saw a "large river" flowing from a "third chain of mountains."

Late afternoon view of the sand dunes from Medano Creek.

Thus he described the Rio Grande descending the San Juans.

The drainage that Pike briefly mistook for the Red River now goes by the name of Medano (Spanish for sand hill) Creek, a stream that quickly drains into the porous sands beneath it. But Pike's description of the area is apt: undulating sand hills bounded to the east by a rugged mountain range and opening on a high-desert valley that sits in the rain shadow of yet another mountain range.

Many other peoples had traveled through the sand dune area before Captain Pike. Archeological evidence suggests that a Folsom-man hunting party killed and butchered a bison at a site just west of the dunes some ten thousand years earlier. In the ensuing millennia, wave upon wave of roaming Indian bands migrated through the area. For centuries Pueblo Indian hunting parties dominated the valley floor until they were displaced by the Utes, who in turn were followed by the Spanish. In pursuit of a New World empire, the Spanish transformed a nomadic high-desert hunting ground into a series of land grants bequeathed by the King of Spain to favored settlers. In due course the dreams of Spanish glory faded, and Pike's visit to the sand dunes was followed by other American explorers. Four decades after Pike's visit, John Frémont passed by the site in search of a transcontinental rail route, and Captain John Gunnison explored the sand dunes area for the same purpose five years later. The August 25, 1853, journal entry in the official report of the Gunnison expedition refers to ". . . gigantic sand-hills, rising above the plain to half the height (apparently, at least, 700 or 800 feet) of the adjacent mountain, and shaped by the winds into beautiful and fanciful forms with waving outlines, for within certain limits this sand drifts about like snow."

During this lengthy period of cultural succession, both primitive man and New-World travelers who followed must certainly have wondered how the accident of geology that we call the sand dunes occurred. The answer to this question begins in relatively recent geologic times. After an extended period of mountain building that created the San Juans, wind and water transported massive amounts of finely ground volcanic sand eastward across the floor of the San Luis Valley. The prevailing southwesterly winds lifted the sand from the arid, thinly vegetated valley, where less than ten inches of moisture fall in an average year, and carried it toward the towering wall of the Sangre de Cristos. The velocity of the winds diminished in the face of this obstacle, and the sand particles drifted to the ground, where further wind action has sculpted them into one of the world's tallest inland sand dunes.

Why did the sand dunes accumulate at the particular location where we observe them and not elsewhere along the border of the valley? For most of their length along the eastern rim of the valley, the Sangre de Cristos form a ridgeline that scarcely drops below 13,000 feet. To the north of the sand dunes, this ridge rises in a cluster of four large mountains, and again to the south three more high peaks thrust up from the valley floor. In between these seven mountains, all more than 14,000 feet high, the Sangre de Cristos dip down in a natural gateway that encompasses several relatively low crossing points: Music Pass, Medano Pass, and Mosca Pass. This drop in the range has acted like an enormous rock funnel, channeling the wind and sand from across the valley. Visitors to the sand dunes wishing to see evidence of this effect should take a trip up Medano Pass, where the wind has carried sand many miles above the floor of the valley into the mountain forest.

The sand dunes are not merely a timeless and sterile monument to the geologic past. Wind and the other forces of nature are continually changing them, as testified to by a strange sight at the northeastern corner of the monument. There, in the Ghost Forest, shifting sands first buried and destroyed, then later reexposed, a stand of ponderosa pine whose barren, sandblasted trunks rise grotesquely from the dunes.

The sand dunes area includes a surprisingly wide array of ecosystems ranging from desert country to a shallow creek bed, arid grasslands, piñon–juniper woodlands, and mountain forests dominated by pine, fir, and spruce. This compact series of ecosystems in turn supports a variety of wildlife. Variations in temperature, moisture, and terrain bring many different species into a limited area. The kangaroo rat, a marvelous study in adaptive development, can exist on the dunes along with blow grass and sunflowers. Hawks, owls, an occasional eagle, and other raptors circle overhead. Coyotes and rabbits populate the area surrounding the dunes; mule deer often wander down to the creek, a small herd of pronghorn inhabits the area, and elk and Rocky Mountain bighorn sheep graze in the mountains above. Contrary to popular imagination, however, the dunes do not support a significant population of snakes or lizards—species ill adapted to a high-desert environment.

Spring and fall are optimal times to visit Great Sand Dunes National Monument. In the spring months, Medano Creek is running at its maximum flow, and the searing summertime heat, which can raise the temperature of the dunes to 140 degrees, has not yet arrived. Autumn brings cooler temperatures along with clear blue skies, lovely fall colors, and a respite from the mosquito hordes that often plague the monument area during summer.

Monument visitors should allow sufficient time for at least three excursions: a tour of the air-conditioned and well-managed monument headquarters, with its informative exhibits; an early morning or late afternoon hike across Medano Creek to the high dunes; and a journey on foot or by four-wheel-drive vehicle (the Park Service provides tours in season) up the creek bed. More intrepid visitors can hike to the Ghost Forest; walk from the monument to the top of Mosca Pass (about seven miles for the round trip) along an historic route of exploration and trade; or travel up the creek to Medano Pass (a twelve-mile route suitable for horseback or four-wheel-drive travel), following the path that Captain Pike probably traveled on his winter crossing in 1807.

Mule deer by the edge of Medano Creek.

23 Rio Grande National Forest

Location: southern Colorado

Size: 2,893 square miles

Terrain: high peaks, forested tablelands, and mountain river valleys

Scenic Value: very high

Historical Interest: very high

External Access: US 160, US 285, Colorado 17, Colorado 114, and Colorado 149

Internal Access: paved highways, improved and primitive dirt roads, and foot trails

Maps: USFS map of Rio Grande National Forest at 1:125,000
Various USGS sheets of Alamosa, Saguache, Conejos, Archuleta, and Mineral counties at 1:50,000

Surrounding the high country above the San Luis Valley, the Rio Grande National Forest stretches in a large, irregular arc from the towering peaks of the Sangre de Cristo Mountains to the top of the San Juan Mountains, along a lengthy stretch of the Continental Divide. The Rio Grande National Forest is aptly named; it includes the headwaters and upper drainages of the Rio Grande del Norte, the Great River of the North, which is the third longest river in the nation.

These two mountain chains, the Sangre de Cristos and the San Juans, represent the southernmost extension of the Rocky Mountains. The area they encompass, the San Luis Valley, was long a buffer land traveled by many cultures competing to hold and gain a territorial base in the New World. The King of Spain's colonial representatives in the New World did little to settle this forbidding land north of New Mexico, but they were the first Europeans to visit it. In 1694 Don Diego de Vargas led a military expedition to the lower reaches of the San Luis Valley. In 1779, while the American colonies were involved in their War of Independence with England, Juan Bautista de Anza led another mili-

View of the Weminuche Wilderness from Big Meadows Reservoir, near the base of Wolf Creek Pass.

tary force through the area. This expedition penetrated deep into the San Luis Valley, noting the headwaters of the Rio Grande and the low crossing point north of the San Juans in the rolling Cochetopa Hills. In 1807 Zebulon Pike traveled through the San Luis Valley in his search for the Red River, and by the 1820s Spanish traders and American mountain men were crossing through the valley and over the Continental Divide by way of Cochetopa Pass.

It was this low route through the forestlands west of the San Luis Valley that John Frémont intended to take on his privately financed fourth expedition in 1848. In an ill-conceived effort to make a winter crossing of Cochetopa Pass to demonstrate its value as a transcontinental railway route, Frémont and his party entered the San Luis Valley in December 1848 and ascended the upland valleys through heavy snow, high winds, and bitter cold. The pack animals began to die of exhaustion, frostbite and hunger set in, and the group retreated to an emergency camp in the La Garita Mountains near the present boundary of the La Garita Wilderness. The stronger members of the party set out to seek fresh supplies; sixteen days later, when they failed to return, Frémont sent out another party to seek aid. By the time help arrived and the stragglers were rounded up, eleven members of the thirty-three-person expedition had died of starvation and exposure. Another two members would be killed by Ute Indians when they returned to collect the supplies abandoned along the route.

Settlement followed in the wake of the early explorers. San Luis, the first permanent Spanish community in Colorado, was founded in 1851, as settlers began growing crops and grazing livestock throughout the San Luis Valley. The discovery of gold deposits in the San Juan Mountains brought the Denver and Rio Grande Railway through the San Luis Valley in 1878 and then over Cumbres Pass, located in the southern end of Rio Grande National Forest. Several years later, prospectors began finding rich ore deposits along Kerber Creek, which is north of Sawatch; near Crestone, located on the east side of the valley; and high in the San Juan Mountains above the Alamosa River. During the 1880s, miners flocked to Bonanza, Platero, Summitville, and dozens of less well remembered sites.

Then, in 1890 Nicholas Creede, a hard-luck prospector looking for ore farther up the Rio Grande, stumbled upon a silver lode of impressive size, and Colorado's last great silver boom was soon under way as miners, merchants, madams, and a host of con men and shadowy underworld figures flocked to the area. By the height of the boom,

Creede's population had swollen to perhaps ten thousand persons, and the town acquired a reputation for lawlessness and violence that rivaled Silverton's reputation in its heyday. Repeal of the Sherman Silver Purchase Act, the Cripple Creek gold strikes near Pikes Peak, and depleted ore deposits eventually restored a measure of normalcy to Creede. Nevertheless, modern-day visitors will still find evidence of the glory days this picturesquely located town once enjoyed.

The upper drainage of the Rio Grande offers a number of additional attractions. Several roads travel north from Creede to various old mining sites. To the east of Creede is the La Garita Wilderness, which was greatly expanded in size by the Colorado Wilderness Act of 1980. At the southern edge of the wilderness, accessible by hiking trail and a four-wheel-drive road, is the Wheeler Geologic Area. Once a national monument but subsequently dedesignated, it offers backcountry travelers some of the most interesting rock formations found anywhere in the state. The little-used forestlands north and east of the La Garita Wilderness include an extensive network of improved—and not so improved—dirt roads that travel through the Cochetopa Hills, crossing the Continental Divide at historic Cochetopa Pass and several other locations.

From Colorado Highway 149 west of Creede, a long Forest Service road continues up the Rio Grande through a lovely recreational area dotted with reservoirs and rich in history. The road travels to Rio Grande Reservoir, set high in the San Juans. From there a primitive road continues over the Continental Divide at Stony Pass, a long and steep but often traveled nineteenth-century route into the gold fields above Ouray and Silverton. The forestlands south of this long route are nearly all included within the Weminuche Wilderness, which spans the Continental Divide, crossing into the San Juan National Forest.

West of Alamosa, in another remote corner of the Rio Grande National Forest, several hundred square miles of fascinating countryside lie hidden in the vicinity of Summitville and Stunner. At the heart of the area is Summitville, a high and forboding ghost town where many cabins, ore-processing equipment, and other mining remains still stand in quiet testimony to the frantic activity that once occurred at this desolate site deep in the San Juans. From Summitville a road leads west, circling above Schinzel Flats and descending through wild and spectacular countryside to the site of Stunner, another former mining town, set near the banks of the Alamosa River. The long, winding, and sometimes rough roads through this remote area should be traversed by passenger cars only under good

All aboard!

weather conditions and with careful attention to detailed maps of the area, as there are rarely other travelers around to lend assistance. But backcountry travelers will be well rewarded with a profusion of lovely valleys, high meadows, steep canyons, rushing streams, brightly colored rock formations, and high peaks.

In addition to the usual methods of travel, visitors to Rio Grande National Forest can also select steam-powered narrow-gauge railroad touring on the Cumbres and Toltec Scenic Railroad. This scenic excursion route between Antonito, Colorado and Chama, New Mexico travels a portion of the old Denver and Rio Grande Railway main line from Pueblo to the San Juan goldfields. After the D&RG abandoned the tracks, the states of Colorado and New Mexico purchased this historic route over Cumbres Pass, along with much of the railway's extensive stock of narrow-gauge cars and equipment. From springtime through the fall, Cumbres and Toltec steam locomotives haul trainloads of delighted passengers through the lush, rolling countryside of southern Colorado and northern New Mexico, returning them to their point of departure by bus over Colorado Highway 17, the modern Cumbres Pass highway. The sight and sound and smell of this more leisurely nineteenth-century mode of travel never fails to entertain modern-day travelers accustomed to looking at the world through the safety-glass windows of an automobile. The experience is particularly enjoyable early in the season, when the heavy accumulations of snow have only recently been cleared from the tracks, and in later September, when the fall colors are at their height.

24 San Juan National Forest

Location: southwestern Colorado

Size: 2,918 square miles

Terrain: dramatic mountain peaks and valleys

Scenic Value: exceptional

Historical Interest: exceptional

External Access: US 160, US 550, and US 666

Internal Access: paved roads, improved and primitive dirt roads, and foot trails

Maps: USFS map of San Juan National Forest at 1:125,000
Various USGS sheets of Archuleta, Mineral, Hinsdale, San Juan, La Plata, Montezuma, and Delores counties at 1:50,000

The San Juan country, in southwestern Colorado, is the most westerly—and also the most dramatic—extension of the Southern Rockies. Nowhere else in Colorado does there exist so extensive a concentration of towering peaks, high meadows, lovely valleys, and awesome canyons as in the San Juan country. In the heart of this region lie the San Juan Mountains, bordered on various sides by the San Miguel Mountains, the Sneffels Range, the awesome Needle Mountains, the La Plata Range, and a southeastward arm of the San Juans, which form the western boundary of the San Luis Valley. Together, these separate mountain ranges and the widely spaced valleys between them constitute the San Juan country, a 10,000-square-mile recreational wonderland carved by repeated geological epochs of uplift, erosion, volcanism, and glacial scouring.

Long before the arrival of white settlers in Colorado, the San Juans were a portion of the homeland occupied by the far-ranging Ute Indians. As immigrants pushed ever farther west into Colorado, the Utes found it necessary to give up increasing territory. In 1863 the Utes ceded the San Luis Valley in return for extensive reservation lands west of the Continental Divide. Encroachment by white settlers continued, however, and five years later the Utes were forced to sign another treaty. This agreement established a new reservation, lying along a north–south line (the 107th meridian of longitude) running approximately through Pagosa Springs and Gunnison.

There matters might have remained for a while, at least among the Southern Ute bands, were it not for two events. The first occurred tens of millions of years ago when successive epochs of volcanic upheaval deposited rich mineral lodes in the San Juan region. The second event took place in more recent times, as a trickle of miners and prospectors climbed the steep valleys and towering rock walls that led into the heartland of the San Juan country. Discoveries of gold and silver overcame any hesitation they might have felt in encroaching upon Indian lands. As the trickle grew to a stream and later to a raging torrent, pressure mounted to push the Utes back once again. The Brunot Treaty, signed in 1873, removed a large rectangular area of the San Juans from Ute control, opening the way to large-scale white settlement. In 1882 the Denver and Rio Grande Railway tracks reached Silverton by way of the Animas River canyon, and in that same year the town of Durango staged its first public hanging. The San Juan mining boom was well under way, frontier law and order and the age of steam locomotion having arrived more or less together in the San Juans.

The San Juan National Forest is a sprawling woodland and mountain preserve that includes the southern portion of the San Juan Mountains, the La Plata Mountains, the Needle Mountains, and the southeastern extension of the San Juans. The northern and eastern boundaries of the forest lie along a high and rugged ridgeline reaching up to 14,000 feet at several points. Access across this barrier has always been by way of mountain pass routes. Still today, only three of the many pass routes (Wolf Creek, Red Mountain, and Lizard Head passes) accommodate paved roads. Several additional pass routes of historical interest, such as Summit Pass, Stony Pass, and Ophir Pass, are open to motorized travel during limited portions of the year, but the majority of crossings remain what they always have been—narrow trails suitable for travel only on foot or by pack animal.

Fortunately for the early San Juan settlers, the principal rivers in the southern portion of the region travel in a north–south direction, providing relatively easy travel routes deep into the mountains. Three of these routes, along the Dolores River (Colorado Highway 145), the Animas River (US 550), and the San Juan River (US 160), remain among the principal transportation arterials in the area. Many hundreds of miles of secondary and unimproved roads along the tributaries of the Dolores and the San Juan provide modern-day travelers with access to a wealth of remote backcountry.

Although the San Juan National Forest is a single continuous unit, for descriptive purposes it can be divided into three separate sections: the western segment, a central unit, and the arc-shaped eastern area.

The western segment of San Juan National Forest, which lies beyond the West Dolores River, is the least mountainous and the most infrequently visited section of the forest. It is bordered on three

View of the upper San Juan Valley from the west side of Wolf Creek Pass.

sides by branches of the Dolores River, which flows southwest through San Juan National Forest to the town of Dolores and ultimately joins the Colorado River in Utah. Starting on Colorado Highway 184 just west of Dolores, a long but well-graded dirt road travels parallel to the main branch of the Dolores River to Narraguinnep Canyon, where one branch of the road exits the forest to US 666 a few miles south of Dove Creek. The other branch of the road climbs steeply to the tablelands above the Dolores River Canyon and continues deep into the forest, with unmarked side roads branching off in

nearly every direction. The Dolores River Canyon, fully a half mile deep in places and richly colored, ranks among the least known of Colorado's major scenic attractions. In addition to the roads on the east side of the canyon, an improved dirt road from US 666 just south of Dove Creek gives access to the Dolores Canyon Overlook picnic ground.

The West Dolores River originates high in the San Miguel Mountains near two 14,000-foot peaks; Mount Wilson and El Diente (the tooth, in Spanish) Peak. The upper portion of the San Miguel Mountains is included within the Wilson Mountains Primitive Area, which straddles the San Juan and Uncompahgre national forests. From Colorado Highway 145 about a dozen miles north of Dolores, another long but scenic and well-maintained back road follows the West Dolores river from its confluence with the main branch of the Dolores to the abandoned mining town of Dunton and the Burro Bridge Campground. From Dunton the road forks both east and west, giving access to additional high forestlands.

The central part of San Juan National Forest, which lies between the Dolores River and the Needle Mountains, is the best known and most heavily used section of the forest. Colorado Highway 145, which parallels the Dolores River from the town of Dolores through Rico to the summit of Lizard Head Pass, is a lovely route with a variety of side roads that wander deep into San Juan National Forest. The Lizard Head, a dramatic 13,000-foot peak capped by a huge volcanic neck, rises west of the pass, and behind it stand El Diente and Mount Wilson.

Bisecting the center of San Juan National Forest is the Animas River, a beautiful mountain stream that flows between Durango and Silverton. The Denver and Rio Grande railroad followed this river route north from Durango in the days when Silverton ranked among the richest and roughest towns in Colorado, a wide-open mining town that did its share, and more, to live up to the reputation of the wild, wild West. Modern-day visitors can travel from Durango over Molas Divide to Silverton on US Highway 550, one of the most spectacular federal highways in the nation. The best way to travel north from Durango, however, is still by narrow-gauge steam locomotive. Every morning during the tourist season, the brightly painted Denver and Rio Grande trains pull out of downtown Durango on their leisurely way through the magnificent countryside en route to Silverton.

Silverton may be the end of the line for the reborn Denver and Rio Grande locomotives, but it is only a scenic way station leading deeper into the San Juan high country. US Highway 550 continues north from Silverton on its way through historic mining districts to the summit of Red Mountain Pass. The main branch of Colorado Highway 110 travels northeast from Silverton up the Animas Valley into a fabled mining region established amidst some of the most spectacular landscapes found anywhere in Colorado. Thanks to decades of intensive mining activity throughout the area, side roads lead up nearly every major valley in the area, providing relatively easy access (though not for passenger cars, in most cases) to a countryside that would otherwise rank as a premier wilderness.

Indeed, a short distance east of the Animas River lies the massive Weminuche Wilderness, where the wild peaks of the Needle Mountains tower above the surrounding landscape. From an ancient, nearly circular peneplain well over two miles high, more than a dozen peaks soar to an elevation above 13,000 feet. Three of the peaks (Windom, Sunlight, and Eolus) reach over 14,000 feet high and rank among Colorado's most remote and challenging large mountains. An aura of awe and mystery has long surrounded the Needle Mountains and the neighboring Granadier Range. The nineteenth-cen-

The Lizard Head seen from Colorado Highway 145.

The San Juans rising above the valley of the East Fork of the San Juan River.

tury Hayden Survey considered the Needle Mountains "almost unequalled in this country in altitude and boldness." Not until fifteen years ago did a trio of Colorado mountaineers manage the first winter ascent of Sunlight Peak and Windom Peak on a nearly week-long expedition, and Mount Eolus resisted a successful winter assault until 1971 – nearly a decade after the first Americans had climbed Mount Everest.

The eastern part of San Juan National Forest stretches from the Needle Mountains to the headwaters of the San Juan River below Wolf Creek Pass and historic Elwood Pass. Reaching across the northern end of this area is a several-hundred-mile expanse of the Weminuche Wilderness, which includes Emerald Lake, one of the largest natural bodies of water in Colorado, and a variety of peaks over 12,000 feet high. South of the wilderness area are three reservoirs: Lemon, Vallecito, and Williams Creek, all of which can be reached by paved or high-quality dirt roads. Vallecito Reservoir, the largest of the three, is located about a dozen miles north of Bayfield on US Highway 160. The Forest Service operates five campgrounds on the reservoir, and two more a short distance to the north. From the road around the west side of the reservoir, several side roads travel north to the edge of the Weminuche Wilderness. The longer of these two routes leads to the site of Tuckerville, once a

small, remote mining camp at the edge of the Needle Mountains. The shorter road, which is paved, ends near the wilderness boundary at the large eighty-eight-unit Vallecito Campground.

Along the southern edge of San Juan National Forest, near the junction of US Highway 160 and Colorado 151, is the Chimney Rock Archeological Area. More than one hundred prehistoric Indian ruins have been identified in this area beneath the towering formation called Chimney Rock. From Colorado 151 a few miles south of US 160, a side road travels through the archeological area to the ruins site. Travelers continuing south on US 160 will arrive at Navaho State Park on thirty-five-mile-long Lake Navaho.

At the far eastern edge of San Juan National Forest, in a pocket of forestlands surrounded on three sides by the meandering course of the Continental Divide, are the upper tributaries of the San Juan River. US Highway 160 travels along the West Fork of the San Juan before climbing to the summit of Wolf Creek Pass. A variety of side roads branch off from the highway, leading up the East Fork of the San Juan and several lesser streams. The very scenic East Fork road crosses over the Continental Divide on a route the upper portion of which is not suitable for passenger cars. Various other roads give access to hiking trails that travel over little-known and unnamed crossings of the Divide into the upper Rio Grande National Forest.

25 Uncompahgre National Forest

Location: southwestern Colorado

Size: 1,473 square miles

Terrain: mountain valleys, high peaks, and plateau lands

Scenic Value: exceptional in the mountain section

Historical Interest: exceptional in the mountain section

External Access: US 550 and Colorado 62, Colorado 141, and Colorado 145

Internal Access: paved highways, improved and primitive dirt roads, and foot trails

Maps: USFS map of Uncompahgre National Forest at 1:125,000
Various USGS sheets of San Miguel, Ouray, Hinsdale, Gunnison, Montrose, and Mesa counties at 1:50,000

The spectacular San Juan country does not end at the boundaries of the San Juan National Forest. Indeed, many people who know the region well would argue that the most dramatic and majestic scenery in the region begins at the northern edge of the San Juan National Forest. Here, in the very heart of the San Juan country, ridge upon ridgeline of high mountains join together in convoluted patterns producing some of the most complex geography found anywhere in Colorado.

This rugged terrain has long delighted tourists and confounded road builders. The first generation of San Juan settlers, intent upon reaching the enormous mineral wealth buried there, spared no cost and ignored most every risk in building an incredible road network that dared the laws of gravity to find the shortest possible routes between the principal communities of the region. Modern highway departments, aware of these early wagon roads but more mindful than their predecessors of geographic considerations, have selected the most practical routes through a complex terrain. The results often frustrate visitors accustomed to flatland-highway travel. Telluride and Silverton, for example, are separated by a distance of only twelve miles, but the highway route between them is seventy-four miles long and takes nearly two hours to negotiate even under good driving conditions. During the summer months, many of the region's historic, cliff-hanging routes are open to backcountry vehicle traffic, offering visitors two separate road networks. Ironically, it is sometimes possible to travel between two points more quickly by primitive nineteenth-century wagon routes than by staying on the modern paved highways.

The northern San Juan country, however, is not merely a landscape of awesome mountain vistas and narrow shelf roads. From the high mountain canyons where the San Miguel and Uncompahgre rivers originate, it sprawls downward into wide valleys that border an elevated plateau. Uncompahgre National Forest encompasses both the mountainous San Juan country and the high forested plateau. The word uncompahgre is a Ute Indian term variously translated to mean red water springs or hot water spring and refers to the area around Ouray, where hot springs occur in the brightly colored rock formations along the Uncompahgre River.

The special appeal of Uncompahgre National Forest stems from two sources. First, it offers a particularly wide diversity of terrain, from box canyons to broad agricultural valleys and from endless mountain landscapes to the quiet beauty of the plateau lands. Second, development of the area during the past century occurred selectively, with the majority of it concentrated in the mineralized belt above the headwaters of the Uncompahgre and San Miguel rivers. Thus Uncompahgre National Forest includes both a heavily impacted segment, where the signs of past and present development are very much in evidence, and relatively pristine wilderness where European man has rarely ventured since his arrival in the New World.

The Uncompahgre Plateau sits toward the relatively undisturbed end of this scale. Ute Indians camped and hunted these forests for centuries, modern hunters descend upon the land for several weeks annually, and local ranchers graze livestock here in an uneasy alliance with the Forest Service. But the absence of significant mineral deposits protects the area from mining scars, and the lack of soaring peaks, prehistoric cliff dwellings, or intricately carved escarpments has retarded recreational use of this land, where paved roads are still non-existent. Since white settlers arrived in this region, the course of civilization has flowed into the valleys lying below the Uncompahgre Plateau.

Fortunately for modern travelers, the upper areas of the plateau have changed little in the past century. What did this land look like a century ago? Henry Gannett, a topographer with the Hayden Survey, was no stranger to the beauties of the West. He visited the Uncompahgre Plateau in the summer of 1874 and wrote the following description of it in the *9th Annual Report of the United States Geological and Geographical Survey of the Territories:*

View of the Sneffels Range from above the Uncompahgre Valley.

Nowhere is the influence of elevation on the character of the vegetation more plainly marked than on this plateau. In the interior, near the crest, the land is, to the Utes, one flowing with milk and honey. Here are fine streams of cold water, beautiful aspen groves, the best of grass in the greatest abundance, and a profusion of wild fruit and berries, while the country is a perfect flower garden. This extends as low as 7,000 ft., below which the scene changes to one in all respects the reverse. Aspen gives way to piñon and cedar. The grasses, fruits and flowers, to sage, cacti and bare rock. The streams become confined in rocky cañons, turn muddy and warm, and gradually disappear . . . Grouse disappear, while rattlesnakes and centipedes assert their proprietorship.

Gone are the days when government scientists and administrators wrote in such a clear, concise, and graceful style. Gannett's description of the Uncompahgre Plateau, however, remains essentially as true today as it was a century ago, despite minor ravages from livestock grazing and some timber cutting.

Fortunately for the modern traveler, a network of well-graded dirt roads now crosscuts the Uncompahgre Plateau. The longest of these routes, known as the Divide Road, is more than sixty miles in length and travels the crest of the plateau nearly from end to end. At the north this road starts on Colorado Highway 141 and terminates far to the south on Colorado 62 a short distance west of the Dallas Divide. A variety of side roads intersect this main route through the plateau. The best known of these routes is the Delta-to-Nucla road, which crosses the crest of the Uncompahgre Plateau at Columbine Pass. From Montrose, two additional roads travel west across the plateau to join Colorado 145 and Colorado 141.

The western side of the plateau, which is more heavily vegetated and less deeply cut by arid canyons than the eastern side, also offers a dramatic excursion along the San Miguel and Dolores rivers. Starting on Colorado Highway 141 south of Grand Junction, the route drops into the steep and colorful Unaweep Canyon, which the Hayden Survey called "grand beyond description;" from there the road continues south of Gateway through additional canyon country carved by the Dolores and San Miguel rivers. North of Uravan, the road passes by the famous hanging flume built nearly a century ago for gold mining; it then continues southeast, taking travelers from this slickrock canyon country characteristic of the Colorado Plateau into the high San Juans.

Visitors who enter the San Juan country by way of the San Miguel River face the pleasant choice of following the San Miguel to its headwaters or traveling east over the Dallas Divide and continuing their journey along the Uncompahgre River. The Dallas Divide route, on Colorado Highway 62, ranks among the most magnificent of Colorado's highway excursions; it travels across idyllic, rolling countryside dominated by a spectacular view of the jagged Sneffels Range rising in the near background. The trip up the San Miguel is an equally dramatic journey into an immense box canyon walled in by a range of peaks reaching up to and beyond 13,000 feet. Squeezed into the floor of this canyon is Telluride, a reborn mining community with a spectacular physical setting unsurpassed by any other town in Colorado.

Now a resort town with some of the most challenging downhill ski runs in Colorado, Telluride was once a hell-bent mining community of five thousand residents. The Liberty Bell, the Smuggler, the Tomboy, and a host of lesser mines produced enough wealth to support a dozen or more bordellos, countless saloons, and the ornate, three-story-high Sheridan Hotel, along with a branch line of the Rio Grande Southern Railroad. Not unmindful of this wealth, George Leroy Parker, a local ranch hand later known as Butch Cassidy, began his bank-robbing career with a stickup of Telluride's San Miguel County Bank on June 24, 1889.

From Telluride, unpaved roads and hiking routes travel steeply upward into the magnificent countryside surrounding the town. Bridal Veil Falls, the highest in the state, the awesome Imogene Pass road, and the road to Alta Lakes are a few of the better-known attractions of the area. Visitors lacking a four-wheel-drive vehicle or strong legs can hire one of the several commercial tour services in the vicinity to see the sights above Telluride. No such effort is needed, however, to reach Telluride's southern neighbor, Ophir. It is a short but highly scenic drive on Colorado Highway 145 to visit this once-thriving community set in a beautiful valley. From Ophir the highway continues south along another beautiful valley, with Wilson Peak and several other high mountains dominating the view.

The route up the San Miguel River may be the most dramatic northern entrance to the upper sections of the Uncompahgre National Forest, but the classic gateway travels along the Uncompahgre River starting at Montrose. From a broad valley view with the Sneffels Range in the distance and the sculptural rock formations by Courthouse Mountain looming on the left, the route ascends a narrow canyon faced with brightly colored cliffs and topped by a sea of high peaks beyond. Near here, in 1875, prospectors found gold lying so close to the surface that it could be prospected with ordinary garden implements. Settlers flocked to the area, founding the town of Ouray in the following year, and additional ore discoveries followed one

Rugged alpine countryside above Telluride.

upon another. The most famous discovery of all occurred about two decades after Ouray was established, when Thomas Walsh hired an old prospector to check out some already developed mining properties. The site, located up Canyon Creek above Ouray, turned out to be one of the richest gold deposits in Colorado history, and Tom Walsh's Camp Bird Mine made him a multimillionaire who went on to become a reknowned U.S. Senator.

Mining activity is still under way in Ouray County, but on a much smaller scale and principally for base metals such as lead and zinc. Tourism has emerged as a leading economic activity, at least during the summer months. Visitors flock to Ouray both for the sights about town and for the backcountry scenery. The attractions around town include the city itself, Bear Creek Falls and Cascade Falls, and Box Canyon, an extraordinary local

gorge that is nearly 300 feet high with a width that narrows to twenty feet.

However, the major attractions of the area lie outside of town. Ouray advertises itself, with justification, both as the Switzerland of America and the jeeping capital of the nation. A few miles south of Ouray on US Highway 550, the Mineral Creek road begins. This four-wheel-drive route travels into the rugged landscape of the Upper Animas Valley, littered with ghost towns and mining structures from a bygone era. From there, spectacular routes wind east over Engineer Pass and Cinnamon Pass to American Flats, Handies Basin, and countless other features in the high mountain countryside above Lake City. To the south, rough side roads ascend the many mining gulches in the area, while the main route travels south to Howardsville and Silverton along a road bordered on both sides by 13,000-foot peaks. Several days of backcountry driving are required to explore even the principal roads in this area southeast of Ouray.

The Uncompahgre National Forest lands southwest of town offer equally exciting adventures. From the south end of Ouray, a steep and exposed but well-graded shelf road (Colorado Highway 361) climbs the cliff side above Canyon Creek to the Camp Bird Mine. A rough four-wheel-drive road branches south from there to Imogene Basin, the awesome Imogene Pass crossing into Savage Basin, and eventually, Telluride. An extension of the Camp Bird road travels east and becomes a four-wheel-drive route as it climbs into the vast expanse of Yankee Boy Basin, an enormous cirque walled in by the Sneffels Range and famous for its profusion of wildflowers. From the top of the basin a hiking trail over Blue Lakes Pass leads to Mount Sneffels, located within the recently designated Mount Sneffels Wilderness.

Directly to the east of Ouray is the highest mountain in the San Juans, Uncompahgre Peak, in the company of another fourteener, Wetterhorn Peak, and a half dozen additional peaks reaching above 13,000 feet. Long a part of the Uncompahgre Primitive Area, this group of peaks is now included in the newly established 153-square-mile Big Blue Wilderness. Access to the southern section of the wilderness is easiest from the Henson Creek road extending west from Lake City. Access from the north to the wilderness and the remaining forestlands in this part of Uncompahgre National Forest is by way of the Owl Creek Pass road. This delightful and well-graded route begins near Ridgeway on US Highway 550, crosses the Cimmaron Ridge, and travels past little-known Silver Jack Reservoir before making a gradual descent down Cimmaron Creek to US 50 by the Curecanti National Recreation Area.

Wildflowers in Yankee Boy Basin.

26 Curecanti National Recreation Area

Location: Gunnison River Valley/between Gunnison and Montrose

Size: 65 square miles

Terrain: plateau and canyon country

Scenic Value: moderate to very high

Historical Interest: moderate

External Access: from US 50, Colorado 92, and Colorado 149

Internal Access: by paved road, by boat, and on foot

Maps: USFS map of Gunnison National Forest at 1:125,000
National Park Service sketch map of Curecanti National Recreation Area at 1:125,000
USGS sheet 4 of Gunnison County and sheet 2 of Montrose County at 1:50,000

For centuries the passage of human history brought little change to the dry, rugged countryside of the lower Gunnison Valley. Ute Indians hunted deer, elk, and other game in the valley when winter snow and cold weather annually drove them down from high mountain hunting grounds. Mountain men, fur traders, and Spanish explorers followed the river route downstream from the high country toward its confluence with the Colorado River. When Captain John Gunnison's expedition journeyed down the river in 1853 to search for a transcontinental railway route, they discovered what many travelers before them had long known. The wide, inviting valley of the Gunnison River leads to a long, steep-walled canyon inhospitable to any form of human passage.

In deference to the awesome terrain of the Gunnison River canyon, no railroad or automobile highway has ever penetrated its heart. However, in the later years of the nineteenth century, one narrow-gauge railroad, the indomitable Denver and Rio Grande, entered its upper canyons. By 1881 the D&RG had reached the town of Gunnison, and the southern branch of the railway was already in the San Juan country, poised to collect revenues hauling ore from the rich mines above Durango and Silverton. To reach the northern San Juan country, Denver and Rio Grande survey crews laid out a route that paralleled the Gunnison River through a canyon five hundred feet and more below the surrounding plateau. At the site of Cimarron, the route exited from the Gunnison and traveled west to Montrose before ascending the Uncompahgre River valley to Ouray.

As agriculture began first to supplement and then to replace mining as the principal economic activity in the region, the demand for water grew proportionately. Starting with the Gunnison Diversion Tunnel in 1910, the federal government has constructed an elaborate water storage and diversion system on the Gunnison in a continuing effort to satisfy the water needs of an arid agricultural region. The result to date has been the completion of three dams on the Gunnison River upstream from Black Canyon of the Gunnison National Monument. The three dams in turn created a series of reservoirs—called Crystal Lake, Morrow Point Lake, and Blue Mesa Lake—which stretch intermittently for dozens of miles along the channel that the river once followed.

In order to capitalize on the recreational potential that this series of reservoirs could offer, Curecanti National Recreation Area was established. The area, which the National Park Service administers, stretches along some thirty-five miles of former river channel from the boundary of Black Canyon of the Gunnison National Monument to the outskirts of the city of Gunnison. The name given to the recreation area honors the Ute Indian chieftan Curicata, who would certainly take slim pleasure in the sight of water-skiers and ice fishermen practicing their respective sports far above his now submerged tribal hunting grounds.

Of the three reservoirs encompassed within Curecanti National Recreation Area, only Blue Mesa Lake is suitable for the full range of recreational water sports. Crystal Lake, the lowest reservoir in the system, is not accessible by road or established foot trail, and its daily fluctuations in water level make it largely unsuitable for recreational purposes. Morrow Point Lake, which is used principally for the generation of hydroelectric power, can be reached only by a three-quarter-mile-long foot trail that starts at US Highway 50 below the Blue Mesa Dam with a dramatic staircase descent of nearly two hundred and fifty steps. Blue Mesa Lake, readily accessible from several points on US 50 and also from Colorado 149 (the road to Lake City), is the largest and best-known body of water in western Colorado.

From the highway, Blue Mesa looks to be a single long reservoir. An aerial view of the area shows it to be comprised of three distinct basins interconnected by channels and extending a considerable distance up its tributary drainages. The three basins, known as Sapinero Basin, Cebolla Basin, and Iola Basin, are each about four miles long, and the four major arms of these basins, called the Soap Creek Arm, the Lake Form Arm, the West Elk Arm, and the Cebolla Arm, extend from two to six

Blue Mesa Reservoir at Curecanti National Recreation Area.

miles up their respective drainages. The total surface area of water within these basins and inlets varies considerably during the course of the year, rising during the season of spring runoff and dropping much lower in the fall. Blue Mesa Lake, however, is sufficiently large to support a full range of water sports during the three seasons of the year when it is not frozen. Rainbow trout are the principal fish found in the reservoir, but Blue Mesa is also well stocked with brown and mackinaw trout and kokanee salmon. Golden eagles, seagulls, and blue herons nest in the area, and the winter wildlife population includes bald eagles, deer, and elk.

The majority of recreational activities at Curecanti National Recreation Area take place around Blue Mesa Lake, particularly at the Elk Creek and Lake Fork campsite areas. But the most interesting sights and the most dramatic scenery at Curecanti are located farther downstream at Morrow Point Lake. Water-level access is gained from the Pine

Creek trail. Intrepid hand-powered boat operators may carry their craft down the trail and enjoy an eighteen-mile round trip to the secluded Hermit's Rest campsite located on the north end of the reservoir, about a mile up from Morrow Point Dam. In addition, the Park Service operates a thirty-passenger tour boat, the *Shavano*, to provide visitors with a two-hour guided excursion of the narrow lake with its towering, fiordlike canyon walls. Reservations for this extraordinary trip are available on a first-come, first-served basis up to three days in advance at the Elk Creek Visitors Center.

Land-based travelers will find two additional attractions in the Morrow Point segment of Curecanti National Recreation Area. At the community of Cimarron, on US Highway 50, a short side road travels up the Little Cimarron River to the base of Morrow Point Dam, a massive double-curvature concrete wall that creates a box canyon. The large underground generating room, excavated from solid rock inside the canyon wall, is open to public tours during the summer months. Outdoor signboards describe additional features of the dam, reservoir, and transmission system. A short distance downstream from the dam, by the roadside, rests an outdoor historic railroad display consisting of a Denver and Rio Grande steam locomotive and several cars sitting on a steel-framed platform.

The other attraction in the Morrow Point area is a little-known but spectacular scenic drive along the north side of the lake. This route, designated as Colorado Highway 92, starts at US 50 by the Blue Mesa Dam, quickly climbs to the mesa top, and follows along the rim, giving magnificent views of the Gunnison River at Pioneer Point Overlook, at Cimarron Overlook, and at several other points. Visitors with only limited time available can travel the scenic drive to the Pioneer Point Overlook by the Curecanti Needle or, alternately, the Cimarron Overlook and return to US 50. Otherwise, Colorado 92 serves as an access road to the Crawford State Recreation Area near the town of Crawford and to the rarely visited north rim of Black Canyon of the Gunnison National Monument.

From both US Highway 50 and Colorado 92, a series of side roads extend north from Curecanti National Recreation Area into a little-used portion of Gunnison National Forest, giving access to the Black Mesa Experimental Forest and the recently expanded West Elk Wilderness, which is among the least-visited wilderness areas in Colorado. Four principal access roads lead into the area, giving travelers an opportunity for extensive exploration off the beaten track.

The Denver and Rio Grande Western railroad display at Morrow Point Dam.

27 Black Canyon of the Gunnison National Monument

Location: western Colorado/southeast of Grand Junction

Size: 21 square miles

Terrain: mesa country bisected by a deep, sheer-walled canyon

Scenic Value: exceptional

Historical Interest: modest

Highway Access: US 50, Colorado 347, and Colorado 92

Internal Access: north and south side rim roads, paved road to the river, and hiking trails

Maps: USGS sheet 2 of Montrose County at 1:50,000

Late in the summer of 1853, Captain John Gunnison's survey expedition was working its way downstream from the Continental Divide toward the Colorado (then the Grand) River. As the expedition drove its wagons through increasingly rough, steep canyon country, advance parties scouting ahead for a suitable route soon observed the river entering an "immense ravine" not practical for the railway route Gunnison was seeking. So Captain Gunnison and his command sidestepped the canyon, taking a more gentle route to the southwest. When the expedition issued its final report several years later, the September 8, 1853 journal account gave a firsthand description of what Gunnison's survey party found: "The stream is imbedded in narrow and sinuous cañones, the dark top outline of which resembles a large snake in motion, as the wavy atmosphere conveys the light to the eye."

In 1874 the Hayden expedition explored the Gunnison country, traversing the north rim of the canyon and providing the first accurate survey of the area. The Hayden party, like Gunnison's expedition, did not venture through the canyon itself. A decade later the Denver and Rio Grande sent a survey crew into the area. This private expedition, led by Byron Bryant, reached the same conclusion as had Gunnison—there existed no feasible railroad route through the entire length of the canyon. The Bryant party pointed out the possibility, however, of diverting water from the river to irrigate the Uncompahgre Valley.

To explore further the possibility of a water diversion from the Gunnison River, another party explored the canyon floor in 1900, using two wooden boats. The swift, shallow waters quickly destroyed one boat, and the survey party failed to

complete its journey through the gorge. The following year, the U.S. Geological Survey authorized another expedition to assess the canyon's water resources. After a number of close calls, A. Lincoln Fellows and William Torrence successfully ran the river in a small rubber raft, collecting the data necessary to engineer a diversion tunnel. The Gunnison Diversion Tunnel, completed in 1910, provided irrigation waters for eighty thousand acres of agricultural land in the Uncompahgre Valley. The tunnel, one of the first in Colorado and an early U.S. Reclamation Service project, has been designated a National Engineering Landmark.

The canyon experienced yet another survey in the 1950s. Wallace R. Hansen thoroughly mapped the canyon's geology for the U.S. Geological Survey. Hansen's study, *The Black Canyon of the Gunnison Today and Yesterday,* is a standard reference work on the geology of the area. In it, the author observes:

> Several western canyons exceed the Black Canyon in overall size. Some are larger; some are deeper; some are narrower; and a few have walls as steep. But no other canyon in North America combines the depth, narrowness, sheerness and somber countenance of the Black Canyon.

This statement summarizes why the Black Canyon of the Gunnison is such a popular tourist attraction, drawing more than a quarter million visitors each year. Not its sheer size, but the dramatic sight of that steep rock incision through an otherwise gentle countryside creates the drama of the Black Canyon. In the twelve-mile gorge section that President Hoover proclaimed a national monument in 1933, the canyon walls soar as much as one-half mile above the river. At the Narrows, the canyon is but forty feet wide by the river and about thirteen hundred feet across at the rim. Especially in late fall and early winter, little sunlight penetrates this dark, winding alleyway of stone, creating the deep shadows that gave the canyon its name. The steep walls and lack of light combine to create another characteristic of the Black Canyon: a striking absence of vegetation throughout most of the gorge. The upper, plateau portion of the monument supports an ample population of birds and other wildlife, but few creatures inhabit the deeper portions of the canyon, which lack habitat to support a significant animal population.

What caused this canyon to occur? The answer, in a single word, is erosion. Volcanic debris accumulating from eruptions long ago in the West Elk and San Juan mountains once covered the area, overlaying a bed of harder rock known as the Gunnison uplift. As the ancestral Gunnison River drained massive volumes of water and debris west from the

Side view of the Black Canyon of the Gunnison.

Bird's-eye view of the Black Canyon of the Gunnison.

Sawatch Range, it eroded the volcanic deposits, eventually encountering harder rock strata formed during previous eras. By this time the course of the river was fixed, its banks were firmly established in the softer rock. So the river cut through the underlying bed as runoff from snowmelt, receding glaciers, and local storms drained downstream.

Many of the forces that created the canyon over a two-million-year period are still at work, but man's intervention upstream from the monument, at Curecanti National Recreation Area, has altered these natural forces. Construction of water storage and electric generating facilities above the Black Canyon has caused a reduction in minimum and peak stream flows, thereby reducing the rate of erosion and allowing increased debris accumulation on the canyon floor. Raging springtime torrents no longer sweep through the Black Canyon.

Other more subtle changes are occurring. The unaltered annual variation in the water level had created a ten-foot-high trim line; within this zone, little but annual vegetation existed. Artificially regulated flows have reduced the height of the trim zone, introducing new plant species to the zone above the low flow line. Summer water temperatures are as much as twenty degrees lower than before because the generating turbines draw water from deeper, and therefore colder, layers of the reservoirs, while wintertime flows are slightly warmer than before. These temperature changes, along with accompanying shifts in the dissolved-oxygen content of the water, can dramatically affect fish and microorganisms on which higher species feed.

Though the long-term cumulative changes that upstream development will bring to the Black Canyon of the Gunnison National Monument are difficult to predict with any certainty, clearly the hand of man has intervened at least briefly in the canyon's natural history. Only the passage of time will tell how lasting or far-reaching these alterations prove to be.

In any case, most Black Canyon visitors do not venture below the rim of the gorge. The predominant pattern of travel at Black Canyon is along the south rim drive from the monument boundary to the headquarters building and the various viewing points on the eight-mile paved road. The Park Service provides a geologic tour guide booklet for this route; it is available at the headquarters building. About a half dozen hiking trails begin at the overlook points and travel partway down the canyon. Another scenic road, starting on Colorado Highway 92 at Crawford, travels along the north rim. This five-mile improved dirt road provides access to a campground and another seven overlook points, but few monument visitors take the north side route. Like the north rim route to the Grand Canyon, it is a little-used yet highly scenic way to avoid the in-season crowds that create a carnival atmosphere at points along the main route.

Experienced technical rock climbers find the sheer canyon walls a challenging experience, but casual visitors should not attempt a foot descent to the river. Fortunately, a paved but steep and little-publicized road descends from Colorado Highway 347 just outside the monument boundary to the river at East Portal. The route provides access to Crystal Dam, picnic facilities, fishing spots, and a downstream hiking trail into the monument.

Travelers visiting this scenic canyon area should bear in mind two cautions, however. First, the East Portal road is one of the steepest paved descents in Colorado. Too rapid a journey will overheat even the best brake systems, causing a severe case of brake fade. If these symptoms appear, stop and take a rest to let the smoke clear and the overworked brake surfaces cool down before continuing. Second, low flow periods along the river may tempt travelers to cross the stream. Be aware that periodic, unannounced upstream discharges can raise the river level rapidly, stranding you on the north side. Therefore, either keep to the south bank or inquire locally regarding high-water periods before risking an extended visit to the other side of the river.

Land of those sweet-air'd interminable plateaus!

Walt Whitman, "Starting from Paumanok,"
Leaves of Grass

IV. The Plateau Country

West of the Rockies stretches an endless no-man's-land, largely arid, long uncharted, and of little apparent economic worth. Father Escalante, the most daring Spanish explorer of the Southwest, passed through this land in the year of American independence while searching for a route to California. Grizzled trappers periodically trekked across the vast plateau wastelands on their way to and from the Green River country in Utah. But for generations of Spanish and American explorers, it was merely a land to be crossed in pursuit of other objectives. As recently as the Civil War era, neither the American public nor the nation's scientific community knew any more about the heart of this country than they did about the face of the moon. When at last explorers penetrated the depths of the plateau country, they found landscapes more extraordinary than anything Jules Verne imagined to exist on the moon. And beneath the surface lay mineral wealth—uranium ores and oil-saturated shale—that a future generation would covet.

For the discovery, exploration, and mapping of the plateau lands west of the Rockies, we are principally indebted to a single man—John Wesley Powell. A Civil War veteran who lost his right arm at the battle of Shiloh, Powell combined the skills of an explorer, scientist, visionary planner, government administrator, and publicist. Perched sometimes on an armchair lashed to the deck of his frail wooden boat, the *Emma Dean,* he led the first expedition to explore the canyons of the Green and the Colorado rivers. Later he would become the first director of the U.S. Bureau of Ethnology and the second director of the U.S. Geological Survey. Not only did Powell navigate the fearful rapids in the Canyon of Lodore and camp at Echo Park, both now in Dinosaur National Monument, but he and his associates named these and many hundred other features of the plateau country. Appropriately, it was a Powell expedition traveling deep in the plateau lands that found the last undiscovered river, the Escalante, and the last undiscovered mountain range, the Henry

Mountains, in the contiguous United States. Those two discoveries, made in 1874, mark the beginning of the end of the western frontier—from then on it was largely a matter of filling in the blank spaces that remained.

Powell's plateau province, as he called it, sprawl across some 130,000 square miles of territory, from the edge of the Southern Rockies to the basin lands of eastern Utah and south into Arizona and New Mexico. At first sight, much of it appears to be a high, denuded plain—the rocky, elevated, and sage-covered continuation of the prairie lands interrupted at the eastern foot of the Rockies. To be sure, the plateau lands do include vast, arid tablelands. But interspaced among them are an astonishing variety and number of buttes, terraced plateaus, escarpments, and canyons, including some of the most spectacular rock gorges and stone cliffs in the world. To describe, classify, and explain these natural phenomena, Powell and his associates expanded the science of physiography and practically invented the modern discipline of physical geology.

The distinguishing geological feature of the plateau country is layer upon layer of sedimentary rock lying more or less horizontally, with few faults and uplifts. Sharp relief occurs throughout the region, ranging from canyon floors below 5,000 feet to mesa crests reaching about 11,000 feet in elevation. The chief cause of the relief, however, is the weathering effect of erosion upon rock layers of varying hardness in an arid climate. This combination of erosion wearing away horizontally-layered sedimentary rock formations, combined with some folding of the strata and scattered volcanic activity, has created the distinctive plateau-country architecture.

Modern-day visitors find it hard to believe that the narrow, shallow rivers of the West could carve such deep and awesome rock canyons. Even the Colorado River, which supplies water to a region much larger than New England, looks tiny in com-

◄ *View of the Grand Valley from Colorado National Monument.*

parison to the Mississippi, the Missouri, or the Ohio rivers. In earlier geologic eras, however, such as warming periods of glacial retreat, the Colorado and its tributaries carried vastly greater volumes of water than is now the case. Additionally, these rivers are far more forceful agents of erosion than their eastern counterparts. The average drop of the Colorado River as it descends through the Grand Canyon is fifteen times greater than the average fall of the Ohio River, and this scouring action is aided by sediment levels thirty times greater than those in the Ohio.

The most famous and spectacular examples of the plateau-land architecture occur in the immense Utah canyonlands and at locations such as Glen Canyon (now inundated) and the Grand Canyon. Only the eastern margin of the plateau country extends into Colorado, occupying about a quarter of the state, but here too are high plateaus, intricately carved escarpments, and steep-walled canyons. Travelers need not leave the state to fish the forested lakes of Grand Mesa, hunt deer on the Uncompahgre Plateau uplands, view the fanciful rock formations at Colorado National Monument, run the rapids below the Gates of Lodore, or visit the canyons on the Gunnison, the Dolores, or the San Miguel rivers.

In addition to the natural wonders of the plateau country, it also contains extensive archeological and paleotological remains. While Powell and his men were studying the landforms of the region, other early visitors discovered to their amazement that an ancient civilization once occupied the mesa tops, cliff sides, and valley floors along the southeastern rim of the plateau province. A government photographic party under the jurisdiction of F. V. Hayden, another of the great Western surveyors, brought back the first pictures of this grand discovery. In the introductory letter of his annual report for 1874, Hayden described the findings:

> From the permanent camp in Baker's Park, [near the present-day Silverton] a side-trip was made into the southwestern corner of the Territory, in search of the picturesque and interesting ruins of the habitations of a long forgotten race. No search was made until the Rio Mancos was reached; but, from this point, ruins without number covered the plateau and filled the valleys and cañons. Through the cañons of the Rio Mancos, were found houses of two stories in height, in the escarpment of the mesa, 800 to 1,000 feet perpendicularly above the valley, of well-dressed sandstone, true in all their angles, laid in a firm and tenacious mortar, and the inside plastered and paneled in two colors. . . . To reach these with photographic apparatus, it had to be hauled up with long ropes taken from the pack-animals. From near the mouth of the Rio Mancos, the party proceeded northwesterly into Utah, find-

ing group after group of towns and isolated watch-towers perched upon great bowlders [sic] and upon the promentories [sic] of the mesas.

Here indeed were the long-lost cities of an earlier civilization, continuously existent in a single area for more than a thousand years and complete with beautifully woven baskets and fine pottery still lying on the pueblo floors.

Several hundred miles to the north, near the confluence of the Green and the Yampa rivers, the evidence of human occupation in caves and rock shelters dates back some seven thousand years to a nomadic hunting and gathering culture that once lived on the plateau lands. In a sandstone formation not far from this site, a turn-of-the-century scientist found startling evidence of still earlier inhabitants— the dinosaurs. They had roamed this countryside more than 100 million years earlier, when the climate was subtropical and swamps lay where piñon and juniper struggle to survive today. Erosion, the prime mover of the plateau lands, had stripped back millions of years of accumulated sediment to reveal the remains of a primordial scene, frozen in time.

Indeed, the entire plateau country sometimes seems a land from the distant past, composed of ancient features elsewhere obliterated in the modern world but preserved here in a province where time moves so slowly. On the vast tablelands and basins, points of visual reference lie so far off and the landscape looks so uniform that a traveler begins to feel that he will never reach his destination. The minutes and even hours continue to tick away, but still there are few signs of progress across this endless landscape. Deep in the canyons, among rock formations buried beneath the earth's surface for hundreds of millions of years, time seems even more ethereal. Only the daily progress of the sun moving across a narrowed horizon provides a sense of time passing.

On the plains the predominant visual reference is linear, while in the mountains it is angular. In the plateau country, it includes horizontal and vertical components, formed by flat mesa tops and steep escarpments, level tablelands and sheer cliffs. No single shape dominates the plateau country, which exhibits a variety of landforms that seems sometimes harsh, often beautiful, sometimes monotonous, and occasionally bizarre. The predominant direction of vision on the plains is across the landscape to the horizon, while in the mountains it is upward from the valleys to the peaks above. In the plateau country, the dominant sights are not uplifted from the surface, but located downward, carved within it.

The mountains long have conveyed to man a perception of freedom. But the canyon country, experienced from below, creates a mood of confinement and even entrapment in the bowels of the earth. Known sometimes as "river fever," this sense of entrapment overtook Major Powell's 1869 expedition down the Colorado River. Powell usually exhibited an insatiable enthusiasm for the canyon country, but his journal contains an entry, made late in the trip, predicting that the expedition would soon be "out of prison." It was this feeling of entrapment in an alien environment, as much as anything else, that drove three of Powell's eight crewmen to attempt a daring escape upward to civilization along a route known ever since as Separation Canyon. By noon of the day following their departure, Powell's expedition reached calm water, but the three escapees were not so fortunate. After climbing up the canyon, they reached level ground again, only to be killed by a party of Shivwits Indians who mistook them for some prospectors who had murdered an Indian squaw.

More than a century after Powell's epic journey down the Colorado River, the plateau country remains a forbidding land physically distinct and culturally isolated from the outside world. During the past sixscore years of Colorado history, the plains were tamed, the front range settled, and the mountains raided. The plateau country, on the other hand, has been neglected, remaining an unknown Colorado whose future seems always to be just around the corner. The settlements existing there are few and far between, separated by lonely stretches of haunting landscape. In this solitary world where isolation is an ever-present fact of life, human association tends toward communal organizations, tightly clustered as at Mesa Verde or closely structured, as among the Mormon communities.

Though recent events have brought new inhabitants to many plateau towns, the land still remains much as it has long been — a little-known and sundrenched sightseer's paradise where extraordinary scenes lie just over the mesa's crest and around the next river bend. It is a special country, requiring a different way of seeing to appreciate it on its own terms and rewarding visitors who do so with unexcelled visual delights.

28 Dinosaur National Monument

Location: northwestern Colorado/northeastern Utah

Size: 264 square miles in Colorado; total size about 326 square miles

Terrain: steeply eroded canyons in arid plateau country

Scenic Value: very high

Historical Interest: exceptional paleontological interest

External Access: from US 40, Colorado 318, and Utah 149

Internal Access: Several short paved roads, several dirt roads, hiking trails, and by river boat

Maps: USGS composite topographic map of Dinosaur National Monument at 1:63,000
USGS sheets 1 and 5 of Moffat County at 1:50,000 (Colorado portion only)
National Park Service sketch map of Dinosaur National Monument at 1:250,000

Dinosaur National Monument, which is actually larger than many national parks, sprawls across a two-state area of deeply cut canyons in the Green River Basin. Most of the monument lies in Colorado, but its most popular attraction occupies an otherwise obscure corner situated in Utah. How this recreational site was created and why it holds such interest for paleontologists and river runners makes an interesting story.

Archeological evidence suggests that early prehistoric people occupied the area as long ago as 6000 B.C. For a number of centuries—the estimates vary considerably—later but still prehistoric members of the Fremont Culture spent time here, leaving a remarkable assortment of petroglyphs. Some of this rock art depicts recognizable objects such as a bison pierced by an arrow, flute players, lizards, and human figures bearing warriorlike ornaments. Other of the rock carvings are wholly obscure. So vast is the cultural gap between the people who carved these figures and our own society that we do not know for certain whether the carvings represent art or language, or perhaps a bit of both, or whether they served some wholly different purpose.

In 1776 Father Escalante led an expedition party through the monument area in the course of exploring a route from New Mexico to California. This group of Spanish explorers also felt compelled to leave evidence of their passage. A member of the expedition, Don Joaquin, carved his name, the year, and two crosses in the side of a cottonwood tree, according to Escalante's journal. John Ashley, an intrepid mountain man and fur trader, made the first known river trip through the present monument almost half a century later, and he too left an inscription, painted on a rock upstream from the monument. The inscription said: "Ashley, 1825." In 1869 John Wesley Powell traveled through the monument on his journey down the Green River to the Colorado River, popularizing in word and picture the sights he saw. Powell's journey, undertaken for a second time in 1871, resulted in the first survey of the area and the establishment of place-names that still identify many prominent features of Dinosaur National Monument. In his journey down the Green River, Powell noted Ashley's inscription on the rock; however, he misread the date and did not know who Ashley was.

The next event significant to this story occurred in August 1909. Earl Douglass, an experienced botanist and paleontologist, was searching for large fossil bones that Andrew Carnegie could install in his museum's Hall of Vertebrate Paleontology, located in Pittsburgh. On August 17, Douglass found eight Brontosaur vertebrae in a sandstone hogback at the site of the monument's present-day Dinosaur Quarry Visitor Center. Over the next fifteen years, some three hundred and fifty tons of bones were shipped from this site to the Carnegie Museum and other institutions.

In order to protect the location from vandalism and souvenir hunters, Douglass prevailed upon the Carnegie Museum for assistance, and in 1915 Woodrow Wilson proclaimed an eighty-acre site around the quarry as Dinosaur National Monument. A portion of the quarry face was incorporated as the north wall of the modern glass-and-steel quarry visitor center, located in the southwest corner of the monument. Today, however, the quarry area is little more than the back door to a large canyon preserve reaching forty miles east and fifteen miles to the north. In 1938 Franklin Roosevelt added an additional 326 square miles of canyon country to the one-quarter square mile originally designated as Dinosaur National Monument.

The present monument configuration is three-armed. The east arm includes the Yampa River east of its confluence with the Green River; the north arm includes the Green River above the confluence; and the west arm extends about twenty miles below the confluence. At the center of the monument is Echo Park, located near where the Yampa deposits its sediment-laden waters into the Green River.

There are two basic ways to travel through Dinosaur National Monument: on the ground or along the river routes. The river routes start either on the Yampa or by taking the Green south through the Gates of Lodore. River enthusiasts argue that a

Steamboat Rock, at the heart of Dinosaur National Monument.

water-level trip is the best way to see the monument, and it is difficult to disagree, since many of the monument's major attractions are not otherwise accessible. Boating on the monument rivers requires, however, the proper equipment and whitewater experience if it is to be done safely. Consequently, boating is permitted only by licensed concessionaires and by private parties who can demonstrate the appropriate skills to obtain a special permit.

By automobile, Dinosaur National Monument is accessible from seven different routes. The majority of travelers enter the monument from Jensen, Utah, taking Utah Highway 149 to the quarry area. The single most popular attraction in the monument, the Dinosaur Quarry Visitor Center, is located here. At this Jurassic-period site of a sandbar that existed some 140 million years ago along an

Cottonwoods along the road to Echo Park.

ancient river, the remains of various animals—most notably the dinosaurs—collected in the silt and eventually were buried by accumulating sand and mud. Subsequent erosion wore down the rock layers of what geologists call the Morrison Formation, exposing the fossilized bones of the creatures that long ago washed up on a sandbar.

The quarry area contains several other attractions including the monument's two improved campsites, at Split Mountain Gorge and Green River, and a short side road to Cub Creek. The only other access to this part of Dinosaur National Monument is by way of a long, rough route called the Island Park Road, which travels to the Rainbow Park Campground and the Island Park segment of the Green River.

The monument includes one other paved route in addition to the Dinosaur Quarry Visitor Center route. This thirty-one-mile scenic drive begins at the monument headquarters on US Highway 40 about two miles east of the town of Dinosaur and traverses the desolate but magnificent countryside along the edge of the Colorado Plateau to Harpers Corner, about six miles inside the monument boundary. An informative Park Service publication called *Journey Through Time* provides a self-guided tour of twenty-three points of interest along the route. At various scenic outlooks beside the road, signboards point out the geological and historical points of interest. Near Harpers Corner, where a vast panorama of canyon, plateau, and mountain country reaches to the distant horizon, a one-mile trail descends to a vantage point on the promontory of the corner itself from which Echo Park, Steamboat Rock, Canyon of Lodore, and various other features are visible.

Only one side road of any significance branches off from the Harpers Corner scenic drive. This route, known as the Echo Park road, leads to some of the nicest scenery in the monument. The Park Service does not encourage the use of this rough dirt road which, like the other primitive roads in the area, is impassable during the winter and when rain soaks into the clay underlying it. With good weather conditions, however, most passenger cars can negotiate the thirteen-mile trip from the pavement to Echo Park.

Travelers taking the side trip to Echo Park should allow substantial time not only since the going is slow, but because the landscape is so impressive. Starting at the Harpers Corner road, the Echo Park route drops steeply through Iron Springs Wash onto a long, arid bench. It then passes by the deep walls of Pool Creek Canyon and descends into the magnificent ivory-colored rock formations of Sand Canyon. The road subsequently winds through a small valley, passing beside stands of cottonwood and a petroglyph carved high on the rock wall. The road ends at a small meadow bordered by the river, surrounded by sculptured rock formations and dominated by the walls of Steamboat Rock. How Echo Park acquired its name becomes immediately clear—sharp sounds come rebounding back from the neighboring rock walls. Yet Echo Park is much more than an amusing acoustical phenomenon. This lovely, lush meadow where grassland, rock sculpture, and two picturesque rivers converge, lies at the very heart of Dinosaur National Monument. And the sense of isolated grandeur it conveys lies equally at the heart of the canyonlands experience. Like any monumental piece of architecture, it leaves in the visitor's mind a lingering sense of awe long after the details of line, form, color, and texture have escaped the memory.

Travelers with sufficient time and the equipment to travel rough backcountry roads need not leave Echo Park by way of the same route they entered. A thirty-eight-mile route called the Yampa Bench Road extends east from Echo Park to Elk Springs, which is located on US Highway 40 about thirty-four miles east of the monument headquarters. The Yampa Bench Road, perched between Blue Mountain and the Yampa River Canyon, is the longest and most isolated motor-vehicle route in Dinosaur National Monument. The eighty-mile trip between monument headquarters and Elk Springs, with a stopover in Echo Park, is a journey through time and space that can only be equalled by a boat trip through the monument.

The northern arm of Dinosaur National Monument is seldom visited except by the water route, following the path of Captain Powell as he passed through the Canyon of Lodore on his journey down the Green River. From Colorado Highway 318 about forty-one miles west of Maybell, a short gravel road enters the monument near the Gates of Lodore. From this popular boat-launching site near historic Browns Park, an interpretive nature trail extends downriver to the Gates. The only other access point in this section of the monument is at Zenobia Peak, which is reached by a long and seldom-used backcountry road that starts at the community of Graystone, located about a dozen miles from Colorado 318.

Dinosaur National Monument is not near any other Colorado recreational sites, but the northern and western entrances to the monument are a short distance from Ashley National Forest, in Utah, and Flaming Gorge National Recreation Area, situated along the Utah–Wyoming border. Travelers can readily combine a visit to one or both of these sites with a trip to the monument.

29 Grand Mesa National Forest

Location: western Colorado/east of Grand Junction

Size: 541 square miles

Terrain: forested mesa with numerous lakes

Scenic Value: high

Historical Interest: slight

External Access: Interstate 70, US 50, Colorado 65, Colorado 133, and Colorado 330

Internal Access: Colorado 65 and an extensive network of improved and primitive dirt roads and foot trails

Maps: USFS map of Grand Mesa National Forest at 1:125,000
USGS sheets 2, 3, and 4 of Mesa County and sheets 1 and 2 of Delta County at 1:50,000

On hot summer days in Grand Junction, residents look wistfully eastward toward the large mesa rising above the Grand Valley, knowing that the cool breezes and wooded lake country there provide respite from the heat of the valley. From Grand Junction, only one small corner of the mesa is visible, for this single plateau, reaching from the Elk Mountains to the confluence of the Colorado and Gunnison rivers at Grand Junction, is among the largest mesas in the world. The forest preserve that later became Grand Mesa National Forest was established nearly a century ago, in 1892, making it the second-oldest preserve in Colorado and the third-oldest forest preserve in the nation.

At first sight, Grand Mesa appears to be the flat-topped remnant of what was once a much higher mountain. In fact, it is the uplifted floor of an ancient lake or inland sea. Long after the waters receded, successive volcanic eruptions formed a cap of hard rock in the area as lava seeped through cracks to the surface. The resulting layer of volcanic rock proved more resistant to subsequent erosion than the surrounding softer rock, leaving an elevated mesa.

The top of Grand Mesa lies almost a mile above the present valley floor, thus producing a cool, moist climate radically different from the warm, dry weather that prevails only a dozen or so miles to the west. The fortunate proximity of Grand Mesa to the fertile valley below provides more than climatic variations and topographic relief. Agriculture is the economic lifeblood of the arid Grand Valley. Irrigation water from the Colorado River supplies some of this need, but it is not sufficient to satisfy the requirements of a water-intensive agricultural industry and a growing population. Local water sup-

plies in the Grand Valley are augmented by a network of some three hundred lakes and reservoirs on top of the mesa; these capture and store moisture for use in the summer.

These many small bodies of water serve recreational needs too, as they are used for fishing and boating. The abundant snowfall and gentle slopes make Grand Mesa a popular winter-sports area, and it is also a wildlife haven that consistently produces among the largest harvests of deer, elk, and bear of any hunting unit in Colorado. The Forest Service estimates that the deer and elk population in Grand Mesa National Forest approximates fifteen thousand head, in addition to a population of several hundred bears. During the summer months, an additional fourteen thousand head of livestock graze on the mesa.

A single paved road, Colorado Highway 65, traverses Grand Mesa National Forest from north to south, providing access to the center of the mesa from Delta and from the town of DeBeque, on Interstate 70. Improved gravel roads climb to the mesa from all four quadrants of the compass. In addition, the top of the mesa is laced by a network of improved and primitive roads, along with a considerable number of hiking trails concentrated in the central and western portions of the mesa.

For travelers who like to stay on paved highways, the Colorado Highway 65 route through Grand Mesa National Forest provides a delightful introduction to the mesa and offers several outstanding views. The northern approach from Interstate 70 between Palisade and DeBeque is a particularly enjoyable trip. As the road turns south from Plateau Creek, a sweeping view of Grand Mesa unfolds, and in a distance of about a dozen miles, the route climbs from the valley to mesa top, traveling from piñon–juniper country through scrub oak, pine, aspen, and fir. The road passes through the flat, open top of the mesa at Skyway Point Overlook and Land O Lakes Overlook, circles around Island Lake, then begins a gentle descent to Delta, located about twenty-five miles beyond the forest boundary.

Travelers willing to venture off the pavement have a bewildering variety of roads from which to select. Many of the more remote reservoirs and backcountry portions of Grand Mesa National Forest can be reached only along four-wheel-drive routes that sometimes become muddy even at the height of summer. Fortunately, there are also many dozen miles of improved dirt roads suitable for passenger-car use during much of the year. The most dramatic of these routes is picturesquely called Lands End Road; it connects Colorado Highway 65 at the top of the mesa with US 50 about a dozen

A pastoral scene on the top of Grand Mesa.

An afternoon scene in a remote corner of Grand Mesa National Forest.

miles south of Grand Junction. From Colorado 65 the road travels through lightly forested terrain at the top of the mesa for about eleven miles to Lands End. From this dramatic overlook, the road spirals downward over the lip of the mesa in spectacular fashion, cutting several dozen switchbacks before it changes from gravel to asphalt at the forest boundary. Spread out below, as if seen from an airplane, is the rolling countryside above the Gunnison and Colorado rivers, which converge at Grand Junction and flow through the broad expanse of the Grand Valley. Although the Lands End Road is a perfectly convenient way to enter Grand Mesa National Forest from Grand Junction or from Delta, it is more properly traveled as an exit route because of the fine view it offers.

Travelers along Interstate 70 who wish to take a leisurely half-day side trip through Grand Mesa Na-

tional Forest can conveniently do so without adding much additional mileage to their journey. At the Silt exit on Interstate 70, a road travels south through ranching country into a remote corner of the White River National Forest, then crosses over a low, unnamed divide into an equally remote portion of Grand Mesa National Forest. The road continues to the town of Colbran, where a paved road climbs to the forest boundary and where improved dirt roads lead to Colorado 65 and the turnoff for the Lands End Road, which exits Grand Mesa National Forest near US 50 and Grand Junction. This extended journey through Grand Mesa National Forest and some of the very attractive adjoining countryside bypasses nearly seventy miles of the Interstate 70 route and is an attractive summertime alternative to the usual trip eastward from Grand Junction.

30 Colorado National Monument

Location: western Colorado/Grand Junction area

Size: 32 square miles

Terrain: canyon and plateau country

Scenic Value: very high

Historical Interest: slight

External Access: from Colorado 340

Internal Access: paved scenic drive and foot trails

Maps: USGS sheets 2 and 3 of Mesa County at 1:50,000

National Park Service sketch map at about 1:40,000

Where the Colorado River Valley meets the Uncompahgre Plateau, natural forces have carved colorful and convoluted sculptures that are intricate in detail and dramatic in scope. Lush, irrigated croplands sprawl across the valley floor. Along the edge of the plateau, however, where man's imprint on the landscape is less evident, an arid climate has preserved scenes of special beauty for millenia.

Viewed from the window of a car, Colorado National Monument appears to be a timeless land of stately and bizarre rock formations, but closer inspection reveals a world of kaleidoscopic change. From morning to late afternoon the shifting angle of the sun alternately mutes and intensifies the colors while shadows that shorten and then grow longer again bring into relief a multitude of sculptural detail. During the course of a single day wind, water, and other natural forces remain at work, eroding materials and depositing them elsewhere. After sufficient time this land, where dinosaurs once roamed in humid swamps, will change again—although we know little of how or when the changes will occur. The science of geology, alas, more proficiently explains what happened in the past than what shape the future will take.

Fortunately for the present generation, a portion of these carved rock formations at the edge of the Uncompahgre Plateau have been preserved and developed as Colorado National Monument. Elsewhere in Colorado and in several other Western states, there are larger expanses of sculptured plateau country. However, most of these locations, like Monument Valley in Arizona and Canyonlands National Park in Utah, are far from the beaten track and accessible only by primitive road. Colorado National Monument, on the other hand, lies within sight of Interstate 70 and is adjacent to a large

town; its paved road remains open year round.

This single access road, constructed during the Depression by the Civilian Conservation Corps, is the only motor route in Colorado National Monument. Starting at an elevation below 5,000 feet on the western side of the monument, the twenty-three-mile-long route climbs through the steeply cut canyons and a short tunnel to emerge nearly 2,000 feet higher on the top of the plateau. The road winds past the monument's only campground and the spacious visitor center. The route, appropriately called Rim Rock Drive, eventually descends to the eastern border of the monument at the edge of suburban Grand Junction.

The western part of Rim Rock Drive, from Balanced Rock to the Coke Ovens, provides the most spectacular scenery. Spread out below is the broad expanse of the Grand Valley, with the Roan Plateau rising above it in the background. A succession of rock formations endlessly varying in size, shape, color, and texture dominates the foreground. Although some of the formations carry formal names like Sentinel Spire, Pipe Organ, Kissing Couple, and Squaw Fingers, visitors are free to let their imaginations run wild, inventing their own names and finding personalized interpretations. For me, the assortment of rock walls, spires, towers, turrets, and buttresses looks like a primeval construction site awaiting the arrival of an omnipotent master architect to assemble these prefabricated components into a netherworld of medieval castles and gothic churches.

Basket-weaving Indian peoples once inhabited the area around Colorado National Monument, and ancient Indians left mysterious cartoonlike carvings on the rock. Antoine Robidoux, that intrepid fur trader who traveled the Rockies between Colorado, New Mexico, and Utah, built his first trading post sometime around 1828 a few dozen miles to the southeast near the present-day site of Delta. Overall, however, Colorado National Monument is of limited historical interest. Until John Otto stimulated interest in the area during the early years of the twentieth century and it became a national monument in 1911, few persons bothered to enter the steep-walled canyons that contain no commercially significant minerals and insufficient vegetation for productive grazing.

Regardless of how you interpret its rock formations, Colorado National Monument remains a monument to time and the weather—an outdoor, three-dimensional geology textbook. A succession of mountain building, erosion, sedimentation, volcanic eruptions, and additional erosion working on rock layers of varying hardness has produced a sculptured history of geological events dating back

Afternoon shadows on the Coke Ovens.

many hundreds of millions of years. A trip along Rim Rock Drive with stops at the various overlook points, combined with a tour of the visitor center, where descriptive exhibits illustrate the natural history of the area, will help convey a grasp of how the monument was formed.

The scenic drive, however, skirts the rim of the canyon, providing an elevated view of most of the formations. Visitors with sufficient time to do so should supplement this experience with a hike to see the formations in a more natural setting and from an angle that enhances their dramatic scale. The rimrock overview provides a sweeping introduction to the monument, but only a hike through the interior will convey a sense of the looming bulk and rich detail of the individual formations. At the Book Cliffs overlook, two short hiking trails skirt the edge of the canyon. From the Coke Ovens trailhead, one route travels a short distance off the road and another longer and more spectacular trail winds down through Monument Canyon, ending at Colorado Highway 340 a few miles upstream from the west entrance to the monument. On the east side of the monument, another route, called the Serpents Trail, travels along the old highway path through

the area before returning to the paved road a short distance from the east entrance. In addition, several longer trails cut through the backcountry of Colorado National Monument.

The desert-canyon terrain of the monument requires that hikers take appropriate precautions for traveling a hot, dry countryside. Fortunately, however, most of the routes are easy to traverse, as the elevation is low by Colorado standards and the majority of the longer trails can be used as one-way downhill routes with a car shuttle or prearranged pickup at the end of the hike. Those persons addicted to driving Colorado's backcountry roads will find no available routes within the monument, but an interesting backcountry trip starts at Colorado National Monument.

From two points along Rim Rock Drive, a paved road and a graded dirt road travel to Glade Park. Starting there, an unpaved road winds south about nine miles to a remote, detached twelve-square-mile unit of Grand Mesa National Forest located near the edge of Unaweep Canyon on the Uncompahgre Plateau. This little-known forest unit, called the Fruita Division, includes a picnic ground and a campground, along with four small reservoirs.

The scenic roadway through Colorado National Monument.

31 Mesa Verde National Park

Location: southwestern Colorado/west of Durango

Size: 81 square miles

Terrain: mesa and canyon country

Scenic Value: unique

Historical Interest: exceptional prehistorical interest

External Access: US 160

Internal Access: paved roads and limited foot trails

Maps: USGS sheets 2 and 4 of Montezuma County at 1:50,000
National Park Service map of Mesa Verde National Park at 1:24,000

Translated literally, Mesa Verde means green table or, more descriptively, wooded mesa. This large, semiarid mesa lying north of the Mancos River includes gently sloping tablelands and steep-walled, rocky canyons formed by erosion working on the sandstone and shale deposited in earlier geologic eras when the area lay in the path of retreating and advancing seas. Windblown soils cover the mesa top, and the 7,000-foot elevation provides more moisture than the surrounding valley receives. Both summer and winter temperatures are milder on Mesa Verde than in the Montezuma Valley directly to the north.

Traditionally the homeland of the Ute Indians, Mesa Verde and the surrounding countryside long lay off the beaten track of exploration and trade. Even the Utes, who were pushed deeper into the area by the Burnot Treaty of 1873 to make way for mining in the San Juans, rarely ventured into the Mesa Verde canyon country, fearing the ancient spirits thought to dwell there. European travelers, fearing the wrath of the Utes, displayed a similar reluctance to penetrate the rugged canyon country

The La Plata Mountains seen from Mesa Verde.

above the Mancos River. In 1859 John Newberry, a geologist with the McComb Expedition, climbed to the top of Mesa Verde, and his field notes remark upon the excellent view of the surrounding countryside. Fifteen years later, William Henry Jackson, head of the photographic division of the 1874 Hayden Survey, visited the Silverton mining district in the San Juans. On hearing of cliff dwellings located in remote canyons to the southwest, Jackson took his party into Mancos Canyon and other remote locations, where they found and photographed dozens of prehistoric Indian ruins. Writing about his expedition in the *8th Annual Report of the United States Geological and Geographical Survey of the Territories,* Jackson said:

> In the extreme southwestern corner of Colorado Territory, west of the one hundred and eighth degree of longitude, are groups of old ruined homes and towns, displaying a civilization and intelligence far beyond that of any present inhabitants of this or adjacent territory.

Then, on December 18, 1888, another major discovery occurred. Two local ranchers, Richard Wetherill and his brother-in-law Charles Mason, were riding through a snowstorm on Mesa Verde rounding up stray cattle. Wary of encountering a sudden dropoff under conditions of poor visibility, they dismounted and proceeded on foot to the edge of the canyon. In amazement, they saw outlined in the falling snow an ancient, multistoried city set in a wall of the canyon. They spent the remainder of that day and the following day searching for—and finding—other dramatic ruins before returning to their winter camp. In that short period, Wetherill and Mason found three of the most famous Mesa Verde cliff dwellings: Cliff Palace, Square Tower House, and Spruce Tree House.

Richard Wetherill, awestricken by his find, enlisted the aid of his brother John to explore further the area, to collect the pottery and other artifacts they discovered, and to guide tourists through the ruins. Their efforts were aided by a young Swede,

The Cliff Palace.

Gustaf Nordenskiold, who had been touring the Southwest and had become equally enchanted with the curious cliff dwellings of Mesa Verde. Nordenskiold helped excavate several of the sites, assembled a large artifact collection for shipment to Sweden, and perhaps most importantly, produced an extensive photographic record of the ruins at the time of their discovery. Virginia McClurg, a New York newspaper correspondent who first began visiting prehistoric Indian dwellings in the 1880s, undertook a vigorous campaign to ensure the preservation of Mesa Verde. Among her other efforts, she formed the Colorado Cliff Dwellers Association, which gained control of the ruins by an arrangement Congress ratified in 1901.

Five years later, following additional lobbying efforts by McClurg, Lucy Peabody, and other persons, Congress enacted a bill creating Mesa Verde National Park; President Theodore Roosevelt signed the bill into law on June 29, 1906. In 1913 a land exchange with the Ute Indians added another nearly forty square miles to the park, bringing it approximately to its present boundaries. So remote was this early national park that a round-trip visit from Mancos, the nearest community, took three days by pack train. In 1913 a wagon road was constructed to the park headquarters, and by the following year the round trip from Mancos to Mesa Verde could be made in one day by automobile.

Nearly a century of archeological exploration and research has revealed an embarrassment of prehistoric remains in the Mesa Verde area. Within the park boundaries, some four thousand sites are known, about six hundred of which are cliff dwellings. To date, the Park Service has excavated, stabilized, and opened for public viewing only a small portion of these sites. The surrounding area, much of which is tribal land within the Ute Mountain Indian Reservation, includes hundreds of additional cliff dwellings and other ruins that have received little or no scientific study.

Archeological research conducted since Wetherill and Mason stumbled on the Cliff Palace that snowy day in 1888 reveals a thirteen-century-long history of human inhabitation in the Mesa Verde area, starting around the birth of Christ. Growth-ring dating of wood samples, archeomagnetic dating of clay fragments, pollen analysis, and a variety of other techniques have revealed a wealth of knowledge about the people who once lived at Mesa Verde.

Evidence of human settlement on the Colorado Plateau—though not specifically at Mesa Verde—reaches back some ten thousand years to a Paleo-Indian group of hunting and gathering people. Sometime around the birth of Christ their successors began to raise domestic varieties of corn, manufacture high-quality basketry, hunt with the bow and arrow, and live not in caves, as their ancestors had done, but in low, semisubterranian pithouses. This era, known sometimes as the Basketmaker Period, lasted about seven to eight centuries. Ruins dating from the latter part of this age, known as Basketmaker III or Modified Basketmaker, are among the earliest archeological sites discovered at Mesa Verde.

During the eighth century a distinct pueblo culture emerged on the mesa tops. The early pithouses underwent a major architectural transformation into vertical-walled living quarters and below-ground kivas, used for ceremonial and related purposes. Cotton fabrics appeared, community water storage and diversion projects were built, and trade with other peoples was expanded. This early or Developmental Pueblo Period lasted some two hundred and fifty years, until the end of the eleventh century. The following two hundred years, from about 1100 to 1300, mark the Great Pueblo Period, during which the Anasazi culture flourished. It began on the mesa tops and then, about a century later, rapidly descended back to cliff-dwelling caves, where a remarkable multistoried communal stone architecture emerged.

It is this last, brief era that created the striking sites for which Mesa Verde National Park is so widely known. During the latter years of the thirteenth-century drought, perhaps compounded by hostile attacks, overpopulation, internal strife, or other, unknown events caused a wholesale exodus south of the San Juan River into New Mexico and Arizona. By the start of the fourteenth century, Mesa Verde had been abandoned. Yet the length of human inhabitation there had lasted longer than the Roman Empire, occupying an era about equal in length to the European Middle Ages. At its height the population of Mesa Verde probably peaked at nearly five thousand persons, or about the same size as a small medieval city in thirteenth-century England or France. Despite what we know about these two very different cultures, it is difficult to say who enjoyed a higher life-style, the late pueblo period cliff dwellers of Mesa Verde or their small-town medieval European counterparts of the thirteenth century.

Thanks to exceptionally skilled restoration and interpretation by the National Park Service, visitors to Mesa Verde National Park can conveniently observe the physical remains of this ancient Indian civilization. From the park entrance, located a short distance south of US Highway 160, a leisurely fifteen-mile drive up Mesa Verde leads to the visitor center, located at Far View. The facilities there in-

Detail of the Cliff Palace.

clude a museum, overnight lodging, and shuttle-bus service to Wetherill Mesa, where private vehicles are prohibited. Wetherill Mesa, the smaller of the two mesas open for public visits, is twelve miles from the visitor center. The major cliff dwelling sites there include Step House, Long House, Jug House, and Kodak House.

From Far View, the main park road continues south past the Far View ruins and Cedar Tree Tower to the park headquarters. The headquarters complex, which includes the archeological museum, a ruins site called Spruce Tree House, and several hiking trails, is well worth visiting. The museum building, completed nearly a half century ago by the Depression-era Civilian Construction Corps, is a lovely example of rustic masonry architecture. It houses both an extensive collection of Mesa Verde artifacts and the much-photographed series of five dioramas depicting the course of human development in the Four Corners area during the past ten thousand years.

From the headquarters complex, two paved roads travel along adjoining arms of Chapin Mesa. These two roads, which skirt the edge of the mesa on one-way loops, lead to the majority of restored ruins at Mesa Verde. The road extending due south from the headquarters gives access to Square Tower House, a variety of pithouses and pueblo ruins, and the Sun Temple. The road along the eastern edge of Chapin Mesa travels to the Cliff Palace, Balcony House, and several lesser sites. The Cliff Palace, with more than two hundred rooms, is the largest prehistoric community in the park, and Balcony House is the best-protected village open to the public. Contrary to the expectation of many park visitors, no paved roads lead directly to the cliff dwellings, and elevator service is not available. Access to the Cliff Palace is by means of a steep steel staircase, and visitors must be prepared for some moderately exposed ladder climbing to reach Balcony House. None of this climbing requires more than modest agility, but it can be strenuous exercise in the 7,000-foot elevation of Mesa Verde and should not be attempted by persons in poor health or with a fear of heights beyond the reach of a footstool.

Visitors to Mesa Verde are advised to concentrate their sightseeing in the afternoon hours. The previous inhabitants were a sun-loving people who oriented their cliff dwellings to the west and recessed them into the canyon walls in order to obtain the maximum winter sun and summertime shade. The mornings and midday at Mesa Verde are fine times to visit the museums or inspect mesa top ruins. Mid- and late afternoon, however, is the appropriate time to see the cliff dwellings in their full glory as the declining sun chases the shadows back and casts a warm glow on the stone walls.

Camping at Mesa Verde National Park is restricted to a single campground near the park entrance, and hiking is permitted only on the park's four designated trails. During the off season, from November to April, no concession services such as lodging, food, or gasoline are available. The Chapin Mesa ruins roads are open all year round, however, as is the museum. The Park Service conducts tours of Spruce Tree House during the winter months as long as weather conditions permit.

32 Yucca House National Monument

Location: southwestern Colorado/southwest of Cortez

Size: 10 acres

Terrain: shallow valley

Scenic Value: moderate

Historical Interest: significant prehistoric interest

External Access: US 666 and Montezuma County Road B

Internal Access: on foot only

Maps: USGS sheet 3 of Montezuma County at 1:50,000

Yucca House National Monument, located southwest of Cortez, surely ranks among the most obscure of Colorado's federally protected recreational and historical sites. Yucca House offers no camping facilities, picnic sites, or the usual amenities; no signs point the way toward it, and the National Park Service actively discourages travel to the monument. In place of the usual visitor center and headquarters building, Yucca House National Monument offers only a guest register and a small sign obscured by chest-high weeds. When visiting the site during the summer tourist season several years ago, I discovered that the most recent entry in the guest register had been made a week before.

The reason for this secrecy and obscurity is clear enough. Yucca House encompasses an unexcavated prehistoric Pueblo Indian village. As there is little of obvious interest to see at the site, the Park Service would prefer to retain it in an unmolested state for future development.

The existence of the Yucca House site has long been known. It was first described by Professor William Holmes more than a century ago, and it was established as a national monument in 1919. The

View of Mesa Verde from Yucca House National Monument.

View of Sleeping Ute Mountain from Yucca House National Monument.

most prominent feature of the ruins is a set of two mounds, designated by Holmes as the Upper House and the Lower House. The Upper House, which may once have been the central structure of this ancient Indian village, rises about fifteen feet above the ground and is surrounded by a scattering of smaller mounds. The Lower House is some one hundred yards distant, suggesting that a community of significant size once existed here. No walls or other masonry structures are still standing at Yucca House, but the ground is heavily littered with fossilized limestone, which previous inhabitants hauled to the site from the base of Mesa Verde, located about two miles to the east.

The setting of Yucca House National Monument was clearly an attractive location for the prehistoric people who hauled their heavy constructon material several miles from its source. The ruins sit in the Montezuma Valley, about halfway between the west rim of Mesa Verde and Sleeping Ute Mountain. To the north a low rise called Aztec Divide provides additional sheltering from the elements, and close by is Navaho Wash, a tributary of the Navaho River. Other prehistoric people apparently found the area attractive for habitation, for many cliff dwellings and pueblo sites dot the mesa rim above Yucca House, and a number of additional ruins lie along the valley floor. These other sites, however, rest on land within the Ute Mountain Indian Reservation and are not open to the public.

The National Park Service distributes a single-page handout on Yucca House, but the directions are not complete or accurate. Since Yucca House National Monument is located several miles from the highway and no signs or road maps indicate the location, detailed instructions are necessary to find the site: travel about nine miles south on US Highway 666 from the intersection with US 160, and turn west on Road B. Take Road B past Road 21; one-half mile beyond this junction, turn north on Road 20.5 (the road number may be missing from the sign) and follow it through several turns for about one mile to a house with a red roof. Park by the corral fence, walk through the corral, take the steel steps over the fence on the west side of the corral, and you are in Yucca House National Monument.

In addition to Mesa Verde National Park and Hovenweep National Monument, several other attractions exist in the vicinity of Yucca House National Monument. To the southwest, along US Highway 160, is the well-known Four Corners Monument, located at the meeting point of Colorado, New Mexico, Utah, and Arizona. South on US 666, slightly more than a mile beyond the US 160 turn-off, an improved dirt road travels up Mancos Canyon, providing an extended journey through a lovely and dramatic stretch of Southwestern countryside. The canyon route, which is located entirely on the Ute Mountain Indian Reservation, parallels the Mancos River, set within towering cliffs that rise 700 feet and more above the valley floor. At a side canyon the road climbs nearly 1,000 feet to the mesa top and finally exits on US 550 at Kirtland, New Mexico, located twenty-five miles from the Colorado border.

33 Hovenweep National Monument

Location: southwestern Colorado/eastern Utah

Size: 345 acres in Colorado and 440 acres in Utah

Terrain: mesa and canyon country

Scenic Value: high

Historical Interest: very high prehistorical interest

External Access: from US 660, US 163, and local roads

Internal Access: secondary roads and on foot

Maps: USGS sheet 1 of Montezuma County at 1:50,000
National Park Service sketch map of Hovenweep National Monument, unscaled

Scattered across the arid plateau and canyon country west of Mesa Verde is a series of crumbling masonry structures that loom above the rough, sunbaked countryside. These towers, turrets, and walls suggest a desert-castle architecture constructed to provide a formidable defense against attack. Indeed, the period in which these structures were built coincides closely with the later medieval period of castle building in Europe. Unfortunately, the inhabitants who once dwelled here left no illuminated manuscripts or epic chronicles to tell us where they came from, why they built these structures, and for what reason they suddenly abandoned them sometime late in the thirteenth century.

We do know that the people who inhabited the area around Hovenweep Canyon and other neighboring drainages were closely related to the larger group of prehistoric Pueblo Indians who occupied the Four Corners area for many centuries. From a hunting and gathering culture, they progressed to the cultivation of corn, beans, and squash and the making of jewelry, baskets, and pottery. Originally they dwelt in cave shelters, then in pithouses constructed of poles and earthen coverings. Like the Mesa Verde residents, the Hovenweep people adopted stone masonry in the tenth century and showed impressive skill in the construction of their communities. The pueblo residents had once lived in small, scattered settlements in shallow valleys and on the mesa tops; but by the start of the thirteenth century, the Hovenweep people moved to the canyon edges, near the location of permanent springs, where they undertook the construction of stone buildings. It requires little imagination to visualize these structures as works of defense for the protection of precious and perhaps dwindling water supplies needed to support a growing population.

As happened at Mesa Verde, abandonment of the Hovenweep communities occurred late in the 1200s during a period of extended drought, as the former residents migrated south of the San Juan River into the Rio Grande basin. Anyone who has also visited the prehistoric cliff dwellings at Bandelier National Monument in New Mexico can well appreciate the difference in environments. In contrast to the parched, exposed locations at Hovenweep, Frijoles Canyon in Bandelier Monument is a lush, protected

Scattered ruins at Hovenweep National Monument, Holly Group.

environment, naturally easy to defend, with better soils and a permanent stream draining into the Rio Grande.

The first person of European descent to report on the abandoned Hovenweep structures was W. D. Huntington, who led a Mormon-sponsored expedition into the area in 1854. William Henry Jackson, the famous Western photographer, visited the ruins in 1874 during the course of the Hayden Survey's expedition through the plateau country. Hovenweep is a Ute Indian word meaning deserted valley, and Jackson applied it to the area. Following an archeological survey of the ruins in 1917–18, the Smithsonian Institution recommended that the sites be designated as a national monument, and the monument was established in 1923.

The present-day Hovenweep National Monument includes six scattered and remote sites. Two are located in Utah, and the remaining four sites lie in Colorado. The principal monument site, called Square Tower Ruins, and an accompanying campground are located in Utah at an isolated spot about a half-dozen miles from the Colorado border. The simplest access route is by way of US Highway 163, turning east about five miles north of Bluff, Utah at the monument sign and proceeding down thirty miles of back road. From Colorado, two long backcountry routes that start on US 666 also lead to the Square Tower sites.

The Park Service provides little encouragement or guidance for persons wishing to visit any of the other five sites, noting only that they are isolated and difficult to reach. Actually, one of the Colorado ruins is the most accessible of all the monument sites, being located less than a dozen miles from downtown Cortez. The other three Colorado sites, which lie in close proximity to each other along one of the backcountry routes to the Square Tower Ruins, are difficult to reach because of inadequate signage and poor road maintenance.

The most accessible of the Hovenweep National Monument sites is called the Goodman Point Group. Unfortunately, it is the least interesting and least developed of the Colorado ruins. To reach it, drive about five miles north from Cortez on US Highway 666; turn west on Road P and follow it along an irregular course for about six miles to a small National Park Service boundary marker located on the south side of the road. The ruins, which must be explored on foot, include several small features and a larger, unexcavated pueblo.

The other three Colorado sites—called the Cutthroat Castle Group, the Hackberry Group, and the Holly Group—all lie along the western edge of Hovenweep Canyon, close to the Utah border. The route to these sites begins just south of Pleasant View on US Highway 666 between Cortez and Dove Creek. Take the graded road indicated by a Park Service sign as the route to Hovenweep National Monument, following it through deserted mesa country with a good view of Sleeping Ute Mountain to the south. The side road to the Cutthroat Castle Group begins inauspiciously at a sign indicating that Hovenweep Canyon is located two miles farther down the main road. The two-mile route off the main road should be taken *only* in dry weather by travelers equipped with a topographic map of the area and a vehicle with adequate ground clearance. The primitive, ungraded road passes through several dry washes impassable during rainstorms, and no signs indicate where to turn along the route.

The access road ends at a cul-de-sac; here a small sign announces that this indeed is the location of the Cutthroat Castle Group of ruins. Several marked trails and paths lead below the canyon rim to the four-acre site. This beautiful but rugged and eerie setting includes a variety of well-preserved masonry ruins that lie baking in the sun, inhabited by lizards and a variety of insects. Visitors to this remote netherworld, located below the mesa top but above the canyon floor, can explore the remains of a pre-Columbian culture at their leisure, unhampered by shuttle-bus schedules and the din of chattering tourists.

To reach the Hackberry Group and Holly Group of ruins, take an unmarked side road that begins about four miles farther down the main route, turning south along a road that deteriorates as it descends below the mesa top. These two ruins, which are located on branches of the same access road, should be approached with the same caution that applies to the Cutthroat Castle Group. The setting is a bit less dramatic than the Cutthroat location, but it is rugged, desolate terrain. Backcountry hiking is required to explore the several-hundred-acre area occupied by the two ruins groups.

Is it worth all this effort to visit the various Hovenweep sites? The answer is probably "no" for persons who believe that getting there—wherever it may be—is less than half the fun. The answer is decidedly "no" for travelers who prefer the blacktop highways and who are unfamiliar with map-navigating techniques. But for the visitor who is traveling through the Four Corners region and who enjoys any excuse to explore seldom-seen backcountry areas, an excursion to the Hovenweep sites offers sufficient reason to roam through a stark, remote landscape where pre-Columbian Indians eked out a hardscrabble existence amidst the endless canyons and mesas of this weathered basin.

Ruins detail in Hovenweep National Monument, Cutthroat Castle Group.

Appendix A

Synopsis of State Recreation Areas

In addition to the State Forest and its state parks, Colorado maintains a system of seventeen state recreation areas. Stretching from the eastern plains to the Denver metropolitan area and to the New Mexico border, these state recreation areas include grassland reservoirs, a river-canyon setting, and mountain reservoirs. The principal focus of most sites is camping, picnicking, and water-sport recreation, but the variety of specialized activities available is impressive, ranging from several nine-hole golf courses to technical rock climbing, riding stables, an archery range, trapshooting, and model airplane fields.

Presented below, in alphabetical order, is a listing of these state recreation areas, with a brief description of each area.

Barbour Ponds State Recreation Area

Location: east of Longmont near Interstate 25
Size: about one-quarter square mile
Terrain: grassland with small lakes
External Access: from Interstate 25 and Colorado 119

Barbour Ponds State Recreation Area, located almost due east of Longs Peak and Rocky Mountain National Park, is a compact recreational area with sixty campsites, a short nature trail, and several pocket-sized lakes open to hand-propelled boats.

Bonny State Recreation Area

Location: eastern Colorado/south of Wray
Size: about 11 square miles
Terrain: high-plains reservoir
External Access: from US 385

This high-plains recreational area surrounds Bonny Reservoir, constructed by the federal government in 1951 to provide flood protection on the South Fork of the Republican River. It is a popular summertime recreational area, providing residents of eastern Colorado and western Kansas and Nebraska with extensive water-sports opportunities amid a quietly scenic grasslands setting. The reservoir ranks among the finest warm-water fisheries in Colorado, and its location on the Central Flyway attracts an impressive array of birds. With a migratory bird population that can reach as many as seventy thousand birds of several hundred species, Bonny receives substantial use during the waterfowl-hunting season. The area's facilities include a grass-surfaced airplane landing strip for visitor use.

Boyd State Recreation Area

Location: east of Loveland
Size: about 3.5 square miles
Terrain: high-plains reservoir
External Access: from US 34 and US 287

This small state recreation area offers a variety of water-sport activities on Boyd Lake, located a short distance east of Loveland in a plains setting with excellent views of the high peaks that dominate Rocky Mountain National Park. Boat rentals are available at the lake during the summer season, and the area offers 200 campsites.

Chatfield State Recreation Area

Location: southwest of Denver
Size: about 10 square miles
Terrain: high-plains reservoir at the edge of the foothills
External Access: from US 85 and Colorado 470

Chatfield Reservoir was constructed by the U.S. Army Corps of Engineers following the disastrous flood of 1965 that swept through the Denver area.

The reservoir honors a former soldier, Isaac W. Chatfield, who farmed the land by the confluence of Plum Creek and the South Platte River in the post-Civil War era. Chatfield State Recreation Area is an intensively used site during the summer months, and it provides an uncommonly broad range of recreational opportunities that includes swimming, fishing, waterskiing, picnicking, camping, horse trails, bicycle trails, a self-guided nature trail, a model-airplane field, a hot-air balloon launching site, and special facilities for handicapped persons.

Cherry Creek State Recreation Area

Location: southeast of Denver
Size: about 8 square miles
Terrain: high-plains reservoir with a good view of the Front Range peaks
External Access: from Colorado 83

Also constructed by the U.S. Army Corps of Engineers, Cherry Creek Reservoir is a heavily used urban recreational facility at the edge of southeast suburban Denver. The recreational area, sited in a shallow valley with a good view of the Front Range peaks in the distance, offers camping, water sports, a short nature trail, a prairie-dog observation area, a ten-mile-long circumferential bicycle trail, a model-airplane field, a firearms range, a dog-training site, and horse stables. In addition, it is equipped with special facilities for the handicapped.

Crawford State Recreation Area

Location: western Colorado/Delta–Montrose area
Size: about 2 square miles
Terrain: upland mesa and valley country
External Access: from Colorado 92

Crawford State Recreation Area is located at Crawford Reservoir on a tributary of the Gunnison River along Colorado Highway 92. Camping (at sixty campsites), boating, and waterskiing are the chief activities available at this state recreation area, located in a valley below Fruitland Mesa and about one mile from the Town of Crawford. Curecanti National Recreation Area is about one-half hour away by auto. The West Elk Mountains section of Gunnison National Forest lies only a few miles east of Crawford State Recreation Area, and the scenic but rarely visited north rim of Black Canyon

of the Gunnison National Monument is about a dozen miles distant by unpaved road.

Eleven Mile State Recreation Area

Location: central Colorado/west of Colorado Springs
Size: about 11 square miles
Terrain: mountain reservoir
External Access: from US 24 and Colorado 9

Eleven Mile State Recreation area surrounds Eleven Mile Reservoir, constructed on the South Platte River in 1932 by the Denver Board of Water Commissioners to provide urban water storage. The reservoir site is at the edge of South Park where the South Platte enters a steep canyon. The terrain in the area varies from high, rolling rangeland to mountain valleys. Eleven Mile State Recreation Area offers three hundred campsites, good fishing and hunting, boating, and winter recreation. Other attractions in the area include the scenic drive along Elevenmile Canyon road, Florissant Fossil Beds National Monument, and the newly created Lost Creek Wilderness located to the north of Eleven Mile State Recreation Area in the Tarryall Mountains of Pike National Forest.

Highline State Recreation Area

Location: northwest of Grand Junction
Size: about 1 square mile
Terrain: valley uplands
External Access: from Colorado 139 north of Interstate 70

Highline State Recreation Area offers camping (twenty-five sites), boating, swimming, and fishing in several small bodies of water located at the edge of the Grand Valley, beneath the Colorado Plateau. Southbound visitors to the area can enjoy sweeping views of the valley as they descend Colorado Highway 139. Other attractions in the area include Colorado National Monument, Arches National Park in Utah, and Grand Mesa National Forest.

Island Acres State Recreation Area

Location: east of Grand Junction/DeBeque Canyon
Size: one-sixth square mile

Terrain: Colorado River canyon
External Access: Interstate 70

This pocket-sized state recreation area provides camping, swimming, fishing, a nature tour, and picnicking for visitors traveling along Interstate 70 east of Grand Junction. The attractive DeBeque Canyon site beside the Colorado River, which includes a small lake and a buffalo herd, was purchased by the Colorado Highway Department in 1960 as Interstate right-of-way and then sold to the Colorado Division of Parks and Outdoor Recreation for park development.

Jackson State Recreation Area

Location: northeastern Colorado/east of Greeley
Size: about 5 square miles
Terrain: high-plains reservoir
External Access: from Colorado 39 to Colorado 144

From the high-plains setting of Jackson Reservoir, the snowcapped peaks of the Rocky Mountains are visible in good weather. Jackson State Recreation Area offers extensive camping facilities (two hundred sites), a full complement of water-sports activities, pleasant sandy beaches, and an undeveloped natural area on the north side of the reservoir. It is the largest eastern Colorado reservoir in the state recreation area system.

Navajo State Recreation Area

Location: southwestern Colorado/New Mexico border
Size: 5 square miles (Colorado section only)
Terrain: southwestern landscape
External Access: Colorado 151 and Colorado 172 from US 160

Navajo Reservoir is a sprawling, man-made lake thirty-five miles long; the principal part lies in New Mexico. The reservoir, constructed by the U.S. Bureau of Reclamation in 1962, dams the San Juan River and several of its tributaries, creating a major water-recreation site in an area of significant archeological interest. The Colorado segment of the reservoir is located about forty-five miles southeast of Durango, adjacent to the site of a former stage-

coach road and the historic route of the narrow-gauge Denver and Rio Grande Railway between Pueblo and the San Juan goldfields.

Paonia State Recreation Area

Location: North Fork of the Gunnison River/ northeast of Delta
Size: about 3 square miles
Terrain: mountain reservoir
External Access: from Colorado 133

This remote state recreation area, located at Paonia Reservoir in the upper valley of the North Fork of the Gunnison, offers water-sports opportunities and limited camping at five sites. The appeal of Paonia State Recreation Area lies in its attractive location below McClure Pass and in its proximity to the Marble–Crystal area of White River National Forest and to the West Elk Mountains and Ruby Range parts of Gunnison National Forest.

Pueblo State Recreation Area

Location: south-central Colorado/west of Pueblo
Size: about 27 square miles
Terrain: high-plains reservoir
External Access: from Interstate 25 and Colorado 96

Located in the rolling grasslands a short distance west of Pueblo, this large plains recreational area has the potential for considerable development in the future. Presently, Pueblo State Recreation Area offers a full range of water-sports activities on Pueblo Reservoir and the opportunity to explore the nearly twenty-five square miles of grassland encompassed by the area. Presently, no camping facilities are available at this site near the Arkansas River.

Rifle Gap and Falls State Recreation Area

Location: northwestern Colorado/west of Glenwood Springs
Size: 4 square miles
Terrain: plateau and canyon country
External Access: from Colorado 325 and Interstate 70

This two-part recreational area at the edge of the oil-shale country north of Rifle includes a reservoir set within sandstone and shale cliffs and, several miles up the road, a wide triple waterfall and some caves. In addition to camping accommodations at sixty sites, Rifle Gap and Falls State Recreation Area provides boating, fishing, swimming, scuba diving in the clear waters, hiking, and a small buffalo herd near the park headquarters. Directly north of the area and easily accessible by improved road is the White River National Forest and the Flat Tops Wilderness.

Sweitzer Lake State Recreation Area

Location: west-central Colorado/south of Delta
Size: one-third square mile
Terrain: shallow mountain valley
External Access: US 50

Sweitzer Lake State Recreation Area is a small picnicking and water-sports site located a short distance outside Delta. Its central location is about equally distant from three national forests (Grand Mesa, Uncompahgre, and Gunnison) and from the Black Canyon of the Gunnison National Monument.

Trinidad State Recreation Area

Location: southern Colorado/west of Trinidad
Size: about 5 square miles
Terrain: piñon–juniper uplands
External Access: Colorado 12

Camping and water sports are the principal activities at this Lake Trinidad recreational site located in typically Southwestern piñon–juniper country at an elevation of 6,000 feet. A hiking trail provides access to an overlook point, with attractive views westward toward the Spanish Peaks.

Vega State Recreation Area

Location: west-central Colorado/east of Grand Junction
Size: about 4 square miles
Terrain: valley and mesa country
External Access: from Colorado 330 off Interstate 25

A favorite local recreational site in summer and winter, Vega is located in a high valley almost totally surrounded by forested mesas. Vega Reservoir supports excellent trout fishing, wildlife is abundant in the area, and overnight visitors have 110 campsites available. A primitive road travels directly from the recreation area onto Grand Mesa, and several improved dirt roads in the area give quick access to the wooded lake country of Grand Mesa National Forest.

$$\text{\textemdash} Appendix\ B \text{\textemdash}$$

Selected Public Recreational Lands of Colorado, by Category

National Parks

Mesa Verde National Park
Rocky Mountain National Park

National Monuments

Black Canyon of the Gunnison National Monument
Colorado National Monument
Dinosaur National Monument
Florissant Fossil Beds National Monument
Great Sand Dunes National Monument
Hovenweep National Monument
Yucca House National Monument

National Recreation Areas

Arapaho National Recreation Area
Curecanti National Recreation Area

National Historic Sites

Bent's Old Fort National Historic Site

National Forests

Arapaho National Forest
Grand Mesa National Forest
Gunnison National Forest
Pike National Forest
Rio Grande National Forest
Roosevelt National Forest
Routt National Forest
San Isabel National Forest
San Juan National Forest
White River National Forest
Uncompahgre National Forest

National Grasslands

Commanche National Grassland
Pawnee National Grassland

State Forests

Colorado State Forest

State Parks

Barr Lake State Park
Castlewood Canyon State Park
Eldorado Canyon State Park
Golden Gate Canyon State Park
Lathrop State Park
Lory State Park
Mueller Ranch State Park (not yet open to the public)
Roxborough State Park (not yet open to the public)
Steamboat Lake State Park

State Recreation Areas

Barbour Ponds State Recreation Area
Bonny State Recreation Area
Boyd State Recreation Area
Chatfield State Recreation Area
Cherry Creek State Recreation Area
Crawford State Recreation Area
Eleven Mile State Recreation Area
Highline State Recreation Area
Island Acres State Recreation Area
Jackson State Recreation Area
Navaho State Recreation Area
Paonia State Recreation Area
Pueblo State Recreation Area
Rifle Gap and Falls State Recreation Area
Sweitzer State Recreation Area
Trinidad State Recreation Area
Vega State Recreation Area

Lowry Pueblo, a twelfth-century religious pueblo near Hovenweep National Monument.

Appendix C

Who to Contact for Additional Information

National parks,
national monuments,
Curecanti National Recreation Area, and
national historic sites

Department of the Interior
National Park Service
Rocky Mountain Regional Office   *and* Individual Superintendents
655 Parfet Street, Box 25287
Denver, CO 80225
(303) 234-3095

National forests, national grasslands,
Arapaho National Recreation Area, and
national forest and grassland maps

Department of Agriculture
U.S. Forest Service
Rocky Mountain Regional Office
11177 West 8th Avenue   *and* District Ranger Offices
Lakewood, CO 80225
(303) 234-4185

Colorado State Forest, state parks, and
state recreation areas

Department of Natural Resources
Colorado Division of Parks and
  Outdoor Recreation
1313 Sherman Street, Room 618   *and* Regional Offices
Denver, CO 80203
(303) 866-3437

Topographic maps and federal
geological information

Department of the Interior	Department of the Interior
U.S. Geological Survey	U.S. Geological Survey
Map Sales, Box 25286	*or* Map Sales
Denver Federal Center	Federal Office Bldg. 169
Denver, CO 80225	1961 Stout Street
(303) 234-3832	Denver, CO 80294
	(303) 837-4169

State geological information and publications

Department of Natural Resources
Colorado Geological Survey
1313 Sherman Street
Denver, CO 80203
(303) 866-2611

State historical sites,
information, and publications

Colorado Historical Society
Colorado Heritage Center
1300 Broadway
Denver, CO 80203
(303) 866-3682
(303) 866-3670

State tourism information

Department of Local Affairs
Division of Commerce and Development
Office of Tourism   *and* Local Chambers of Commerce
1313 Sherman Street, Room 500
Denver, CO 80203
(303) 866-3046

Weather, snow, and
road conditions

Colorado Travel and Recreation Weather Information
(303) 639-1515

Road Conditions, I-25 and East
(303) 639-1234

Road Conditions, Denver and West
(303) 639-1111

Aviation Weather
(303) 321-1032
(303) 388-3653

Ski Country Snow Reports
(303) 837-9907

Suggested Reading

These selected publications offer the reader an opportunity for further armchair exploration of Colorado people, places, and events, both past and present:

Guidebooks

Borneman, Walter R. and Lampert, Lyndon J. *A Climbing Guide to Colorado's Fourteeners,* Pruett Publishing Company, Boulder, Colorado. 1978.

Brown, Robert L. *Jeep Trails to Colorado Ghost Towns,* The Caxtun Printers Ltd., Caldwell, Idaho. 1963.

————. *Ghost Towns of the Colorado Rockies,* The Caxtun Printers Ltd., Caldwell, Idaho. 1968.

————. *Colorado Ghost Towns, Past and Present,* The Caxtun Printers Ltd., Caldwell, Idaho. 1972.

Eberhart, Perry. *Guide to the Colorado Ghost Towns and Mining Camps,* Sage Books, Denver, Colorado. 1969.

————. *Treasure Tales of the Colorado Rockies,* Sage Books, Chicago, Illinois. 1969.

Grout, William. *Colorado Adventures: 40 Trips in the Rockies,* Golden Bell Press, Denver, Colorado. 1974.

Hagood, Allen. *Dinosaur: The Story Behind the Scenery,* KC Publications, Las Vegas, Nevada. 1981.

Koch, Don. *The Colorado Pass Book: A Guide to Colorado's Backroad Mountain Passes,* Pruett Publishing Company, Boulder, Colorado. 1980.

Norton, Boyd and Barbara. *Backroads of Colorado,* Rand McNally, Chicago, Illinois. 1978.

Ormes, Robert O. *Guide to the Colorado Mountains,* published by the author, Colorado Springs, Colorado. 1979.

————. *Tracking Ghost Railroads in Colorado,* Century Press, Colorado Springs, Colorado. 1975.

Stegner, Wallace (editor). *This is Dinosaur: Echo Park Country and Its Magic Rivers,* Alfred A. Knopf, New York, New York. 1955.

Trimble, Stephen A. *Great Sand Dunes: The Shape of the Wind,* Southwest Parks and Monuments Association, Globe, Arizona. 1978.

U.S. Forest Service. *Guide to High Country Auto Tours: Rio Grande National Forest,* Rocky Mountain Region, USFS, Denver. No date.

Wenger, Gilbert R. *The Story of Mesa Verde National Park,* Visual Communication Center, Inc., Denver, Colorado. 1980.

Yandell, Michael. *National Parkways, A Photographic and Comprehensive Guide to Rocky Mountain and Mesa Verde National Parks,* World-Wide Research and Publishing Co., Casper, Wyoming. 1975.

Historical Books

Bueler, Gladys R. *Colorado's Colorful Characters,* The Smoking Stack Press, Golden, Colorado. 1975.

Goetzmann, William H. *Exploration and Empire: The Explorer and Scientist in the Winning of the West,* Alfred A. Knopf, New York, New York. 1966.

Hayden, F. V. *Annual Reports of the United States Geological and Geographical Survey,* Government Printing Office, Washington, D.C. 1873 through 1876.

Jackson, Donald (editor). *The Journals of Zebulon Montgomery Pike, with Letters and Related Documents,* Volume 1, University of Oklahoma Press, Norman, Oklahoma. 1966.

Lavender, David. *Bent's Fort,* Doubleday, New York, New York. 1954.

Powell, John Wesley. *The Exploration of the Colorado River,* University of Chicago Press, Chicago, Illinois. 1957.

Reps, John W. *Cities of the American West: A History of Frontier Urban Planning,* Princeton University Press, Princeton, New Jersey. 1979.

Sprague, Marshall. *A Gallery of Dudes,* Little, Brown and Company, Boston, Massachusetts. 1967.

———. *The Great Gates: The Story of the Rocky Mountain Passes,* Little, Brown and Company, Boston, Massachusetts. 1967.

———. *Colorado: A Bicentennial History,* W. W. Norton Company, Inc., New York, New York. 1976.

Stegner, Wallace. *Beyond the Hundredth Meridian: John Wesley Powell and the Second Opening of the West,* Houghton Mifflin Company, Boston, Massachusetts. 1976.

Ubelohde, Carl; Benson, Maxine; and Smith, Duane. *A Colorado History,* Pruett Publishing Company, Boulder, Colorado. 1972.

Natural History

Bailey, Alfred M. and Niedrach, Robert J. *Birds of Colorado,* 2 Volumes, Denver Museum of Natural History, Denver, Colorado. 1965.

Costello, David F. *The Prairie World,* Thomas Y. Crowell Company, New York, New York. 1969.

Chronic, Halka. *Roadside Geology of Colorado,* Mountain Press Publishing Company, Missoula, Montana. 1980.

Chronic, John and Halka. *Prairie, Peak and Plateau: A Guide to the Geology of Colorado,* Colorado Geological Survey Bulletin 32, Colorado Geological Survey, Denver, Colorado. 1972.

Fenneman, Nevin M. *Physiography of the Western United States,* McGraw–Hill Book Company, Inc., New York, New York. 1931.

Hylander, Clarence J. *Wildlife Communities from the Tundra to the Tropics in North America,* Houghton Mifflin Company, Boston, Massachusetts. 1966.

Knight, Clifford B. *Basic Concepts of Ecology,* The Macmillan Company, New York, New York. 1965.

Larkin, Robert P.; Grogger, Paul; and Peters, Gary L. *Field Guide: The Southern Rocky Mountains,* Kendall/Hunt Publishing Company, Dubuque, Iowa. 1980.

Pesman, Walter M. *Meet the Natives: An Easy Way to Recognize Wildflowers, Trees, and Shrubs of the Central Rocky Mountain Region,* Denver Botanic Gardens, Denver, Colorado. 1967.

Stokes, William Lee. *Scenes of the Plateau Lands and How They Came to Be.* Publishers Press, Salt Lake City, Utah. 1973.

General

Clawson, Marion. *Uncle Sam's Acres,* Greenwood Press, Westport, Connecticut. 1951.

Lavender, David. *David Lavender's Colorado,* Doubleday, New York, New York. 1976.

Momaday, Scott N. *Colorado,* Rand McNally, Chicago, Illinois. 1973.

Peirce, Neil R. *The Mountain States of America: People, Politics and Power in the Eight Rocky Mountain States,* W. W. Norton Company, Inc., New York, New York. 1972.

Sumner, David. *Colorado/Southwest: The Land, the People, the History,* Sanborn Souvenir Company, Inc., Denver, Colorado. 1973.

Tilden, Freeman. *The National Parks: What They Mean to You and Me,* Alfred A. Knopf, New York, New York. 1951.

National Park Service Mail Order Catalog, Parks and History Association, Washington, D.C. 1979.

About the Photography

The photographs included in this book were taken by the author with Hasselblad camera equipment and Zeiss T* lenses with focal lengths from very wide angle (38mm) to mild telephoto (150mm). Hasselblad cameras, in this case a 500 CM and a SWC/M, are of single-lens reflex design, with detachable film magazines, and produce an image two and one quarter inches square. Most shots were taken hand held, but a tripod with mirror lockup and remote shutter release was used when necessary to employ slow shutter speeds and minimum aperture to achieve maximum depth of field. Moderate filtration, usually with an orange filter, was used to preserve cloud detail and enhance the sky—a necessity in high-altitude black-and-white photography.

Kodak Plus–X pan professional film was used exclusively for the black-and-white photography and was hand processed with Kodak Microdol–X developer. Ektachrome 64 professional transparency film was used for the color photography. All enlargements were made on a Bessler enlarger equipped with a Schneider Componon S 90mm lens. Burning, dodging, and other image manipulation techniques were kept to a minimum, and most enlargements were printed as closely to full frame as the dictates of the subject matter permitted.

About the Author

Don Koch, born in Pittsburg, was educated at the Nichols School, Brandeis University, Princeton University, and the University of Colorado. An avid sports enthusiast and an occasional planner and consultant for government agencies, he has traveled extensively throughout the West. His writings include three books; more than forty articles, essays, and reviews; and a variety of technical documents on land use and environmental matters, economic development planning, and human resource development.

Index of Recreational Areas

(Note: entries in italics refer to chapter headings in this book.)